BARBARIAN'S HEART

Berkley Titles by Ruby Dixon

Ice Planet Barbarians

ICE PLANET BARBARIANS

BARBARIAN ALIEN

BARBARIAN LOVER

BARBARIAN MINE

BARBARIAN'S PRIZE

BARBARIAN'S MATE

BARBARIAN'S TOUCH

BARBARIAN'S TAMING

BARBARIAN'S HEART

Royal Artifactual Guild

BULL MOON RISING

BARBARIAN'S HEART

RUBY DIXON

BERKLEY ROMANCE
New York

BERKLEY ROMANCE
Published by Berkley
An imprint of Penguin Random House LLC
penguinrandomhouse.com

Book design by Kristin del Rosario

Library of Congress Cataloging-in-Publication Data

Names: Dixon, Ruby, 1976– author. | Dixon, Ruby, 1976– Aftershocks.
Title: Barbarian's heart / Ruby Dixon.
Description: First Berkley Romance edition. |
New York: Berkley Romance, 2025. | Series: Ice planet barbarians |
Barbarian's heart and Aftershocks were originally self-published in 2016.
Identifiers: LCCN 2024039010 | ISBN 9780593954768 (trade paperback)
Subjects: LCGFT: Science fiction. | Romance fiction. | Novels. | Novellas.
Classification: LCC PS3604.I965 B3765 2025 |
DDC 813/.6—dc23/eng/20240903
LC record available at https://lccn.loc.gov/2024039010

Barbarian's Heart and "Aftershocks" were originally self-published in 2016.

First Berkley Romance Edition: January 2025

Printed in the United States of America
1st Printing

For Alex Conkins, because you've been such an amazing inspiration!

AUTHOR'S NOTE

Hello there!

Thank you so much for reading! This book wouldn't have been possible without all of the readers who have continued to demand more Ice Planet Barbarians. You want everyone's story, and I aim to deliver (as best I can).

That being said, a lot of you were upset at the earthquake in the last story and at Pashov's injury. Our alien tribe was happy and healthy, and why did I have to go and ruin it??!!?? Because I'd talked for many (many) books about how it's a dangerous planet and yet I'd shown none of it. I wanted real consequences for the characters and a reminder that nothing is a given.

Plus, it gave me the perfect opportunity to slide in two of the best romance tropes: amnesia and a marriage in trouble. I wanted Stacy and Pashov to fall in love all over again, but this time on-screen instead of off-screen like many of our earlier couples. I wanted to show that, and I wanted to show Stacy's struggle with having her life "settled" and then being forced to deal with changes. I wanted to show Pashov dealing with the very strangeness of waking up one day to find out you have a fated mate and a child and you don't remember either.

SPOILER ALERT FOR *Barbarian's Heart*

In the end, I opted to make Pashov's memory recovery vague. I did a lot of research on traumatic amnesia as I wrote this, and I learned that it's not a "snap your fingers" sort of scenario. Some people might get their memories back slowly, and others might not get their memories back at all. Never getting those memories back isn't ideal, of course, but I wanted to show more than anything that this is okay in a relationship. That people change or have things happen to them, and they can still recover and find (or rediscover) love. Sometimes things don't work out perfectly, but that doesn't mean there isn't a happy ever after. Also, as a reader I would have found it a little too simple if he just woke up one day and suddenly remembered everything again. It would have taken away from the gravity of what they'd just gone through.

I'm absolutely not in the business of being deliberately cruel to my characters, but one of the big themes in my stories is that people are flawed and imperfect. Imperfect people are capable of loving, being loved, and having fantastic, sexy, wonderful relationships. I hope I leave you feeling that way, too.

END SPOILER ALERT

I've also included the novella "Aftershocks" in this particular book, as I felt it was an important part of the storyline of the cave collapse overall, and I wanted readers to have it. Even though it's tucked behind *Barbarian's Heart*, if you're a timeline purist, you can and should read it first. It's a quick story about various people in the tribe and how they're dealing with the changes they've been going through, and I personally loved the glimpse into the broader tribal life as they struggle and survive. (And thrive! We are always thriving!)

Until next time!

Ruby Dixon
August 2024

CONTENTS

BARBARIAN'S HEART

CHAPTER ONE

Stacy

Pashov's arms go around me and he nuzzles my neck, all affection. He's always very affectionate around breakfast. And lunch. And okay, dinner. The man's ruled by his stomach, and today is no change. He presses a kiss to my neck and then peers at my frying pan. "Are you making those for me?"

"No," I say, teasing in my voice. "This is for Josie. Are you hungry again?"

"I am always hungry, female." His hand slides to my butt and he gives it a squeeze. "Perhaps throw one of your cakes on there for your suffering mate?"

Suffering? I snort with amusement, but I get out a scoop of the mash I use for the not-potato cakes. "Sweet or meat?"

"Meat, of course."

Of course. He likes sweets about as much as the next sakhui, which is to say not at all. I open my pouch of spices for the peppery flavoring he likes so much. "Oh, shoot. I'm out. I need more of the spicy stuff. Do you think your mother has more?"

"There is some in the storage cave," he tells me, pressing a kiss to my cheek. "I will go and get it for you."

"Leave Pacy with me," I tell him, setting my pan down. "He needs to eat, too."

He shrugs off the baby sling and sets my son down near my feet, touching his nose. "Do not eat all of the cakes. Save some for your father."

Pacy giggles and tries to catch his father's big finger with his tiny hands. My heart squeezes with affection at the sight. "Hurry up," I warn Pashov. "I need those spices if you want to eat." I'm not trying to nudge him too much, but my mate can get distracted at times, and if I leave my pan on for too long, it'll get too hot and scorch the cakes.

"I am going," he says, uncurling his big body and getting to his feet. He tugs on my braid, grabs my ass again as he leaves, and then jogs away into one of the back tunnels.

The ground shifts.

I drop my pan into the fire, ignoring the crash of sparks it makes, and grab Pacy instead. I don't understand what's happening. I look around, wondering if I'm imagining things, but then the ground shakes again.

"Out of the cave!" someone bellows, and then hands grab me and pull me blindly after them. I think it's Haeden, and he's got Josie in one arm and drags me with the other.

"Wait!" I cry out. "Pashov!" He's in the storage cave.

I look over . . . and then the ceiling collapses.

"PASHOV!"

I wake up in a cold sweat. Every inch of me is slick with it, and I rub my arms briskly to get rid of the dampness before it can crystallize to frost. Next to me in the nest of furs is Pacy. He's got one fist in his mouth, and as I watch, his little mouth works as if he's nursing in his sleep. Normally the sight of my son in sleep brings me immense joy, but today . . .

All I can see is the velvety pale blue skin, the dark lashes that frame his eyes, and the nose with the bump right in the middle of the bridge, just like his father's. He's the spitting image of him, and it hurts me.

I've lost my mate.

Even though Pacy's asleep, I pick him up and pull open my tunic, settling him to my breast. He latches on sleepily and then begins to nurse, pushing a small hand against my skin. The nursing's to comfort me more than him, I think. I need to hold him close. I need to feel the calm that motherhood brings with it.

I need to feel the touch of someone who loves me and whom I love.

Because right now, I'm losing control.

I glance across the small tent. Georgie's sleeping curled against her mate, Talie in a basket of furs nearby. They've been nice enough to let me stay with them for the last week and a half, but I know it can't be easy on them. It's not easy on me, either. Every time Vektal pulls Georgie close, I think of Pashov. Every time they exchange a look, I think of Pashov. Every time he steals a kiss from her, I think of Pashov.

And I hurt all over again.

Tears threaten, but I close my eyes and force myself to be calm. It does no good thinking about my mate right now. Right now, he is not my mate. He doesn't remember me. Doesn't remember the last two years we've spent together, or the baby we made together. Doesn't remember resonating to me.

Doesn't remember me at all.

To him, I'm just another faceless, puzzling human. He doesn't remember our crash here. He doesn't remember Vektal mating to Georgie, or me resonating to him the first day we met. He doesn't remember the birth of our son. He remembers his sister and his brothers. He remembers his family and the rest of the tribe.

Me? I'm just a big fucking blur.

No matter how many times I tell myself that it doesn't matter, that he's alive, that all I ever wanted was for him to be alive and whole, I'm lying to myself. He *is* alive. He *is* whole. I *am* grateful. I'm just . . . miserable. I feel like I lost him.

The moment those rocks came down, I lost everything. I didn't think I could feel worse than I did during those endless days wondering whether or not he would live, but back then, I had hope. I don't even have that now.

I stroke Pacy's brow as he nurses. It's been eleven long days. Eleven long days since Pashov woke up, and fifteen days since the cave fell to pieces. For the first few days, I had hope that Pashov's memory would come back. That he'd look at me and recognition would dawn. That he'd grab my ass the way he always used to, and he'd be himself again. I kept that hope up for well over a week.

And then as each day passed and he grew a little more distant, a little more uncomfortable each time I looked at him, I realized that I was hoping for too much. My mate is alive. My mate is healthy.

He's just not my mate anymore, and I have to figure out how to go on without him. I won't push him into a relationship—hell, a mating—when he doesn't feel a thing for me. How can he? All of our memories are gone. Me crying over him just makes it worse.

So I'm avoiding him. I'm doing my best not to make him uncomfortable. Maybe it's not the best way to handle it, but it's the only way I can. I'll break if he looks at me in that empty, polite way again.

"You lost your frying pan?" Josie asks me, aghast. "I thought you weren't cooking because of . . . well, never mind." The look on her face gets awkward.

I shrug and spread the leaves I'm trying to dry on a hot stone, then cover them with a second stone to flatten them. I don't have a closed-in, windless spot to dry more spices, so I'm hoping that squishing them between two hot rocks will do some of the trick. Mostly I'm just guessing and trying to stay busy. "When the cave shook, I think I threw it into the fire by accident. And then after that . . ."

The knot forms in my throat again and I can't speak. After that, my world was destroyed.

"Shit. I'm so sorry for bringing it up." Josie grabs my hand and rubs it. The expression on her face is concerned. "What are you going to do?"

"There's nothing to do." One of the leaves is sticking out from between the rocks and I absently tuck it in—and then jerk my hand, my fingers burning. Ouch. Hot already.

"This is bullshit!" she whispers at me. "I can't believe he's acting like nothing happened! He should be here with you, Stacy! I can't imagine what it'd feel like if I didn't have Haeden right now! Aren't you scared? We don't have a home and food to eat for the winter!"

I know Josie's trying to help. It's the only reason I don't take my hands and wrap them around her neck. She means well. She does. Her mouth just runs away with her. "I'm scared," I admit. "I think we all are."

"And you don't even have your mate to lean on!" She's outraged on my behalf. "Even right now, he's over there hanging with Bek and the other hunters like you're not here by the fire with his baby! What the ever-loving fuck already!"

"Shh," I tell her, because she's getting louder with her indignation. "Really, Josie, it's all right." I just feel defeated. Tired. I have for days. It feels like I haven't relaxed or slept in weeks, though I know that isn't true. And I just don't have the energy for Josie's outrage. "I chose to stay away from him, not the other way around."

"You what? Why?"

Why? How can she sit here and ask me that? Because my heart is breaking every time I look at him? Because he should be relaxing and recovering, and me shoving myself and my baby under his nose and demanding that he remember us will be stressful? Not just to him but to me? "I just can't right now, okay?"

From the look Josie gives me, it's clear she doesn't understand. How can she? Has anyone ever had to deal with their mate just not remembering them at all?

Pashov

On the outskirts of the encampment, I tie sinew to a new spearhead and try to keep my head down. I can feel eyes on me, watching me, waiting to see how I react. To see if I fall over, clutching my head.

It is all very strange. I do not feel like a hunter who has nearly died. I do not feel like a male who survived a cave-in. I feel . . . normal. I just do not remember anything that has happened.

When they first told me, I thought it a joke. A cave-in? At the tribal caves? Everything lost? Old, peaceful Eklan dead?

Surely I would remember that.

But I search my mind and search my mind, and there is nothing there.

Yet the fact that there was a cave-in cannot be denied. My people are here in the snow before the elders' cave, homeless. I have seen many tears and much frustration since I awoke. I have seen people carefully doling out soup to make meat last. And I have seen the elders' cave, flung onto its side, resting in a gorge that was not in my memory, either.

It feels as if I closed my eyes and have woken to a strange new world, and it unsettles me.

Most unsettling of all?

The human females.

I can remember the first dvisti I killed, and the first time my father took me hunting. I remember my sister's birth and what a squalling, strange thing she was. I remember how my first taste of sah-sah burned the tongue. But I do not remember the humans.

I am told that they came to our world on a strange black cave, not unlike the elders' cave. That Vektal mated with the curly-haired one, and she brought him to the others. Now, everyone else in the tribe has mated with one. Several have young, and at all times, there is the sound of a kit wailing in distress.

And I am one of the ones that is mated.

The strangeness of it gnaws in my belly and makes me sick. Not that I am mated to a human, but that I cannot remember it at all. The humans have been here for three seasons—two bitter, one brutal. Long enough for the human that is "mine" to bear my kit. They are a welcome, happy part of the tribe.

How can I not know of this? How can my mind betray me so?

I scan the smaller forms huddled near the fire and see two humans talking. The one they say is my mate has a flat face with no bumps, a very tiny nose, and no horns. Her mane is a strange furry brown. Other than that, I remember nothing about her. Normally I recognize her amongst the tribe because she carries her kit—our kit—on her back in a strange pack. I do not see a human wearing that today, so I squint at the females by the fire. Not the small one—the other. It is Stay-see. The one that is my mate.

Was my mate.

She is pressing something between rocks and talking to the tiny one, who waves her hands and speaks angrily. They seem strange to me, with their pasty pale coloring, lack of horns, and small build. If I were to stand next to Stay-see, she would not come to my shoulder. She bends over to pick something up, and there is no tail, a sight I find unnerving.

The other female says something, and then they both look over at me.

I busy myself with my spear again, not wanting to be caught staring. I have tried talking to Stay-see a few times since I awoke in the healer's tent, but each time it goes badly. It always ends with her weeping and running away, and I do not wish that to-day. Perhaps her tears should upset me more than they do. They bother me, but only because when she cries, I feel confusion. I do not like to cause distress in another. I want to comfort her, but I have no words of comfort to give.

"Are you sure they will let you out of the camp with that, brother?" Salukh drops to the ground next to me, crossing his legs. He pulls out his favorite sharpening stone and his knife, and begins to scrape it. "If Mother sees it, I am sure she will come running."

I snort. My mother has been coddling me as if I were a fussy kit and not a grown hunter. "It is a spear. Surely they cannot stop me from making weapons if I am not allowed on the hunt."

"I suspect you will be allowed soon," my brother says. "All hands are needed to gather food." He scrapes his stone along his knife, unruffled. Salukh is always calm. Always possessed. He does not look as if worries over mates and the brutal season ever cross his mind, though I know he has a human mate now, too, and her belly is big with kit.

"I am tired of lying about, doing nothing. I am glad to be out of the furs."

"I am glad you are out, too." My brother gives his knife a long scrape and then offers the sharpener to me. "How is your head?"

I take it from him and run it along the sides of my spearhead, even though it is already sharp. "It does not hurt today."

"A good thing. And your memory?"

I shake my head. "Same."

"Mmm. It will return. How is Stay-see? Tee-fah-nee says she cries much."

I shrug, and the unhappy feeling returns to my gut. "We do not speak today. She is busy, and I have much to do."

My brother is silent. I know if I look over, I will see his look of disapproval.

I continue to sharpen the spearhead, and then add, "When I talk to her, it upsets her. I am trying not to distress her."

He grunts. After a moment, he adds, "She cares for you very much."

"I know." I do not offer more than that.

"And you remember nothing of your resonance?"

"Nothing." I hand him back the whetstone.

Salukh has a pitying look on his face. "Your khui was one of the first to sing to the humans. I remember being envious of your happiness. You smiled so much in those days, brother."

"Why are you telling me this?" There is an edge to my voice.

He puts a hand to my shoulder and squeezes it. "I am glad I did not lose you in the cave-in, but . . . I would like for you to smile again. Stay-see as well."

I flick his hand off my shoulder. It feels like judgment. Does he think I do not want to remember? A mate is the greatest thing a hunter can hope to acquire, and mine cannot look upon me without weeping. "You think I do not wish these things?"

Salukh sighs. "I know you do." He claps my shoulder again and then gets to his feet.

He leaves, and I am alone with my thoughts and a spear with a point so sharp and thin that it will likely shatter when thrown. I toss it aside in disgust. Just another thing I cannot seem to do right lately. Maybe I should do more. Talk to Stay-see and try to convince her to stop crying. Gaze at my son and see if his face stirs my memories.

I glance over at the fire again. Stay-see is gone, along with her friend.

Perhaps it is for the best. My mood is dark and I would just make her weep again.

Hassen and one of the yellow-haired human females return to the tribe that afternoon, speaking of a strange encampment in a new canyon. The area they describe is deep in metlak territory, which worries me, but it is large enough to house all of my people. I watch my chief as I eat my watery soup around the fire with the others. I have seen the worry on Vektal's face, and I know we are in danger. The cold tang of the brutal season is in the air, and we are in the open, in tents. The humans look frail and wear many furs, and they will not be able to withstand the chill of the brutal season. They must be sheltered.

Some are excited by the prospect of a new encampment, though I think we all worry that it is not protected like our cave. We gather near the fire, waiting for our chief to tell us what will happen. I glance over at Stay-see as I eat, but she is pointedly ignoring me, her focus on the kit in her arms. She lifts one side of her tunic and tucks him underneath to nurse, and I find myself curious what she looks like without her leathers.

Why do I not remember even that?

Vektal gets to his feet, gazing into the bonfire. The tribe hushes, the evening growing still. Everyone watches him, waiting.

"This has been a difficult time for us," he begins, voice grave. "Never have our people been cast out from their home by an earth-shake. We have lost everything we owned, our memories there, and even some of our tribesmates." He looks over at Warrek, whose eyes shine with tears. "Since that day, we have been searching for a new home. But the South Cave is gone. The elders' cave is unfit to live in. And Taushen, Raahosh, and Leezh have said that the great salt water is too high and covering the caves. We are low on options. We can split up for the brutal season and each family take a hunter cave."

I tense at the thought. Would I go with my father and mother, or would I go with Stay-see, who does not look at me? Who cries whenever I am near? The thought is worrying. I will care for her and the kit, of course, but I do not know how she will feel, and the brutal season is long.

"I have thought about this," Vektal continues, "and I do not feel it is the right way to go. We are strongest when we are together, and therefore, we must stay together. All of us. One kill can feed many mouths, and we ensure that all will be fed through the brutal season when we have many hunters to provide for the tribe. So, I will take two of my fastest hunters with me and we shall investigate Hassen's new place. We will make sure it is safe to bring our families to such a place, and then we will all go. It will not be an easy journey, but if it is as safe and peaceful as it sounds, it will be a good place to stay."

A low murmur sweeps through the tribe. I see several people nodding approval. I agree. The thought of spending the brutal season split from each other is a lonely one. Our tribe is close-knit. There is no way we would do well spread apart.

Raahosh speaks up. "It is a good plan. Let me go with you, my chief, to investigate this new place."

Vektal nods. "Hassen will guide us. It took him several days to journey there with Mah-dee, but with fast hunters, we can run for very long distances without tiring, and make it there and back quickly. I would like for Harrec to go as well. He is swift on his feet."

Eh? Harrec? I am twice as fast as he is. I jump up. "I wish to go, my chief. I am fast. You know I am." I also need to prove myself once more—not just to my tribe, but to my own mind. That I am not as broken as everyone thinks I am. Also, I want time away from Stay-see and her sad, accusing looks. I do not say this aloud, though.

It grows silent once more.

Vektal crosses his arms, frowning at me. "You are newly healed, Pashov."

"I feel fine." I do not look over at Stay-see. I cannot. But I must do something. I am restless and unhappy around camp. "Let Maylak put her hands on me. She will see I am well."

Vektal gazes at me for a long moment and then shakes his head. "You will stay. If the healer says you are well enough, you can hunt for the tribe."

I sit down again, frustrated.

At my side, Salukh nudges me. "Give yourself time, my brother. We will all be going there soon enough."

He is right. I do not like it, but he is right. I nod.

"We will leave in the morning," Vektal says. "Until then, pack everything you can. We will need sleds to carry our gear and for the pregnant females to ride upon when they get tired. Make no mistake, it will be a difficult journey, but I think we will find our home at the end of it."

Vektal's human mate breaks into a smile, showing her square white teeth. It makes me think of my human mate. I glance over at Stay-see. She is not smiling. Her gaze meets mine, and she stares at me long and hard, and then looks away.

It is almost like she knows I wanted to escape, and it fills me with guilt.

CHAPTER TWO

Stacy

TEN DAYS LATER

Of all days to be fussy, my little Pacy picked today. Moving day.

He's normally so good. He loves to hang out in his sling, he naps like a pro, and when it's feeding time, he's not picky. He's a good baby. He really is. But he *is* a baby, and he's prone to the occasional fit . . . and he seems to want to have one right now. He screams in my ear, banging a fist against my jaw as I hold him. Right now? He doesn't want to eat. He doesn't want to nap. He wants to crawl around and explore, but it isn't the time. Everyone's packing the last of their gear on sleds as we prepare to leave.

The hunting party checked out the new city, found it a good place to live, and has returned. So now, it's time to go. Everything's being bundled up and we set off today.

I'm trying to pack my tent while holding my child. My screamy, screamy child. And I love the little bugger with a fierceness and intensity, but right now, I wish someone would walk a little closer so I could pass him off. My sled is tiny compared to some of the others. Kemli and Borran are helping Farli pack, arguing about whether they can squeeze more furs onto their already laden sled. Georgie and Maylak are talking nearby and juggling their own kits while their mates prep their sleds. Two of the hunters are butchering a carcass as a last-minute meal, and in the distance, I see Raahosh hastily putting together another sled because, even though we're homeless, we already have too much crap. Ironic, that.

Theoretically, the supplies are a good thing. Even in a short time frame, we've managed to recover and remake a lot of our missing stuff. It helps to have the small things again, but when you have to carry them across the snow to a place god knows how many miles away? You start wishing you had less gear. And babies? Babies need so much gear. There's Pacy's favorite teething rings. His nappies. His *extra* nappies. The dishes that have the rounded edges. Cups. Blankets. Booties. More nappies. Hell, half my sled is his crap, and I'm pretty sure the other half is my tent.

Pacy screeches like he's in pain, yelling again.

"What, little man? You want into your sling?" I start to put him in there, but he only cries louder and waves his arms, indicating I should hold him. All right. I give up on packing for now and hold my son, who decides that I'm still holding him wrong and continues to wail in my ear. Heck, give me a few minutes and I'll probably be ready to start crying, too. We haven't even taken step one to the new campsite and I'm already mentally and physically exhausted. I don't know how I'm going to do this. I don't know what other choice I have.

"Do you need help?"

My heart thuds. One beat. Two beats. The blood races through my body, drowning out sound. I turn, and there he is, tall and strong and handsome, his appearance unchanged except for the fact that one of his horns is now broken off near the brow. My Pashov. My mate.

A stranger.

Nerves curl in my belly. Pacy grabs a handful of my hair and screams louder. I stand there like a doofus, not entirely sure what to do. I want to fling myself into Pashov's arms, but I know that won't be well received. I'm still a stranger, and the wary, cautious look he's giving me tells me that. It hurts to see. My Pashov would have made lighthearted jokes about my packing skills, and grabbed my ass while he did so. He was completely free and open, a bit of a rogue at times, but always knew that even when I laughed and smacked his hand away, I didn't mind.

That's not the person that stands before me. There's a question in his eyes, but that's it. No warm affection, no amusement. No teasing flirtiness with his mate.

"Hi," I say. I sound breathless, but the truth is that I'm so tense I don't know if I'm going to be able to do more than speak in monosyllables. Please remember me, I silently beg. Please. Remember who I am. Remember your son.

He gestures at the sled. "Do you need help packing?"

Oh. I nod, prying Pacy's hand free of my hair. "That would be wonderful, thank you."

Pashov kneels in the snow next to the sled, and his tail gives a little flick. He gets to work, tightening straps I didn't do a very good job with and straightening the gear. I watch him as he works, full of longing. There are so many things I want to say to him. That I miss him. That I'm hurting without him. That Pacy's cutting teeth and should have his first one poking through his little gums soon. That being a single parent is hard as heck and I'm struggling. But I wouldn't say any of that to a stranger, and I'm pretty sure I'm a stranger to him. So I just try to smile and rub Pacy's little back even as his tail thrashes against my arm.

Pashov works quietly, silent as he fixes the sled up. That's not like him, either. My mate's a cheery one. It must be me that's making him quiet, and of course, that just makes me feel lousy. Like I'm a problem. Like my baby is a problem. And okay, that's making me get all emotional again. I turn away . . .

And realize that people are staring.

Okay, it's a small tribe. We don't have TV, don't have books. Gossip is the order of the day, and I get that. But do they have to stare right now? Shouldn't everyone be busy with something else?

"Is this all?"

"Hmm?" I turn back to Pashov.

He gets to his feet, all graceful motion, and my mouth goes dry at the beauty of him. I thought I'd never see that again—never see his smile, his eyes crinkle at the corners when he's amused, never look at something as simply gorgeous as his big muscular body flexing as he moves. "Your sled is small. Is this all you have with you? Or is there more?"

I'm vaguely insulted by the question, even though I know it's asked innocently. "I lost everything in the cave-in. Just like everyone else."

"Yes, but . . ." He pauses, rubbing his jaw.

"But I have less than the others?" I guess, filling in the blanks. "I don't have anyone to hunt for me," I point out. No one's going to let me starve, of course. But the extras that come with living with a hunter—extra skins, bones for utensils, all the stuff that makes life here easier—haven't been coming my way. The mated hunters bring them home for their families. I'm sure if there were extras, they'd bring some to me. But that's the thing—right now, there are no extras. I'm not going without, I'm just . . . not as geared up as some of the others. And the unmated hunters haven't approached because a gift to me in my current state might come across as a courting gesture, and no one wants to do that.

He flinches as if I've hit him, and I immediately feel guilty. "Of course."

"I'm not saying it to be a jerk," I explain quickly. "But you asked."

"I . . . have not yet been cleared to hunt alone," Pashov says, words measured and careful. His gaze flicks from my face to Pacy, then back to me. "I did not realize I was to hunt for you. I should have guessed . . ." He trails off.

Great, and now I feel like an even bigger asshole. Of course he wouldn't think to hunt for us. Half the time he can't even remember us. My bitterness threatens to overwhelm me. I don't want to nag him, because if that's his only memory of me, that's terrible. But I'm hurt. So hurt. "You didn't know. Don't worry about it."

"But I should be looking after you, yes . . . ?"

Should he? I don't even know anymore. "It's not important. Really. And the small sled means I can drag it along behind me more easily—"

The look on his face is aghast. "You are going to drag your own sled?"

I snap at that. "Do you see anyone else that's going to do it for me?" I hold up Pacy. "Maybe our son?"

Pacy makes a high-pitched baby squeal and reaches out for Pashov.

Pashov, meanwhile, is frozen in place. I don't know if it's because I just lost my temper or because I'm holding a baby up in front of him that's half his. He looks over at me and then puts his hands out. "May I . . . hold him?"

Did I think my heart was done breaking? It's breaking all over again right now. "Of course."

I hand over Pacy and watch to see how Pashov holds him. Will it be with the casual effortlessness of a father accustomed to slinging his son onto his hip? Or will he hold him gingerly like he's never held a baby before?

As I watch, Pashov pulls the baby against his chest and studies him for a long moment, face solemn. Pacy, of course, is just thrilled at the familiar face and gurgles happily, smacking a little four-fingered hand against Pashov's chin. Pashov looks surprised and then laughs. "He is strong!"

"He is." My voice catches a little. "You always used to joke that he was going to wrestle Vektal for the chiefdom."

"Did I? It sounds like something I would say." He grins, a dimple flashing as he touches Pacy's little nose.

Seeing them together, I can't decide if I'm filled with joy or anguish. I should be able to tell the two apart, but they seem to be inexplicably intertwined nowadays. The smile on Pashov's face is pure delight, though, and I hold my breath, hoping that he's going to remember something. Anything.

"Why is his name Pay-see?" He trips over the syllables.

Just like that, my hope is extinguished again. "We've taken on the custom of mashing two names together. Part human, and part sa-khui."

He nods slowly and grabs Pacy's little hand in his own, gazing down at the four fingers there. "It is odd to see the elements combined."

"Odd? My son isn't odd. Your son isn't odd!" I reach forward and snatch my baby back out of his arms.

Pashov looks surprised at my reaction. "I only meant—"

I hug Pacy close. He wails and tries to push away from me, wanting to go back to his father. I don't blame him. I'm overreacting. Being a jerk. It's just that everything Pashov says feels like a dagger right to the freaking heart. "I know. I'm sorry. This is all very hard for me."

He nods slowly. "I will not bother you anymore. I am sorry."

I close my eyes and turn my back to him. Did he think he was bothering me? I'm going to fall asleep tonight dreaming of that smile when he held his son. I want to tell him that he's not bugging me, that I want him to stick around so we can talk and maybe get to comfortable ground somewhere in the middle. But the knot in my throat sticks, and it takes me a long moment before I can compose myself enough to speak.

But when I open my eyes and turn around, Pashov is gone. He's walked away with the others, my sled tugged along behind him. He doesn't want to hang around me, then, but he also won't forget his duty. I ache at the sight and wish I'd said something. That I want him to stay.

Perhaps when we stop for a rest tonight, I'll talk to him. I'll have all day to think of something to say that won't trigger defensiveness on either side. I just have to figure out what.

"Come on, let's get you bundled up and into your sling," I tell Pacy, pressing kisses to his tiny brow. This one, at least, I can shower with love.

Pashov

I grip the small sled I have taken from Stay-see and try to find a measure of calm. Up ahead, Vektal is waving us forward. The journey begins, and those with the heaviest sleds take up the lead. They will set the pace, and we will all stay together. Some of the unmated hunters move toward the back of our group, waiting to help out when necessary, and to protect us as we leave a trail wide enough for a blind metlak to follow.

And even though I am trying to calm my mind, I watch Stay-see. She moves forward, adjusting her hood. Her kit is on her back, strapped into the strange carrier. He is sleeping, his face little more than a blue circle surrounded by plush white dvisti fur. I watch her move, her steps strong and steady as she plunges ahead. She follows the rutted trail left behind by Vektal's sled at the forefront. She is moving fast now, but most of the other females are riding on the sleds of their mates. Leezh walks alongside her mate, but he carries their kit and hauls the sled. Jo-see chatters happily to her mate from her seat behind him, on their sled, and my brother Zennek is taking one last moment to tuck an extra fur blanket around his mate. The females are tended to and cared for. Of course they are. The walk will be a long one, and Stay-see will tire soon enough.

I feel another pang of guilt. Why did I not create a sled big enough to pull her along? Is it because she bites at me with her words and cries when I try to talk to her? Even so, I should have thought of this. I should have realized she would have no one to look out for her . . . except me.

When we stop, I will make a new sled, a bigger one, and I will let her ride for the rest of the way. She should not be forced to walk. I am strangely protective of her, even though she will likely get angry at me. I figure she will be angry at me either way. I might as well keep her rested. It will be a long journey, and longer still if she is exhausted.

My sister trots up beside me, a frown on her face. "Why are you back here?"

"Eh?" I watch the little creature bouncing around at her feet. I have no memories of it, either, though I am told that Salukh's mate tamed the dvisti kit and gave it to Farli. My sister spends more time with the animal than most of the tribe, and I find it strange to invite food to dwell in our encampment.

But lately I suppose I have found a great many things strange, with the large gaps in my memory.

"You are back here," Farli emphasizes. She nods in Stay-see's direction. "Should you not be there with her? Keeping her company?"

"I doubt she would like that," I tell her. I nod at the small pack on her shoulders. "Do you want me to take that?"

She shrugs and immediately dumps it on my sled with a grin. "If you are offering, I will take it. But you should still go to Stay-see's side."

Her pet bleats at me.

I grow irritated that everyone has opinions on what I should be doing with Stay-see. "You think I have not offered?"

"Oh, I think you offered." The look she gives me is far too clever. "But I do not think you are trying very hard to make her happy."

I bare my fangs at my sister, and she bounds away a step, laughing. "You do not know what you speak of."

"I bet I do."

My sister is full of spice this morning, and instead of being amusing, it is irritating. "Is that so?"

She shrugs her shoulders. "I am just saying . . . I remember how often you and Zennek and Salukh used to speak of mates. How jealous you were when Hemalo and Asha mated, and then Maylak and Kashrem. You wanted nothing more than to have a mate of your own." She raises a hand, gesturing ahead to where Stay-see plods behind Shorshie and Vektal. "There she is. Your mate. And ever since you woke up, you have stayed away."

"She has stayed away from me!"

"And your feet do not work?"

I growl low in my throat, growing angry. "I have been unwell—"

"Not so unwell you were not the first to volunteer to go with Vektal," she points out. "And you seem to be fine now, except for your memory."

"Stay-see does not wish me near."

"Of course she does. She is emotional. All of the humans are. Plus, she nearly lost you. And she has a small kit to think about. There has been much for her to worry over, and yet I see her alone constantly."

My sister's words shame me. Does she not understand that both Stay-see and I do not know how to go forward? "I do not know how to speak to her. I do not remember how we were, as mates. I look at her, and I remember nothing." It makes my chest ache just to think about it. "She is disappointed."

"She would be far more disappointed if you were dead," Farli says sharply. She bats at my arm. "Go talk to her."

I spoke to her earlier and she grew upset. "She does not want to talk."

"You are not trying."

Have I not? "It is a . . . strange situation."

"And you make it worse! You do not talk to her!"

"I am trying."

"Try harder."

Why is my young sister lecturing me on my relationship? What does she know of these things? "Leave it be, Farli."

She throws up her hands in a gesture that makes her seem very human, and storms away, the dvisti dancing at her heels.

My sister. I snort to myself. What does she know of mates anyhow? She is yet too young to even think of such things.

Everyone travels with speed and determination early in the day. By midday, when we stop for a break and a meal, several groups are straggling behind. Some of the heavier sleds are repacked and their goods redistributed amongst others, and the sled I am carrying nearly doubles in size because Kemli and Borran are growing tired and I do not wish them to struggle. By the time everyone begins to walk again, the enthusiasm is gone. Now, everyone is just tired. Now, the true hardship begins.

I hear a human female crying, complaining about exhaustion. Her mate soothes her, and her tears are quickly silenced. No fire is made, so meat is eaten raw. Some cry over that, too. I watch Stay-see, but she does not seem to have much of an appetite. She feeds her son, lingers near Jo-see and Shorshie, and then gets to her feet, stretching.

I watch her as she stands. She does not move like a sa-khui female does. Her movements do not have a hunter's grace. Her hips are, well, they are more rounded, her teats fuller. I watch them jiggle as she flexes one arm over her head, talking to Salukh's mate. I should not be staring at her teats. I should not.

Nor should my body be responding.

I force myself to look away. If I am to admire her body, I should remember it, should I not?

"Time to go again," Vektal calls out, moving toward his sled. "Make ready!"

Stay-see shrugs on her carrier, adjusting the straps over her shoulders. She tugs her cloak on tighter and begins to walk, but her steps are slower than before. I hesitate, then abandon my sled, jogging to her side. "Ho," I call. "Stay-see, wait."

She stops and turns to me. The look on her face is wary. "What is it?"

"You look . . . tired. I wish to help."

Her brows draw together. "Help?"

"I will carry your kit. Or let you sit on the sled as I pull it. Come."

The expression on her face is not friendly. Her eyes narrow. "*My* kit? He is yours, too."

I have made a mistake. "Of course."

She presses her fingers to her mouth and gives a deep, tired sigh. "I . . . actually I don't think I want to talk to you right now, Pashov. I'm sorry. Please leave me alone."

"But you are tired—"

She puts a hand up, pushing me away. "Not that tired. I'm fine. And I'm going to carry my son."

"Very well." I watch her storm away, pulling her fur wraps tight around her body. The low feeling in the pit of my belly is guilt, and I ignore it. It will do me no good right now. I march back to my sled and pick up the leather straps, tugging it forward. I will keep pace with Stay-see even if she does not want me around. It is the least I can do.

Time passes. The afternoon suns grow high in the sky and then disappear behind clouds. Stay-see walks on, but she is slowing down. First, she walked near Shorshie and Vektal. Then she was in the middle of the pack. Now, she hangs at the outskirts, and her steps grow slower all the time. I am careful to keep my sled a safe distance behind her so she does not feel like she is slowing me—or the tribe—down. But my steps have been growing smaller and smaller, and I have been pausing, waiting for her to catch up to the others. I am not tired. I can run all day. My arms ache from pulling the sled, but it is a good ache.

But Stay-see is exhausted. I watch her struggle, frustrated.

I am concentrating on her and do not notice when a figure rushes up to my side and bangs one large hand against my broken horn. It startles me so much that I fling myself to the side, only to topple over one of the handles of the sled and collapse on my back into the snow.

It grows deadly quiet. Someone gasps.

"Pashov!" Stay-see screams. She rushes forward, even as Harrec appears at my side, a sheepish look on his face.

"I am sorry," Harrec says, looking at the frantic human moving to my side. "I was not thinking clearly—"

I ignore him, because as I lie on my back in the snow, Stay-see leans over me. Her mane tumbles around her pale face, and she is suddenly . . . not so strange. Her flat features become appealing, and I remain still as she runs her hands over me, worried.

Well, most of me remains still. My cock responds to her touch, eager for a caress.

I suddenly realize that she is carrying my kit on her back. I have seen her carry him plenty of times, but it has never sunk in until now: We are mated. I am Pacy's father.

That means I have mated with a female and forgotten it.

This is terrible.

"I am fine," I murmur, my tongue feeling thick in my mouth. All of the blood in my body seems to have surged to my lower half. "I was merely startled."

She swipes at her face, and I can see her cheeks are damp. "Right. Fine." She jerks to her feet and huffs away, her kit wailing in his backpack.

My kit. My son.

My mate.

I am truly cursed if I cannot remember such things.

I watch her leave, and Harrec shakes his big hand in my face again. I grab it, haul myself to my feet, and then punch him in the shoulder. "You startled me, fool."

He just grins like the big idiot he is and taps my broken horn. "Losing this has thrown you off balance, has it?"

I shove him away, and he chuckles. I watch as Stay-see marches onward, fascinated by the sway of her hips. Harrec regards me and then turns to look in the direction she has gone. "You still do not remember, do you, friend?"

"I do not."

"What do you recall of the last few seasons?"

I shrug. "I do not feel as if I am missing anything. Clearly I am, but I cannot say what it is." My memories feel like a jumble. Certain ones are clear, and certain ones are hazy and distant. As a people, we dwell on the here and now, so it should not bother me.

But the fact that I cannot remember Stay-see or her touch? It bothers me. It bothers me very much.

"Do you remember that Asha and Hemalo have broken? That they no longer claim to be mates?"

"Eh?" I try to think about this, but my mind is blank. "They do not?"

"They have taken separate caves." He nods as if pleased. "I feel for Hemalo, but . . . perhaps Asha will return to her flirty ways. Remember how we used to stare longingly after her?" His mouth crooks into a smile. "She is not half so pleasant to be around, but she is female."

All of the hunters in the tribe once panted after Asha. I remember Harrec was wildly attracted to her, and yet she resonated to another. Perhaps Harrec, my friend, sees this as an opportunity. It feels distasteful to me. Hemalo is a friend to both of us, and even if he and Asha have split, in my mind they are still together. "Will you pursue her?"

Harrec shrugs. "In time, if no one else appears? I suppose I must." He bats a hand at my shoulder. "I have a secret hope that a new cave of humans will drop on our heads."

"Mm." I pick up the poles of my sled again and heft them. I check Stay-see, but she is still a fair distance ahead, her anger and worry over me having sped her steps.

"You watch her a lot," Harrec comments, smirking at me.

I look over at him, trying to figure out where he is going with this.

He nods at Stay-see. "Do you not remember?"

"None of it."

"You do not remember resonating?"

"No."

"Or the birth of your kit?"

"No." I am growing irritated at his questions. I have said I do not remember, have I not? What is he getting at?

Harrec makes a noise of agreement and is silent for a moment. Then he continues. "What about the foot and ball game we played last hawl-ee-deh?"

"I do not remember. I have said this."

"Or . . . the time you shared your mate with me? In the furs?"

I growl low and stop in my tracks, sudden fury sweeping over me.

Harrec stops, too. He raises his hands into the air, grinning. "It is a joke, friend. Merely a joke. I was testing you."

"It is not funny." Another hunter walks up and gives Harrec a push on the shoulders, indicating he should walk. It is Bek. "Your jokes are as poor as your hunting skills."

"At least I know how to joke," Harrec counters, and he looks wounded at Bek's criticism. "I am just trying to make my friend laugh again."

We start to walk, and it takes several steps before my blistering rage at Harrec's words begins to filter out of my thoughts.

Share.

My mate.

With him.

With another male.

My mate.

How long have I wanted a mate? A family? And to think of letting another male touch her? I know that three-pairings have happened in our tribe in the past, with two males agreeing to be the pleasure mate of the same female. I watch Stay-see as she walks, her back stiff, her hips swaying. I cannot imagine how it must have been to touch her.

But I know I would never share.

I tamp down the urge to fling myself at Harrec, horns first. I must not. He meant no harm. The last thing I need is another head wound. And still, the thought of him touching Stay-see fills me with possessive rage.

"Why do you move so slowly, Pashov?" Harrec asks after a few moments have passed. "We are falling behind the others."

Clearly he does not sense my foul mood. I watch Stay-see as she walks, a good distance ahead of me. If I catch up, she will march even faster, angry, and she is already exhausted. I do not wish to tire her more than she already is. "I have my reasons."

Bek sighs, the sound exasperated. "He is a fool, Harrec, just like you."

Eh? I glare over at Bek, who has not changed in the slightest. "Me, a fool? What do you know of this?"

"I know that you have a mate," Bek bites out. "And a kit. And you should be with her right now. Protecting her. Walking at her side."

"Let me handle this," I snarl at him. Is everyone going to harass me about my mate?

"You are pissing this away," Bek retorts, the look on his hard face cold. "You have a mate. A resonance mate. A kit. It is everything any hunter has ever wanted. She is your heart. You should not throw her away."

"Advice from you? What do you know of mates?" I scoff.

Bek's nostrils flare. He storms away.

Harrec coughs, though it seems as if he is trying to hold back a laugh.

"What?" I ask. Is there something no one is telling me? "Did Bek resonate and no one has told me?"

"No, he has not resonated," Harrec says. That is all he says, though. He grins at me. "I think I shall go talk to the chief, see how long we will be walking today. The humans are already growing slower by the moment." He jogs away, ever full of energy. I watch him, and my eyes narrow as he approaches Stay-see. He slows his steps and talks to her for a moment. I cannot see her expression, her face hidden by her large fur hood. Harrec glances back at me, grinning, and then continues forward, heading toward the front of the group.

Which is good, because now I do not need to throttle him.

I resume my steps, keeping my pace slow so I remain carefully behind Stay-see.

Still . . . was she pleased to have him talk to her? She has fallen behind all the other humans and walks alone. Would she enjoy company? Should I move to her side?

I decide that perhaps I should. I pick up my pace, watching

her as I surge forward. Her steps are always careful and measured, even though it is clear she is tired. She holds on to the straps on her pack, and as I approach, I can see Pacy's round face swathed with furs, his small mouth slack with sleep. A fierce surge of pride rushes through me. Strange that I should feel this way at the sight of a kit, sleeping.

Not just any kit, I remind myself. He is mine.

My sled bounces over an ice-covered rock, making a loud cracking noise. Stay-see turns, surprise on her face. "Everything all right?"

I move to her side, straightening my sled. It pulls to the left now, but nothing I cannot handle easily. "A little mistake, nothing more."

She nods slowly, then turns away, concentrating on the trail in front of her. A short distance ahead, there are a few of the heaviest sleds, Aehako dragging one behind him as he talks and laughs with his father. Farther up the snowy hills, more sleds and more fur-covered forms stagger along in a thin line. If this was a hunting party, our chief would be ashamed. But these are families, females, young children, and much more gear than any hunter could ever think to bring with him on a hunting run. The travel will not be the same.

My footsteps crunch in the snow, and it is the only sound other than the quick rasp of Stay-see's panting breaths. She is breathing heavy, I realize. This must be difficult for her. "Do you need to stop for a time? I will keep you company."

She turns to me, surprised. "What? No, I'm fine. I'm just . . . not used to all this physical labor." She pants between words. "I forgot I've been sitting in a cave for almost two years now. I'm out of shape."

"Your shape is appealing." I have been staring at it all afternoon.

It is a good shape, for all that she is small and human and solid in places the sa-khui females are not. I am still deciding if I like the differences, but I think I do. I am especially intrigued by her round, full teats.

Her face scrunches in a curious expression, and then she laughs, the sound breathless but pleasant. "Thanks, I think?"

I smile at her. This is good. We are talking. She is not upset. In fact, she laughed, and I feel the warmth of it down to the tip of my tail. I want to do more. I want her to say more, but she is struggling to keep her breath. "Shall I take Pacy and carry him? You seem tired."

"No, I'm all right. I don't want you to wear yourself out." Her smile is faint and apologetic as she looks over at me and the sled I'm dragging. "You're already carrying a lot of stuff."

And she thinks a tiny kit will somehow cause me to collapse in the snow? The idea is laughable. "I can carry him easily."

"So can I. And you need to heal."

My frustration begins to bubble over. Why will she not let me help her? "I do not need to heal. I am whole."

She stiffens, silent.

I realize I have spoken wrongly to her, again. In Stay-see's eyes, I am not whole.

I am not whole at all.

CHAPTER THREE

Stacy

In some part of my mind, I knew that the trek wasn't going to be, well, a cakewalk. Of course, it's a lot of walking, and the weather is crappy. But I didn't really stop to think about just how much walking it was going to be.

And this is only day one. God help me now.

I'm exhausted. I'm utterly drained, and my feet feel like wet blocks of ice. The wind—brisk and pleasant when it floats in from the cave entrance—is relentless out in the open. It feels like my face is scoured raw, and my lips feel tight and painful. My shoulders ache from where the straps on Pacy's carrier are cutting in through the warm layers of fur.

And this is only day one.

Day *one*.

How am I possibly going to last until we get to the new camp? How am I going to do this? I don't have a choice, though. So I put one foot in front of the other and try to think of happier things. Like chocolate bars and freshly baked cake with a buttercream frosting. Scrambled eggs. Pashov's hearty belly laugh when he's delighted.

But then that makes me hurt, and so I go back to thinking about food.

I'm daydreaming about a spinach and feta cheese frittata when I realize I'm about to run into Aehako's enormous sled. Kira's perched atop it, Kae in her lap. Kira smiles at me, and she looks so happy and refreshed, and here I am, sweaty and gross and exhausted . . .

And for a brief, uncharitable moment, I really want to punch her. Or someone. Anyone. Everyone who got to hitch a ride today and I had to hike with a fat infant strapped to my back.

Well, I amend, I didn't have to hike. Not exactly. Pashov would have pulled me on a sled. And probably tried to talk to me the whole time. And I'd probably have cried all day. And it would have been miserable.

But more miserable than walking? That's debatable right now.

"Are we stopping?" I wheeze. I want to put my hands on my knees—or just collapse, because collapsing sounds nice—but I've got a baby strapped to my back. So I just put my hands on my hips and try not to pass out. Two years sitting around a fire hasn't done me any favors at all.

"We are. Vektal put out the call a short time ago. They're going to build a fire, and we'll have some stew tonight." Kira gives me a look of concern. "You all right, Stace?"

I'm still busy catching my breath, so I give her a thumbs-up.

Suddenly, the weight on my back shifts, and I panic. Pacy gives a wail of surprise, interrupted out of his sleep, and in the next moment, I hear a low, firm "Shhh."

Pashov.

My heart hammers in my chest, and I force myself to remain

completely still as he pulls our son free of his carrier. "Do you have him?" I ask, breathless in so many ways.

"I do," Pashov says. "He is quite heavy."

"He's a big boy," I say, and it feels like a boulder has been lifted off my back. I feel so much lighter. Almost better, but I'm still exhausted. I want to collapse right here in the snow and sleep for a week.

Pashov moves to where I can see him, and the sight of him with Pacy tucked high against his shoulder makes my girl parts go pitter pat with longing. Does he remember? Has the hike jarred his mind?

But the smile he gives me is tentative, and I suppose I'm still hoping for too much.

"Thank you," I murmur.

He nods at Aehako, who is slightly sweaty from his day of hauling but still looks like he could go for miles longer. "Where will you set your tent?"

Aehako shields his brow and gazes up the hill. There's a cluster of people gathered together, I see, and between there and here, a few hunters are digging out a pit for a bonfire. "Here is fine. Kira?"

"This works for me," she agrees, and gives me a curious look. "Do you want to stay with us, Stace? I'm sure we can make room—"

"No need," Pashov says in a firm voice. "I will make a tent for Stay-see."

I'm just as surprised as everyone else. "You will?" A tent of my own? It seems like such a luxury after days and nights of bunking with other people. A moment later, I feel strangely vulnerable. Is he planning on sleeping with me? Is that why he's been determined to talk to me today?

I don't know if I'm hurt or amused. It's like the man I love more than anything is a stranger . . . and yet not. It's the most confusing thing I've ever experienced, and it's hurting my heart so very much.

Pashov nods at Pacy, swinging him around to make him laugh. "I will make a tent for you next to Aehako and his mate. I will sleep with Harrec and the other hunters." His expression darkens, and then he adds, "Not Harrec."

"Thank you," I tell him. I don't know if I'm disappointed that he's bailing out. It's probably for the best that he does.

I must be having a weak moment, though, because the thought of sleeping curled up next to my mate makes me want to weep. I want that again. Someday.

But it's clear that right now I am just a duty to him. Until we can be more—or his memory comes back—I need to keep him at arm's length.

The evening is a blur.

The bonfire is lovely and warm. People are piled up around it, laughing and talking and passing around bowls of warm soup. I nurse Pacy and just hold him quietly, stroking his rounded, sweet baby cheek. When I'm feeling jittery or antsy, just looking down at him sleeping calms my mind. I've been staring at my baby a lot lately, but I don't mind it. In his face, I see both Pashov and myself, and someone entirely new. I see a sweet little soul entirely dependent on me, and it both worries me and makes me that much more determined to keep him safe.

Someone pushes a bowl in my direction, and I sip the soup as I hold Pacy. There are several fussy babies by the fire tonight, but my Pacy is sleepy and content. Thank goodness. Poor Ariana looks ready to tear her hair out in frustration as Analay screams in her ear. I'm so exhausted it doesn't even fray my nerves. I just stroke Pacy's little face and make sure he's not panicking. As long as he's happy, I'm happy.

A warm blanket is tossed around my shoulders.

I look up, surprised out of my stupor to see Pashov. I don't know why I'm surprised, but I am.

"You were shivering," he says in a low voice, dropping in the snow to sit next to me. His gaze moves to Pacy, who is sleeping cradled against my breast. "Can I get you anything? Or Pacy? Tell me what you need and I shall find it for you."

I want my mate, I want to say, but even I know that's childish. He's trying right now, too. So it'd be bitchy of me to slap him down. "I'm fine, really." He has to be tired, too. I study his familiar face, suddenly worried. He was in his sickbed for so long that I thought I'd lose him. Even now he's not quite the same as before—his cheekbones are a bit more prominent, his eyes a little hollower. And I can't forget the missing horn . . . "Are you all right?"

He nods, gazing into the fire. "Today was a good journey. We did not make it as far as I expected, but I am not used to traveling with so much." He glances back over at me. "It is going to take many days for us to make it to the new place. You must save your strength."

What, does he think I'm deliberately trying to wear myself out? I'm just trying to freaking keep up. I bite back my sarcastic retort. We don't have the comfortableness between us that we used to, and I ache with missing it. With the old Pashov, I would have snarked back at him. But this man's a stranger, wearing my beloved mate's face. "I'll keep that in mind." I pull the fur tighter around my shoulders and deliberately stare into the fire.

He sits next to me for a moment longer and then leaps to his feet. "I will ready your tent."

I should say something back to him, but Pacy wakes up and smacks his sweet little mouth, looking up at me with glowing eyes, and I focus on him. I lift my tunic, snuggle him against my breast, and let him feed. It seems easier than talking to Pashov, when everything he says feels like it's carving my heart out.

I know he's trying. I know he is. But I also know that everything he says reminds me of the fact that I've lost my mate, and it hurts so much.

Sometimes I feel like my life ended when the cave-in happened.

I sigh at myself for being so dramatic. I've had it easy, really. I didn't suffer through the "week of hell" that the six original girls did when they landed here. I was in a tube. All I remember is waking up and seeing blue faces. And Pashov. My sweet, sweet Pashov. I've leaned on him ever since I got here. I've never had to do anything on my own, never had to be independent.

Maybe this is the universe telling me not to depend on one person too much, because everything can change in the blink of an eye. Maybe this is karma telling me to be a stronger person. Maybe it's fate shaking me out of my complacency.

But I don't want to be shaken out of it. I liked the way things were, damn it. Loved it, actually. I don't care that we don't have toilets or real frying pans or legit vegetables. Or eggs. That I'd lost my job that I loved in a little bakery. I had my mate and then my baby. That was all I needed.

Or so I'd thought. Because as it turns out, I need more.

I focus on hugging Pacy close. This will hurt less in time, I tell myself. It's just new right now, and raw. That's why it's so painful.

Time heals everything.

I must have fallen asleep by the fire, because I only have vague memories of the rest of the night. Of someone taking Pacy from my lap and helping me get to bed. Of wrapping me in blankets and tucking my baby's basket next to me.

When I wake up the next morning, it's to a strange clacking noise. I sit up, my head brushing against the roof of the small leather tent, and I realize that the clacking noise is my teeth.

It's absolutely freaking freezing.

My breath puffs in front of me, and there's ice crystalized on the corners of my mouth. I wipe it away, confused. It's still dark outside. Why is it still dark if it's morning? I push at one of the flaps at the front of the tent—

And snow cascades into the entrance. Faint light spills in, but not much. Ugh. I shudder, scooting to the back of the tent. I'm shivering despite the fact that I'm rolled in blankets. It's wickedly cold, and I remember that the brutal season is almost here. Last year, it barely bothered me because I didn't leave the cave much. I guess I get to experience it in all its glory this year.

Lucky, lucky me.

I pull my furs tighter around my body and check on Pacy. He's sleeping peacefully, even though his diaper stinks to high heaven. The cold doesn't bother him nearly as much as it does me, because he's half sa-khui. More than half, really. He's the same dusky blue as Pashov, has knobby little horns and a flippy tail. Most all that he's gotten from me are extra fingers and the little dimple in his chin. He's sucking on his fingers right now as he sleeps, oblivious to the fact that it's positively Arctic. Or Antarctic. Whichever is colder.

I eye my little tent. It must be new, because I don't remember having one. I touch the interior wall and find it's the soft leather hide of a dvisti, probably waterproofed in the last two weeks of frantic leathermaking. Did Pashov make it for me? If so, when? Or is this just borrowed from another family and I'm reading too much into things?

Probably. Still warms me a little, though.

I dress in as many layers of furs as I can squeeze on, and I'm still cold. Shivering, I nurse Pacy quickly, wrap him in double blankets, and then emerge from my tiny tent.

Snow is falling thick and heavy, the pale twin suns completely obscured by cloud cover. It's not a blizzard, not quite. But it is going to make traveling a bitch. Snow is piled high around the front of my tent, and I realize as I stagger out that it must have snowed several feet overnight. Just walking is a challenge.

"Ho," calls someone, and then Pashov is right there, taking Pacy in his arms and offering me a hand. "Can you walk?"

"I don't know," I admit, staggering through the hip-high snow. My heart's fluttering at the sight of him, and I'm feeling schoolgirlishly giddy that he seemed to be waiting for me. "I see we got a bit of weather overnight."

"This is but the beginning," he says, and sounds cheerful over it. Crazy man.

The landscape is completely changed, thick white powder blanketing everything. There's a small fire built and a group of humans huddle close to it to warm up. I join them, and we sip hot tea and chew on dried meat to try and breakfast before the day's travel begins. I eat slowly, taking time with each bite. Not because it tastes good—it doesn't—but because I'm dreading the thought of walking today.

Eventually, my tea gets cold, no matter how I wish it wouldn't, and people start to get up. Vektal comes to the group to retrieve

Georgie, and he's full of energy. The snow and cold aren't bothering him or the other sa-khui. For a moment, I'm bitterly jealous of his immunity to the chill. It seems unfair that even with a cootie in my breast, I should be so darn cold.

"Let us put the fire out," Vektal says to our small group. "Finish your meals, and then we must go. This nice weather will not hold up for long."

"Nice weather?" Josie chokes out.

"A storm will be rolling in soon," Hemalo offers, pointing at the sky. "Look at how dark the clouds are."

A chorus of female groans meets his comment.

I get to my feet slowly. Everything aches and feels knotted up, and the prospect of more foul weather makes me want to scream. I settle Pacy on my hip and turn toward my tent, only to find that it's gone.

In its place is a much larger sled, with Pashov securing a large leather cover over its contents.

I struggle to wade through the snow over to his side. "Is my tent gone?"

He turns and looks at me, then rushes over to grab Pacy from my arms. "I packed it for you."

"You did?"

Pashov casually tucks Pacy against him and grins at me. "Of course. I made it for you. I will pack it up for you." He grabs Pacy's waving little hand and gives it a small shake. "How is this little one today?"

"He's great." I'm a little wary of Pashov's mood . . . but pleased. In this moment, he feels so much like his old self that it's making me ache. "His mommy is struggling, though."

Pashov immediately turns, surprised. He moves to my side, wading through the deep snow as if it is nothing. "What is it?"

I shake my head, sorry I complained. "Cold. It's all right. I just need to adjust."

He gestures over at the sled he's packing. "I have more furs—"

"I'll be fine once I start walking."

He turns back to me, surprised. "You wish to walk today?"

Huh? "Um, I can't stay here."

"I thought I would pull you on the sled. Like others are pulling their mates." His voice is almost bashful. Is that a hint of a dark blush spreading on his blue cheeks?

Is my mate . . . shy?

I can't help but be startled. It's never occurred to me that because he's missing huge gaps in his memory, he won't know how to act around me. It's always been about me and how wounded I am.

Oh my god. I'm realizing that I'm a huge jerk. He's trying, isn't he? He's trying to figure out how he fits into this, and I'm making it difficult. I didn't realize. "I don't want to be a burden," I whisper.

"You? You are light and airy, like Pacy. You weigh no more than a spindly scythe-beak," he scoffs.

I raise an eyebrow at that. I'm pretty sure that amongst most humans I'd be labeled as "solid," and that hasn't changed after giving birth. But if he wants to think that, he can. "Your sled grew overnight."

"I realized I could carry more." He extends a hand to me. "And I made room for my mate, as I should have yesterday."

I slowly put my hand in his. "If you're sure you don't mind . . ."

"It would give me great pleasure." His eyes gleam as if the thought of hauling my weight on top of a supersized sled is indeed the most exciting thing he's thought about all dang day.

"Well, you don't have to twist my arm."

Pashov gives a little shake, and then his expression is aghast. "Twist your arm? Is that what humans do?"

I don't know whether to laugh or cry. "You don't remember anything about humans, do you?"

Some of the brightness dulls in his eyes. "I am relearning what I can."

"I know. And thank you."

Pashov

This is what I need, I realize, as Stay-see gives me a tentative smile. My mate's happiness. It feels as if something shifts into place inside my mind. This is what I am meant to do. This is my mate. It is my job not only to care for her, but to make her happy. And I have been doing a poor job of it lately.

That is changing as of now.

I eagerly help her atop the sled. I have packed it carefully so that the softest furs are stacked on top, and there is a small nest at the front of the sled where she can curl up and relax while I pull her. She sits down, and I can see the surprise on her face when she pulls her legs under her. "This is really comfortable."

"I am glad." I pull out one of the thickest furs and tuck it on her lap, juggling my son in my other arm. "Will this do? Should I change anything? Repack anything?"

"No, this is fine. Really." She smooths the blanket over her legs and then reaches for the kit. "Are you sure it won't be too much for you to pull?"

"Not at all. I am strong. Very strong."

"You are also still recovering." Her voice is mild with rebuke, but there is a smile on her face.

I am fascinated by that small curve of her mouth. Her lips look so soft. So pink. My cock rises in my breeches, responding to her pleasure, and I force myself to remain busy until it calms once more. There's a low rumble in my chest that I don't recognize at first.

It's resonance.

I rub my chest, surprised. I should not be. Of course I am resonating to her. She is my mate, and even now, my kit is in her lap. I hear a soft sound and realize that she is singing back to me, her khui responding to mine. I remain still, waiting for the unbearable need to sweep through me. For the song to become so consuming that I have no choice but to respond.

Instead, it is just . . . pleasant. It is a remnant of past resonance, a resonance that has been erased from my mind.

I am disappointed.

I should not be, but resonance is one of the rare gifts of life, and to have experienced it and forgotten it feels like a loss. Is this how Stay-see feels every time she looks at me? Like she has lost something enormous? I want to hug her and comfort her at the realization. But I do not. I just tuck the blankets tighter around her body and chuck my son's cheek. "Ready to go?"

"I think so." Her voice is soft. Shy. There's a vibrating in her throat coming from the resonance between us, and it makes her sound different. I like it.

I like a great many things about Stay-see, even her odd little face. I pull her hood down to protect her head and then turn around to grab the poles of my sled. I test the heft of the sled and then begin to pull it along. Her weight on the sled is slight, unnoticeable. I am pleased that I am able to make the journey easier for her. "Speak if you need me to stop," I call over my shoulder.

"Are you sure this is okay?" She sounds worried. "I can walk."

I turn my head and mock growl at her. "You will not walk."

A giggle escapes her, and it is the sweetest sound I have ever heard. I need to make her laugh more often.

I keep the sled to the edge of the group, near the back with Aehako and his enormous sled, and the hunters who guard the rear and watch for stragglers. It is not that my load is too heavy, but rather that I prefer to be back here, on the fringes.

It feels almost as if I have Stay-see to myself this way.

We talk back and forth through the morning, about small things. We talk of the weather and the snow. We talk of the tooth Pacy has cutting through his little blue gums. We talk of my mother and father, and my sister, Farli. We talk of my brothers Zennek and Salukh, and Stay-see tells me all about their mates and Mar-layn's kit. How Salukh courted Tee-fah-nee and she is now rounded with child. How Zennek and Mar-layn resonated mere days after us, but Mar-layn gave birth to her little Zalene nearly two hands of days prior to Pacy's birth. Of the fact that two of the humans—Mah-dee and Li-lah—were not with them at all, but had come in another one of the spays-ship caves. Of how Hassen stole one sister away, only to end up taking the other as a pleasure mate and then resonating to her days later. There is much to talk about, but we keep the conversation on others and not on our situation.

It is easier that way.

As we travel, snow continues to pour from the skies, and the day remains cold and dark. The kit fusses, and she nurses him off and on. He grows more irritable as the day goes on, and I can tell Stay-see grows tired. How she can carry him all day and not grow frustrated shows me how patient she is. My mother would happily take him for a few hours, and I make a mental note to ask her about it tomorrow. Perhaps I can give Stay-see time to take a nap during the day while we travel. I am lost in thought for a time, trying to figure out a way to bring my mother or my sister back to us so Pacy can—

"Pashov!" Stay-see's voice is full of terror.

I halt, dropping the sled handles into the snow, and turn around. "What? What is it?"

Stay-see presses a hand to her chest, her face as white as the bone handles of the sled. "D-do we have to s-stay so close to the cliff?"

Eh? I look over to the side. We are skirting a low, narrow valley where the snow will be thicker. Instead of going through it, we are moving along the cliff's edges. I am following the others as they leave a trail, and we naturally walk where the snow is less deep, usually along the top of a sloping hill. "You are safe, Stay-see. I will not let you fall."

She bites her lip, and I am surprised to see her mouth is the same color as her square little teeth. All of the cheery pinkness is gone from her small face. "I'm scared," she whispers.

I try not to frown with worry. "You wish me to go into the valley? It is dangerous in this weather."

"I . . . no, I guess not." She is breathing quickly. Her eyes flick back and forth, and I realize she is panicking. "It's just . . . do we have to be so high?"

Pacy wails, pulling at her braid, his little face screwing up with frustration. I know she is not herself when she raises a trembling hand to her mouth, and she keeps looking over at the valley below.

"Stay-see," I say, my voice calm. "I will not let you and Pacy fall. This I promise."

"I know. I just. I can't. High. Really high." Her words are quick and pulsing, her movements twitchy. I begin to worry that she will lose her grip on Pacy, who is already squirming. I pluck him from her lap, and his wet leathers slap against my arm. "He needs changing."

"Yes. Of course." She blinks rapidly, but her face is still bone-white. She cannot stop staring at the valley below.

I must get her away from this. "Stay-see." I keep my voice calm. Is her fear of heights something I have forgotten? Am I a terrible mate because I am torturing her by bringing her this high? I eye the cliff, but this path is the best one, already rutted with the sleds that have gone before us. It will be quickest if I continue forward instead of taking her to fresh snow. "I am going to change Pacy's leathers," I tell her. "And then I am going to carry him for a while. You must calm down."

"I'm calm," she snaps, and sounds anything but. Her trembling hand goes to her brow. "I'm sorry. I'm trying to be calm. I know it's stupid. I just—"

"No," I tell her. Greatly daring, I reach out and brush my knuckles over her cheek. Her face is ice cold, but she looks up at me with big, glowing eyes and a frightened expression that makes my heart ache. "It is not stupid. You are frightened, but I am here. I will not let you fall."

Her hand brushes over mine, and she rubs her cheek against my hand. I feel a surge move through my body—protective, possessive, and full of need. "I trust you," she whispers.

I gaze down into her eyes and feel a connection to her. Something deep inside—

"Why have you stopped moving?" Bek bellows, storming up to the side of our sled. He moves along the edge of the cliff, and plants his hands on the side of my sled. Stay-see jerks away with a whimper, and the moment is lost.

I want to snarl at Bek, but my anger at him will not bring the connection with Stay-see back. It is gone. "We need a moment."

"Why? We are traveling. You can have many moments when we stop for the night." Bek raises a spear, gesturing at the caravan of sleds far ahead of us. "You will lose sight of the group if you go any slower."

"We need a moment," I repeat, a low growl rumbling in my throat. I adjust my son on my arm. "Unless you wish to change my son's leathers for him?"

Bek gives a constipated frown, then glares at me. "I do not think so."

I flick a hand at him. "Then go on. We will move again soon."

He snorts and mutters something under his breath, storming forward.

I toss my light shoulder wrap onto the snow and set my son down on it. He makes a burbling sound and raises his hands into the air, reaching for me. His tail flicks wildly back and forth, and there's a bright, gummy smile on his face that makes me laugh with sheer joy. When he makes that face, he looks like Farli did when she was young. Does he look like me? I touch his small features. I have never seen my own face, but I must look somewhat like my sister.

His legs wiggle in the air and I peel one corner of his leather breeches off. It is hot and wet, and a horrible stench rises.

"Faugh!" I bury my nose in the crook of my elbow, trying to protect it from the smell. "Is he sick?"

Stay-see gives a small laugh—still fragile, but sounding more like herself. "No, he's just a baby."

"Does his dung always smell so foul?" I return the scrap of leather to its place at his belly in an attempt to cut the stench.

"Not always." After a moment, she adds, "But a lot of the time, yes."

I glance over at her. She's lying down on the sled, and the hood is pulled over her face. Maybe she feels better now that she cannot see the cliffs. Good. I will fix the problem of my son's leathers, and I will carry him so she can relax for a time. "What do I do with the dirty one? I have never changed a kit's leathers . . . or if I have, I do not remember."

"You have," she says, and her voice is so soft. "But I can walk you through it."

For some reason, I feel sad. It is just leathers . . . I look down into my son's happy face as he waves his arms and legs. And I wonder what else it is I have missed.

CHAPTER FOUR
Stacy

Today makes my heart hurt so much. For a little while, it was almost like having my Pashov back. Not the Pashov with the single horn and the confused smile on his face when he changes diapers. For a brief, shining moment, we felt like husband and wife. Or mate and mate, I suppose. Like nothing had ever come between us.

But something always comes along to burst that bubble.

I hear a happy giggle and peer out from under the hood of my fur wraps. I've been keeping my head down and my eyes closed ever since we started traveling along the cliffs. I'd forgotten—safe and cozy in the tribal cave—that this land is nothing but peaks and valleys and snow as far as the eye can see. There's not a lot of flat surface, and I've got a killer fear of heights, which means that when it gets rockier, I get freaked out. I want to go down low, where it feels safer to me, but Pashov says it's not as safe or fast to travel there, and I trust him.

I don't like the answer, but I trust him.

I glance out and see Pacy wiggling in his sling, strapped on

Pashov's big, broad shoulders. Pacy's small hands are waving in the air, and he's laughing that happy, careless baby giggle that just makes you feel good all over to hear it. I don't see what he's laughing at, though. Then, a moment later, a long strand of leather with one of Pashov's decorative feathers comes flying over his shoulder. Pacy gives another shrill giggle of delight and tries to grab it as Pashov pulls it slowly back. He's rigged his sled to where both handles are strapped across a chest harness and it leaves him one hand free. I guess he's using it to tease Pacy with a feather toy. It reminds me of someone playing with a cat, and I smile. I've never thought to entertain my baby while he's on my back. He's going to be spoiled, but I can't find it in my heart to chide Pashov.

For a man that doesn't have any memories of his son, he's really, really good with him.

I look out at the sky, but the snow's still coming down in thick, heavy flakes. They're so big they're practically cornflake-sized . . . and now I'm hungry for a bowl of cornflakes and some warm milk. Sigh. I know that's a pipe dream, but right now I'd settle for it to stop snowing. The world looks like one big gray-and-white blur, and the wind is picking up. My face feels hot and windburned under the cloak, and I'm sure it's just going to get worse as we continue on. Nothing to do about it but suck it up, I suppose. "Is it almost time to stop?" I call out. I'm exhausted, and all I've done is ride all day.

"Not quite yet," Pashov calls over his shoulder. "If you are yet tired, sleep longer. We have another valley to cross soon."

Which means more walking along the ridge instead of in the valley itself. Eek. The thought makes me anxious as hell, but there's nothing I can do. The sa-khui know the safest route of travel and are familiar with these lands. If it's safer walking along a cliff instead of in a valley, I'll take their word for it. And it's not like I plan on ever making this journey again.

I just have to stick it out. I bury my head back under the blankets and hope I can fall asleep.

Seems like I must be pretty tired, because I do fall asleep. Right away.

When I wake up later, it's bitterly cold and dark. Pacy isn't crying, and I'm still exhausted despite riding around all day like a queen on her chariot. I sit up on the sled, peering around in the darkness. "Pashov?"

"I am here," he says, and footsteps crunch in the snow before a warm hand touches mine. "Your tent is ready."

"Where is the bonfire? Where is Pacy?" My breasts feel heavy with milk, and I resist the urge to put a hand on them as I yawn. "God, why am I so tired?"

"It is a taxing journey," he says, and his hand goes under my thighs, his arm around my back, and then I'm being lifted into the air as if I weigh nothing. "Pacy is asleep. My mother fed him a mash while you slept, though he will probably be hungry in a short time. And there is no bonfire tonight. The weather is too bad."

"Oh." I huddle closer to his chest, because it's petrifyingly freezing out here in the wind. "That sucks. I'm freezing."

"I will stay with you tonight," Pashov says in a low voice, and I feel his body bob and move as we duck into the tent.

"You don't have to," I begin to protest, but it's not much warmer in here. The furs are spread on the snow, and as he sets me down, I begin shivering all over again.

"Yes, I do," he says. He picks Pacy up out of his basket and hands him to me.

I take my baby, but he's fast asleep, his body a heavy, solid weight. He doesn't wake up even when being shifted, so he must not be hungry. I lie down and settle him next to me.

A moment later the tent flap closes and the wind becomes muffled. I can hear nothing but the sound of my own breathing. Pashov shifts in the darkness, and I feel his big body move onto the furs next to me. Not too close, but close enough that I can feel the warmth radiating from his skin. "Are you hungry?" he murmurs. "I have some rations—"

"Not hungry. Just tired."

"Then sleep. Everything is taken care of."

I lie down. In the darkness, I can feel the blankets shift. Pashov's body brushes against my arm, and I realize he's lying down on the other side of Pacy. It's almost like we're a family again, and I'm hit with a bolt of such intense longing.

Please get your memory back soon, Pashov, I pray silently.

The wind picks up in the middle of the night, the walls of the tent shaking. The temperature drops again, and even with Pashov's big body providing heat, it's still chilly. Pacy wakes up to feed, but then goes back to sleep, completely unaffected by the wintry storms.

Me? I feel like a Popsicle. And I'm drawn impossibly to all that heat. I tuck Pacy into his basket at the head of the bed, and slide a little closer to Pashov under the covers.

His arms go around me, and he pulls me against him. I'm enveloped in warmth, and his skin is touching mine, and it feels so good that I want to cry. My eyes well up, but I work on composing myself. The last thing I want to do is freak him out. It takes several minutes before my eyes stop pricking and the knot in my throat recedes enough that I can relax. I've missed my mate so much.

Here I keep thinking I'm being strong, and all it takes is a brush of his skin against mine to make me collapse again.

I rest my head in the crook of his arm, and my hand goes to his chest. He's shirtless. I shouldn't be surprised. Even the worst of the weather seems to roll right off of the sa-khui and their velvety blue skin. I should pick my hand up and keep it to myself. I tell myself this, but I can't quite seem to lift my fingers. He's so warm, and familiar, and I'm hit by a wave of arousal.

Oh boy.

It's been weeks since Pashov and I last had sex. Weeks since I've felt the touch of my mate. My body's craving him, hungry for his touch. For affection. For love. For connection. And so, even though I know I shouldn't, I trace my fingertips lightly over his stomach muscles. One of my favorite things to do when we're in bed is just to touch him. To feel the differences between his skin and mine. To explore every hard muscle with my fingers and get to know every intimate inch of him. Even when I was a jillion months pregnant with Pacy and completely uninterested in sex because I was so uncomfortable, we'd lie in bed for hours and just touch. His fingers would move over my skin, caressing me, and I would explore him with my hands, and we'd talk.

We've always been a handsy couple. That hasn't changed since the day we met. After the first time we had sex, Pashov grabbed my ass and jiggled it with one big hand. "No tail," he'd said, as if both awed and surprised by this fact. And I had laughed, because it seemed such a ridiculous thing to say. Of course humans don't have a tail.

That little ritual has continued for us. He always grabs my butt and jokes about my lack of a tail. He says it's because he likes to make me laugh. It's just a silly, corny moment between mates, but god, I have missed it so stinking much.

For now, though, I'll take the touching.

"Is this okay?" I ask as I trace my fingers along his ribs. I can feel they're a bit more prominent than they were in the past, but I know that's because he was sick. He's better now, and other than the horn, there are only small changes left behind.

In response, his hand covers mine. His thumb strokes over the back of my hand, and it's such an easy, affectionate gesture that I'm lost. This is my mate, isn't it? That's how Pashov always comforts me, with caresses. Touches. Simply grounding me with a caress of his hand.

In that moment, I really, really want sex. My khui fires up in my chest, thrumming. I can feel the need spreading all through my body. This isn't resonance; this is just me responding to my mate, his nearness, my need.

So I stroke my hand over his chest, gliding over one of his nipples to see how he'll react. He immediately pulls me tighter against him, nuzzling at my hair. My mate. My love. "Touch me?"

He groans low in his throat, the sound nearly muffled by the howling wind, and then he's pushing me onto my back, tearing at my leathers. Yes! I want this! I undo the tie at the front of my tunic, letting it fall completely open.

His hands are immediately on my breasts, caressing my skin and rubbing over my nipple.

I whimper, because they're extremely sensitive, especially while nursing. I can feel a bit of milk dribbling down each breast, but in the next moment, his mouth is there, lapping at the nipple, and I don't even care. I grab a handful of his hair and hold him to my breasts, so aroused and wild that my hips are arching up from the furs.

Pashov's mouth is everywhere, nipping at my breasts, his tongue moving over my nipples, licking at the valley between them. There's no subtlety in either of us, just need.

He licks lower, moving down my belly. It's a little jiggly post-baby, and covered in stretch marks, but it also doesn't matter. He flicks his tongue at my navel, then tugs at my leggings, hauling them down my hips.

I try to help out, wiggling, lifting my butt into the air to free the leathers when he pulls down on them, and I kick them off. Almost feels like a stupid move because it's so damn cold, but in the next moment, Pashov slides his big body down, and his arms cover my hips and thighs. He pushes them apart, moves even farther down in the tent, and then buries his face between my legs.

A sobbing gasp escapes me. "Yes!"

He growls low in his throat, and his hands tighten on my hips. He licks my folds, exploring me with his tongue, and the broken shaft of his horn jabs against my thigh. I don't even care. I just want him to keep licking. He moves all over, his tongue with all those fantastic ridges dragging up and down my pussy. It's like he's deliberately avoiding my clit to make me crazy, and when he starts to lick my core again, I get impatient and slip a hand to my clit, desperate to get off. He gives a possessive growl and bats my hand away, and in the next moment, his mouth and tongue are there, licking and sucking at that tiny bit of flesh.

And oh god, this is exactly what I needed.

My toes curl, and I cry out. He makes another growling sound and redoubles his efforts, until I'm writhing and squirming on the blankets. The pattern of his mouth is impossible to figure out, and just when I think he's about to speed up and push me over the edge, he changes tactics and begins soft, slow licks that make me even crazier. Frantic to come, I try to push his mouth aside so I can touch my clit myself, but he growls and shoves my hand away again. God, that should not be nearly as hot as it is. He's so . . . possessive of my pussy.

He licks me with renewed enthusiasm, and then it's just too much. I've gone too long without release, and it's all built up in my system. The moment he pushes a big fingertip against my core, my entire body jerks, and I come. I come so fast and so hard that I cry out, startling Pacy awake.

Pashov doesn't even lift his head, just keeps licking and tonguing me, lapping up every last drop of juice between my thighs. And I keep coming like a freight train, my entire body trembling.

Pacy hiccups in his basket, then is silent, and I bite down on one of the leather blankets, trying to muffle my whimper as another fierce ripple of pleasure surges through me. Oh my god, he won't stop licking. He just keeps going on and on. My eyes roll back in my head, and he just grips my hips tighter, going in for another round. I'm going to be unable to stand in the morning if he keeps this up. I tap his shoulder, and when that doesn't get his attention, I yank on his good horn.

He lifts his head, bright blue eyes glowing in the darkness. "Mine," he says thickly.

I shiver at how ferocious he is. "Want you," I pant. "Inside me."

Pashov moves over me, his big body settling over mine, and I eagerly wrap my legs around his hips. His tail lashes against my leg like a mad thing, and it just makes me even more riled up. He braces his hands next to my shoulders and looks up at Pacy's basket. "The kit—"

I shake my head, pressing a finger to his lips. "Back to sleep,"

I whisper. No second crying after the first initial noise means he's fine.

Pashov nods and touches my face. For a moment I think he's going to kiss me, but instead, he bends his head and shifts his hips. The head of his cock pushes against my entrance, and I cant my hips to welcome him. It's been far too long since I've been filled. Pashov thrusts into me, so hard that my body jolts across the blankets, but it feels incredible. I can feel every inch of him seated deep inside me, his spur rubbing in that maddening way against my clit.

I wrap my arms tightly around him and nod, encouraging him to go on. He thrusts again and then is pumping into me, fast and furious and so good that I'm biting down on my lip because I know I'm going to start crying out again. Another orgasm is about to blast its way through me, thanks to his spur, and I decide not to fight it. I just let go and totally give in, losing myself to the moment. One endless orgasm crashes into another, and I'm barely aware of Pashov straining over me.

He comes in the next moment, and I'm surprised by how quickly he gets his release. It's all right, though. Right now it's all about connecting again. And I've come so many times, so fast and so hard, that I don't mind that he got his in a flash.

Pashov collapses on top of me, all sweaty, velvety skin, and I cling to him with arms and legs, desperate to keep every inch of our skin touching. I need this. I need my mate's touch. I'm worn-out, exhausted, but this is the best I've felt in weeks. And a happy, sated little smile curves my mouth when he rolls onto his side and pulls me along with him, letting my smaller body sprawl over his chest.

Now, it'll come, I think drowsily. He'll remember that he always grabs my ass right about now. No tail, he'll say, and spend the next half hour petting and stroking my butt like it's something special.

But he doesn't.

He touches my hair, panting, and seems content to let me lie on top of him.

And as one moment ticks into the next, my skin prickles with just how . . . different this is. This isn't our normal MO. At all. Pashov and I, we have a ritual. We're not the most inventive or imaginative, and I like it that way. I like it that my mate kisses me for what feels like hours before he moves on to my breasts, and then licks my pussy before penetration. It's like he's going down a menu, and I enjoy that.

Except tonight . . . he didn't kiss me. At all.

And he's still not grabbing my butt. His hand rests at my waist.

My heart hurts all over again.

I can't help it. I start to cry. At first it's just a sniffle, but as one moment passes, and another, I feel more alone.

I feel . . . like I cheated on my mate.

Which is so stupid, but this wasn't my Pashov. This wasn't my kiss-hungry, loving, silly, and grabby-handed mate. This was a stranger wearing his face, and I slept with him because I miss my mate so fucking much.

"Stay-see?" His hand moves against my waist, and I can hear the question in his voice. "Are you . . . well?"

Am I well? I press a hand to my mouth, trying to stifle my sobs because I don't want to wake Pacy up. I want to push off of Pashov and retreat to the far side of the tent. I want to bury my face in his chest and let him stroke my hair and tell me everything's going to be all right. "I wish you could remember," I choke out. "Something. Anything. About how it used to be with us."

I feel him suck in a breath. "Me as well. I would give anything to remember."

And that somehow makes it worse.

Pashov

The greatest moment of my life is followed by my lowest.

Being inside my mate? Sharing pleasure with her and feeling the sated release that comes with mating? The low thrum of my khui in my chest? The feel of Stay-see's small human form resting on top of me? I feel like the strongest male in the world.

It all means nothing when she begins to cry.

Her shoulders shake with weeping, and even though I ask what is wrong, she can't speak between her sobs. Only *I wish you could remember.*

To her, I am still a stranger. This is why she cries. She misses her mate. And I feel . . . like half of a person. For the first time since I woke up and was told the strange news that two turns of the seasons had passed and I had forgotten them, I feel like I am missing. Missing something big.

Before now, it was just strange. To look at Stay-see's odd human face and try to fit it into my memories was a game. Pacy? My son? Interesting, but I did not feel strain or worry when I did not remember him. It was just an oddity. It would come back in time. Nothing to worry over.

But now? I worry.

Now, I feel like less. I have mated with her wrong, and she realizes it.

I have mated *wrong.*

I have no memories of mating before this. How can I have forgotten something that feels so important? So primal? So perfect? Yet I have clearly mated with Stay-see many times in the past, and I have done it wrong this time, and this is why she weeps. It is yet another reminder that I am not the mate she thinks I am. And it hurts her.

Her tears pain me. They wound my heart. I want to be whole, for her. I want to remember what I have lost. I want it so badly that my fists clench at my sides and my entire body strains with frustration.

On my chest, my small mate trembles, and her tears wet my skin. Even though she lies atop me, I feel Stay-see is more distant now than ever. I do not want that. I want to be close to her. I want to remember.

I need it.

I must comfort my mate, though. Her distress is destroying me. Hesitant to bother her more, I stroke her back. Once. Slowly. Tentatively. When she does not push me away, I continue to run a hand up and down her smooth back, petting her. She is so soft. Her entire body feels like a gentle clasp. Even her back is nothing but pink suppleness and a hint of bumps underneath her skin along her spine. There is no bony plating to protect her softness. There is no tough, sinewy muscle. She is . . . fragile.

She is mine to protect. From everything.

I hold her as she cries, her tears wetting my chest, and every one of them feels like an icicle pressed to my heart. I must fix this. I must. But how? I worry over this, wondering, even as she slowly cries herself to sleep. Even when she no longer shudders with tears, I still hold her.

I want to hold her forever. I want back what I lost.

I did not realize until now just how much I had lost.

Even in her sleep, Stay-see turns to me for protection. She shivers and huddles against me in a deep slumber, and I wrap my body around her to keep her warm. Pacy is undisturbed in his crib, but the cold troubles my frail human.

She is mine now. I do not care that I do not remember her. She is mine, and I am not going to give her up. I will fight with every breath in my body to make her happy.

I do not sleep that night. Even though I am tired, I cannot. I push my mind, trying to recall every small thing that I can. My sister's bald head when she was born. The first time Zennek and I went hunting with our father, Borran. My first taste of sah-sah. The crushing moment when Hemalo resonated to Asha and I lost my last hope of having a resonance mate. Of hunts, both good and bad. I remember so many things.

But of Stay-see, there is nothing but blankness. Of Pacy, my son, nothing.

And it makes me angry.

I have lost her. I thought, when she reached for me, that we would mate and it would be pleasurable. I did not realize that in doing so, it would wound her. I never want to hurt her again.

In the morning, the storms have cleared from the skies and the snow no longer falls. The ominous clouds are in the distance, and the weather has warmed. It will be a good day for travel. Not for me, because the snow will be thick and slushy due to the suns, but for my mate, who cannot stand the cold. I get up from our shared furs and dress, watching her. She is a small bundle under the furs, still sleeping heavily.

I will get her food and let her sleep for a bit longer.

I emerge from the tent and use a handful of snow to wash

myself, gazing about the campsite. There is a fire this morning, the faint scent of smoke permeating the air. Several human women sit around it, and everywhere the camp is full of sa-khui packing gear, sharpening weapons, or grabbing a bite to eat before setting off on the trail again.

I must find the healer. I must have her put my memories back somehow.

A tiny sneeze and then a gurgle catches my attention. Pacy. Quickly, I duck back into the tent and pull him out of his basket. His lower half is damp, and the smell of piss makes my nostrils burn. For a moment, I think about waking Stay-see, but then I feel shame. Surely I can change my own son. It cannot be that difficult. I pull off his filthy wrap, ignoring his wiggling and trying to remember how Stay-see did it yesterday. Her hands moved so fast. I find a square piece of leather that looks like it has been washed many times, with cords on the sides. This must be it. I toss his filthy wrap aside and try to put the new one on him, but he wiggles and bounces and makes it nearly impossible to do so. Exasperated, I wrap one of my own cloaks around his lower half, tuck him under my arm, and head into the encampment to seek the healer.

I head to the fire first, where there are many kits and females. Surely Maylak will be with them. She has a new kit of her own. But the faces that look at me are curious blanks. I do not recall their names. I try to focus on one. Ah, that one. With the black hair and the pale face. My brother Zennek's mate with the funny name and the odd voice. I focus on her. "Have you seen the healer?"

Her black eyebrows go up and she looks worried. "Are you hurt? Shall I get Zen-nahk?"

I squint at her. It takes me a moment to realize that in her strange, rolling voice, she is speaking of my brother. Zennek, not Zen-nahk. "No, I merely wish to ask her a question."

"Um, I don't mean to point out the obvious, but your son is naked," says another female. A chorus of giggles meet this announcement. "You want me to go wake up Stacy?"

"Stay-see must sleep," I tell the giggly females and glance over at Pacy. My wrap has moved off of his shoulders, and his tiny tail is waving in the breeze. He gives me a delighted smile and taps a little hand on my face, and I chuckle to myself. How is such a small being mine? I feel a fierce, protective surge and hug him closer, rewrapping him. "I will keep looking for May-lak. My thanks."

"Check by Vektal's tent," offers a quiet female. Aehako's mate, I think. She points in the direction of the far end of the encampment.

I nod and head toward the cluster of tents there.

At this end of the camp, Vektal crouches over a stone, spear in hand. He is using it to trace a map into the snow for Bek, Taushen, and the other hunters. Perhaps he is sending them off on a hunt while we travel. Days ago, I would have been the first to volunteer. Hunting is a source of pride, and I take great pleasure in it. But days ago, I was not thinking about my mate, Stay-see, or my small son, who even now is relieving himself on my arm and my favorite wrap. I adjust the leathers to try and find a dry spot, and when I do not find one, swap it out for the wrap I am wearing. I rebundle him, tuck the filthy leather under my arm, and move to the other side of the camp, where the chief's mate is talking with Asha as they pack their gear.

"Have you seen the healer?" I ask.

Asha frowns at me and moves forward, taking Pacy from my

arms. "Why is your son naked, Pashov? Did you hit your head again?"

The chief's mate gasps. "Asha!"

"I did not know how to tie his clothing," I admit, and a flash of memory pulses through my mind. Of Asha, weeping over her small daughter, born too soon for even a khui to save. My gut clenches. It is a fresh memory, though it must be many seasons old by now, because I have my own son. I let her take Pacy, noting how her eyes light up at the sight of him. "Can you watch him for me for a moment, my friend? I wish to talk to the healer."

Asha pulls Pacy close and holds her cheek to his, a peaceful smile on her face. "Of course. I am going to dress him properly, though."

"If you do, you have my thanks." I offer her the wet, pissed-on leathers I am carrying. "What do I do with this?"

"You take it back with you and clean it when we arrive at our new home," Asha says.

The chief's mate grimaces. "My laundry pile is growing enormous, too. If we stop near a hot spring, I'm going to ask Vektal if we can take a day and just clean clothing. Babies go through so many changes, and there's no time to set out anything, much less dry it." She turns her gaze to me. "Does Stacy have enough clothing for Pacy? Do you need extras? I know she lost everything in the cave-in."

"I . . . did not think to ask. I will talk to her." I feel shame. How have I not thought about my mate's comfort? Every time I turn around, there is another task I am failing at. I must do better.

"Go find the healer," Asha says, bouncing my son and making him laugh. "She is in the small tent near the end."

I nod at the females and head toward the tent indicated. The flaps are closed, and so I clear my throat, unsure how to signal that I am waiting outside. I do not wish to be rude if she is mating with Kashrem.

Esha's tiny head sticks out of the tent a moment later. Maylak's kit. So small in my old memories, but a gap-toothed toddler now. I grin at her. "Is your mother inside?"

Maylak emerges, moving Esha gently aside. "Pashov. Are you well?" Worry crosses her face. "Does your head trouble you?"

"It does not hurt, but it does trouble me," I tell her. "May we sit?"

"My tent is full." Her smile is apologetic. "But there are endless amounts of snow we may sit in. Kashrem, watch Esha, please," she calls into the tent and straightens, gesturing at the snow. "Shall we?"

I follow her a short distance away, to a rocky outcropping overlooking the valley below. It is peaceful here, the snow thick and a herd of dvisti staining the snow in the distance. I take a deep breath, inhaling the crisp air. Normally I enjoy the turn of the weather toward the brutal season, but now, with a mate and kit and no shelter, it fills me with a vague sense of dread. I glance at the healer, but her expression is as calm as ever.

"Tell me what is bothering you," Maylak says, voice gentle. "Perhaps I can help."

I extend my hands toward her so she can touch them and use her healing magic on my khui. "My memories. I need them back."

Maylak looks startled, pausing before she takes my hands. She grips them a moment later and gives me a gentle squeeze. "I have done all I can for that, and your horn. Some things take time to heal, Pashov."

"Try again," I demand. When she frowns, I realize I am being unfair. "Please," I ask her. "I want to remember my mate. My kit. I . . . there is nothing there when I think of them. I should at least remember something, should I not? The memories must be there. Can we just try to find them again?"

She must sense my desperation, because she gives my hands another squeeze. "You were very hurt when they pulled you from the cave," she murmurs. "Your brain was very damaged. It took everything your khui had—and mine—to keep you alive. I am pleased that all that happened to you was memory loss, Pashov. Do you realize how close you came to dying?"

"I am still dying." My voice cracks. "My mate's pain is destroying me. Help me, Maylak. Please. Try again."

She nods and closes her eyes. I close mine, too, waiting for her healing to sweep over me. I feel it a moment later—a subtle warmth that pours through my body. My khui shivers in my chest, responding to hers. I force myself to relax, to slow my breathing, to let my khui speak and tell her of the pain I am in. I need my mate back. I need my life back.

There must be a way.

The warmth recedes, and I open my eyes, frowning. That was . . . fast. I rack my brain, trying to think of the first time I saw Stay-see. Of memories of how she arrived and our quick resonance.

But there is . . . nothing.

My disappointment is obvious to Maylak. Her expression is apologetic as she releases my hands. "Your mind is as healed as I can make it. Only time can say if your memories will come back, Pashov. Be gentle with yourself."

I rub a hand over my brow, frustrated. "Can you try again in a few days?"

"There is no further injury to be healed," Maylak tells me, and there is a firmness to her voice that wasn't there before. "Your memories will either come back, or they will not. I must save my healing for emergencies."

"And what of me?"

Her hand briefly touches my shoulder as she stands. "Perhaps you must learn to live without those memories."

The thought is unbearable.

CHAPTER FIVE

Stacy

Even though the weather is nice, the day is long. The ease I felt around Pashov yesterday is gone. I'm silent and withdrawn, no matter how much he tries to talk to me. I know it's not his fault, and it just makes me feel worse. Last night was a mistake. I was weak, and needy, and it can't happen again. Not until he gets his memories back. I'm not trying to punish him . . . I just can't let my heart break into any more pieces than it already has. I can't take it.

Pashov senses my bad mood and leaves me alone, for the most part. Of course, that's not surprising, given that I cried myself to sleep on his chest last night. Awkward. He won't understand why, I don't think, because he doesn't know me. He hasn't lived with me for the last two years. In his mind, he's only known me for a short period of time. I'm a stranger. And it sucks. It's best for both of us—and Pacy—if we figure out how to be a team without the messy entanglement of sex.

Especially sex that leaves me hollow and aching for what we used to have.

I know I'm being unfair to him. I love him. I know he's trying. I just . . . I just can't. Every touch that doesn't have our old routines behind it feels like a betrayal. Maybe that's crazy of me, but until I can shake it, and until he gets his memories back, that's how it has to be.

I still feel like the bad guy, though. And I cry a little under the blankets as we travel, riding on the sled that he's pulling. Because I'm stupid and weak and human and get too tired and slow on my own. So I hide under the blankets and nap, because napping's easier than holding a conversation.

I sleep all through the afternoon and wake up toward evening, when the sleds stop and tents are unpacked. There's a bonfire being prepared, but I don't feel much like being chatty. I slide out of my nest tucked between bundles on the sled, and my muscles groan a protest. I've ridden for the last two days. Why is everything so sore?

Then I realize I'm sore between my thighs, and I'm both embarrassed and sad.

"Are you all right?" Pashov asks, worry on his face as he sees me waddle forward a few awkward steps. "Do you need to see the healer?"

"I'm okay." I pull my cloak tighter around my shoulders. "Where's your mother? I should feed Pacy." Kemli, bless her heart, has had my baby all afternoon. Maybe she sensed I wasn't feeling like myself, but the moment she volunteered, I handed him over. Of course, then I felt guilty that I was passing him off to his grandma, and I might have cried a little over that, too.

Man, I've been a weepy mess lately.

He tries to take my hand. "They are setting their tent near the others. I will show you."

"I can find it," I say quickly, and pull my hand from his.

Pashov nods, his expression carefully blank. "I shall set up our tent, then."

I hesitate. It's on the tip of my tongue to beg him to go sleep somewhere else tonight. That even if it's cold, I don't think my heart can take another round of this. I glance away, and he turns his back. His tail flicks, and I realize he's agitated. That's one of Pashov's little tells—he's good at hiding his emotions sometimes, but his tail always gives him away. The side-to-side flick it's doing right now tells me that he's waiting for me to kick him out. And then what? Force him to sleep alone by the fire? Shiver by myself? I need to be a mature adult. His shoulders don't seem as broad today, now that I look at him again. They're slumped, as if he's disappointed.

And that makes me ache all over again. He expects me to reject him. He knows as well as I do that something went wrong last night.

Why does that surprise you, idiot? The moment he came, you cried like a fool for an hour and then fell asleep. That has to sting.

God, I'm just making things worse. I've never wanted to hurt Pashov. Ever. I watch him as he unties a strap on the sled, and I bite my knuckle. Should I say something? That I know he's doing his best? That the problem is in my head? But will that even help? I watch him for a moment and retreat to the fire, because I'm a coward.

I see Kemli's sharp face before I make it to the fire. Pashov's mother has a face like a hawk, all pointy chin and strong nose. She's the opposite of Sevvah, who's round everywhere, with looping gray braids. Kemli's hair has streaks of white mixed in with the black, but she doesn't look much like the mom of three adults and one almost-adult. She's a fantastic mother-in-law, though, for how fierce she looks. I see her holding Pacy on one hip, talking to Farli and bossing Borran around as he spits what looks like a fresh-killed quill-beast over the newly made fire.

When she spots me, her eyes light up with pleasure, and she waves me over. "My daughter! Just the person I wished to see."

I smile at her and hope I'm hiding my heartache well. One of the best things about resonating to Pashov the moment I arrived was that I had a ready-made family to greet me and make me comfortable here. Other girls haven't been so lucky, and I adore Kemli and Borran. I just worry I'm disappointing them now with how difficult this has all been for me. "Sorry if you've been looking for me. I was asleep."

"Not a worry. I am used to going to the community fire and seeing you there, cooking for someone." She beams. "That will have to wait for a new community fire, I think."

I do like to cook for people. My instincts lean heavily toward nurturing, and when we first got here, the other girls struggled so much, and I never seemed to struggle. Not with Pashov and his family at my side. So I took up the "mother" role (even though I'm the same age as everyone else) and cooked for people. Two years later, everyone still looks to me for treats, and I admit that I enjoy spoiling everyone in the cave. I miss my janky makeshift skillet. I miss the firepit.

I miss my mate.

Ignoring the grief rising in my chest, I put on a brave face. "Was Pacy bad today?" I hold my arms out for him.

He clings to Kemli's tunic and hides his face, which makes the older woman beam with pleasure. "Not at all. He loves visiting! And he was so good! He sat in my lap all afternoon, and we watched the dvisti herds move through."

"I'm so glad he behaved. I know he gets restless." I grin at my little son. "Has he eaten?"

"He has been chewing on fresh meaty bones to get his little teeth ready for good meat." She smiles at me, and indeed, there's a long, rounded vertebra in my son's hand, still slightly bloody. As I watch, he pushes one end into his mouth and begins to gum it.

Yeah, so there are some aspects of ice planet life I'm still not a hundred percent all in on. I inwardly wince at the sight but don't pluck it from his hands, because it would offend Kemli. "You're good to take him, Kemli. I appreciate the break."

"But of course. He looks just like Pashov at this age." She pokes Pacy's nose and beams at him when he giggles. "Handsome and full of smiles."

My own smile grows tight. Normally I love hearing Pashov-as-an-infant stories, but right now, I just can't.

Kemli isn't stupid, though. Her smile becomes bittersweet with understanding, and she looks over her shoulder. "Is my sled still nearby? I have something for you."

"For me?" I'm surprised.

"Yes. Come." She hands Pacy to Farli instead of to me, and waves me forward.

I follow, curious. I should feed Pacy to get the milk out of my breasts, but Farli's surrounded with people and they're all gathered near the fire. My baby isn't going anywhere. I follow in the path Kemli wades easily through the snow, and when we get to their half-dismantled sled, she begins to pick through her herb satchel. Pashov's mother is the tribe expert on herbs and plants, and I'm not surprised when she pulls something out of her bag and hands it to me. I am a little surprised to see it's a horn, though. A small one, with a bit of leather stuffed into the end. "What's this?"

"A balm for your face," she tells me. "Animal fat with a paste of dranoosh leaves boiled in."

I dab my finger in the yellowish sludge and then sniff it. It smells awful, but I'm not going to tell her that. "My face?"

She nods. "Pashov says human skin is too soft for this weather. That your face gets red and sore. He does not like to see you hurting. He asked if I had anything, so I boiled that this morning and let it set."

I'm surprised, not only at her thoughtfulness, but at Pashov's. "I . . . thank you."

"Of course." She rubs my arm, her voice lowering. "You are in pain, aren't you? How can I help?"

I have to blink rapidly to fight back more tears. "My face?" I repeat stupidly.

"Not your face." She taps at my chest. "Here. I know you struggle. I care for you as my own little Farli. I see how you and your mate act together, and today, you seem distant." Her proud face is full of worry for me. "Forgive a nosy old female."

"You're neither nosy nor old," I tell her, sniffling. She puts an arm around me, and I lean against her. God, it feels so good to be hugged. To be comforted. Of course, then I feel like an even bigger asshole, because I know Pashov would comfort me. "It's just . . . really hard."

"Of course it is," she soothes, rubbing my back.

"He doesn't remember anything of me. Of Pacy. It feels like we're starting from scratch. I don't want that. I want what we had back. I miss my mate." I hear my voice, and it sounds petulant. "Sometimes I think it's him, and then . . ."

"And then he says something and you realize he does not remember?" she guesses.

I nod, swiping at my runny nose. She nailed it.

"I share your pain, Stay-see. I worried at his bedside for all those long days and nights that Maylak worked on him. We shared our grief. We hoped he would wake up and waited for that moment. Sometimes it seemed as if it would be a dream to see him smile again." She hesitates, then gives me another hug. "Is it not enough that he is alive and well?"

"I tell myself that." I clutch the little horn of face balm in my hand tightly. "Sometimes I feel like I'm being unfair. That I'm not giving him a chance. That it's my Pashov despite everything and I'm being ridiculous." I think back to last night, to the sex we had that was so good . . . and yet so wrong. It was like having sex with a completely different person, and it hurts me deep inside to think about it. "I don't know what I should do," I tell her. "How would you feel if your mate woke up and had forgotten everything you had ever shared? All your memories, your habits, your name . . . your kits you had together?" Just saying it makes me hurt all the way down to my bones. "If when he looked at you, he saw nothing of what you'd shared?"

Kemli rests her chin atop my head and strokes my hair. "I would feel the same as you do."

Pashov

She is distant around the fire.

Stay-see joins the others, sharing soup and smiling as stories are told by the warmth of the firepit, but she does not speak. She does not look at me, either. Our eyes meet by accident at one point, and I see a flash of pain and the shimmer of tears in her gaze before she looks away, hugging her kit tight to her chest.

Eventually, most drift away from the fire except for Harrec, who has tonight's early watch. When Stay-see gets up from her seat and cradles my sleeping son against her, Harrec smirks in my direction. I know he is thinking about his joke. It has been days and I still do not find it funny. Even now, it churns in my gut like bad food. I scowl at him and put a protective arm around Stay-see, and am glad when she does not push me away.

Inside the tent, though, she ignores me. When we go to sleep, I try to pull her against me to share warmth, but she gently pries herself out of my grip. "I'm sorry," she whispers. "I can't."

And she puts a rolled bundle of furs between us.

I spend most of the evening staring up at the tent walls, fighting my frustration. Mating with Stay-see should have brought us closer together. Instead, it feels as if she is pushing me even further away.

Something must change.

I am up before the dawn, and I can tell the day will be a cold one. Snow is falling again, and the brutal season will be upon us in a mere handful of days. Maybe two handfuls at the most. I can smell it in the air. It will be another hard day's journey for Stay-see, and that worries me. I want to protect my mate from the bitter cold, but I have no choice. I think of her red face, burned by the cold wind, and the circles under her eyes. She needs to rest for a few days. The other humans struggle, too, but Stay-see seems to be having a rougher time than most. Is it because of me? Because of her sadness? It fills me with deep concern and eats at my thoughts.

If I could, I would put up a shelter for her right here and let her rest for days, but we do not have that time. The brutal season is nearly upon us, and when it arrives, the snow will not break for endless turns of the moons. She cannot be trapped out here. Not when it grows so cold that the air burns to breathe. She will not survive it.

I must think of her and my son.

I head to the fire to gather food for Stay-see to eat, but there is no meat cooking for the humans yet. It will be a few minutes. I turn away, and I am surprised to see my mother waiting for me.

"My son. There you are. I wish to speak to you a moment." Her smile is bright, perhaps too bright. I suspect I am about to get a lecture like a young kit.

"Mother." I lean in and rub my cheek to hers in greeting. "How are you and Father faring in your travel so far? Is your tent comfortable?"

"We are fine," she says, patting my arm and pulling me away from the gathering crowd. "Your father can sleep through anything, and Farli takes after him. It is me that must endure their snoring." Her mouth turns up in a faint smile. "But I wish to talk to you of something else."

"Stay-see?" I guess.

"Yes. My son, I feel you are not very patient with her."

Patience? I do not have enough patience? I feel as if I have been nothing *but* patient. I ignore the anger burning in my throat, because my mother is only trying to help. "What makes you say that?"

"Stay-see is very upset with you—"

"Stay-see is always upset with me lately," I counter. I think of her tears after we mated, and it feels like a knife in my gut. "How can I know how to please her and make her happy when all she does is cry?"

"You are not trying to understand her. She is a young mother who has recently lost her mate—"

"I am her mate," I protest.

"In her eyes, you are not. You do not remember her. You do not remember your kit. The fact that she is a stranger to you hurts her deeply."

"I went to the healer," I say, frustrated, and rake a hand through my mane. "She tells me my mind is fine. That my memories will either come back, or they will not, but she can do nothing else for me."

My mother reaches up and taps my cheek. "You are alive and you are whole, my son. If you lose those memories, make new ones with her. You are both young. Do not let this pull you apart."

"She does not want me."

"She will give you another chance," my mother says, self-assured. "But you must try harder."

"Try harder?" How can I give more than I already am? "When she looks at me, she sees a stranger. Just as I see when I look at her. She wants back a mate that I am not sure I can ever be again." I shake my head. "You think I do not want to be her mate? She is everything I have ever wanted. Her and my son both."

"Then you must fight for them." My mother puts her hands on my shoulders and looks me in the eye. "Stay-see is hurt and feels she has lost the love you shared. You must prove to her that it yet exists. That it does not matter if you have lost your memories. That you are still the same Pashov here." She points at my heart.

My mother's words sting me. Am I not fighting for my mate? Do I not do everything she asks? Have I not shown her that I care? How is that not enough? It stings, even when my mother gives my shoulder another sympathetic touch and then moves back to the fire.

And I am left with nothing but questions and worry.

I must stay busy. Above all else, I must think of my mate and the small kit that is mine as well. I must think of their comfort. I move to the sled and begin to repack it. I will leave the tent for last so my mate can continue to sleep, but some of the gear must be rearranged so Stay-see is comfortable. I tug on one leather knot—too hard—and it snaps, sending me flying backward into the snow. I bite back a curse of frustration.

"You seem troubled." Rokan appears at my side and offers me a hand up. "Is all well?"

Is everyone seeking me out today? I grip his arm and haul back to my feet. My mood is foul, and I wait for him to begin to lecture me, but the look on his face is contrite. I sigh and dust the snow off my leggings as I stand. "I am not paying attention. This weather concerns me. Stay-see struggles with the cold."

"All the humans do," he agrees, a distant look in his eyes. No doubt he is thinking of his mate, the one that talks only with her hands. He focuses on me after a moment and smiles. "The weather should hold up for the next moon, though. This is just bad luck. After this storm, all will be quiet for several more hands of days, until the next full turn of the moon." He claps my back. "Plenty of time to settle into our new home."

I grunt acknowledgment of his words. I think about our new home, like the other hunters do, but I am more focused on my mate and her well-being. I cannot relax while she is struggling so. "It is good to hear the weather will hold out." If today is the last day of storms and snow for a time, I will take it. There are so many other things to worry about . . . like the way Stay-see and I are fracturing like an old bone.

Or were we ever strong and whole? I have no memories of it, but surely we were happy. Surely I cherished her. My mind has not changed; I am just missing parts of my memory. I cannot help but feel panic as she grows more and more distant, though. Being around the others, in this journey? It is just making it worse. There is not much privacy, and she is exhausted. If only we had time alone together, to talk in private and learn to understand one another again—

I pause, thinking. The wind howls, and Rokan gestures at his own distant sled. "My mate will be up soon and wanting to eat before we travel. I will speak with you again soon, friend." He raises a friendly hand. "Good day to you."

I repeat the words back to him and focus on my sled, but I am not thinking about it. I am thinking about the weather and how it will hold for several more hands of days. Weeks, as the humans say. I am thinking of a hunter cave tucked into a nearby valley, a brisk walk from here. It is big enough to house a small family for several days, and there is a cache nearby that could feed us for several *more* days, even if the weather is too poor for hunting.

Am I brave enough to steal my Stay-see away like Raahosh did with Leezh? Like Hassen tried when he stole Li-lah? People have told me of these things, and I am both shocked and fascinated. No one disobeys the chief . . . and yet two males have in such a short period of time, simply because of the human females.

To break the tribe's rules seems wrong to me . . . and yet I need to be alone with my mate. To connect with her again. To get an answer to this problem between us. But just running away does not seem to be the answer. I think of Rokan's words, of how the weather will be clear.

Do I dare . . . ? It would be an easy thing to let the sled drop back behind the others in the midst of the snow, to veer off the trail and take her toward the hunter cave. But the hunters would follow us. And my chief would be furious. I think for a moment . . . and then I stand.

I will not run away like a coward. I will let my chief know my wishes. Surely if I go to him first, he will understand.

I check the tent, but Stay-see is still sleeping. Good. I have time to speak to my chief, then. I jog through the encampment, a fire burning in my belly. The more I think about this decision, the more it feels right. I can keep my mate safe. All I need is a handful of days for her to rest, for us to establish ease between us once more. Then I can take her on to join the others.

I find Vektal breaking down his tent with his mate, Shorshie. She is bundled heavily against the weather, the furs making her body seem twice as round as it is. The chief gives me a curious look as I approach. "Is all well?" he asks. "You look . . . troubled."

Shorshie is watching me with great curiosity. "Did you remember something?"

I shake my head, hating that I will see disappointment in their faces. "My chief, I must speak with you. I have a request."

Shorshie puts down the corner of the tent she is holding up. "Why don't you two talk and I'll go grab Talie from Asha." She gives her mate a meaningful look and walks away, hugging the hood of her cloak tighter to her face.

I watch her as she leaves. "Does your mate struggle with the cold?"

"All the humans struggle," Vektal says, picking up one corner of the tent again and gesturing for me to take up Shorshie's place. "Some more than others. I think my Georgie hides it because the other females look to her for strength." He pauses. "Stay-see suffers?"

"She does."

He looks thoughtful. "A few of the females have taken to hiking or learning to hunt. Stay-see has always been content to remain in the cave and look after the others. She cooks for them, you know."

"She does?" I am surprised. Stay-see has not shown much enthusiasm for any of the soups doled out on the journey and little interest in the meat, raw or charred. I grab the side of the tent and pull it from its moorings. "What does she cook for them?"

"All kinds of terrible things." Vektal gives a full-body shake, as if even the thought disturbs him. "Cakes and meat rolled between cakes and roots added to it. The humans are fascinated with these cake-things. I tasted one once and it was sickly sweet, like bad meat." He reaches forward and grabs a knot, untying it, and the tent collapses. "The females love it, though. They always come to Stay-see and ask her to make things for them. And she does. She is very kind, your mate."

I do not know if I am upset by this information or pleased. I knew my mate has a big heart—I have seen her be gentle and pleasant to others even when she is tired. But I have also learned more about her in the last few moments than I have in the last hand of days.

All because Stay-see does not talk to me. She does not share her thoughts with me. She does not cook for me. I would eat everything she put in front of me, even her terrible cakes that taste like meat gone bad. "She is the reason I have come to speak to you, my chief."

"Then speak."

"I want to take Stay-see away."

His face grows thunderous. "Explain yourself."

"She will not talk to me. She carries her hurt like a cloak and will not let me see what is underneath."

"And you think taking her away will solve this?"

"I think if she has no one to talk to but me, perhaps she will choose to speak to me more." I can see my chief does not agree, so I rush on. "The more I try to talk to her, the more she pushes me away. I could live with that, I think, and be a patient male . . . except the travel is hard on her. It pains me to see her suffer."

"You have feelings for her?"

"Of course. She is my mate." I am appalled he would even have to ask.

"But you have no memories of her."

This makes me pause. What he says is true. And yet, the thought of parting from Stay-see makes me ache. Even if I cannot remember our resonance, there is no doubt in my mind that we have a connection. She is mine, just as much as Pacy is, just as much as my hand or my tail belong to me. They are part of who I am, and to lose them would leave me less than whole. Even the thought of Stay-see parting from me causes me agony. "I may not have them here," I say, pointing at my temple. "But I have them here." I put a hand over my heart. It makes me think of the words my mother gave me. Was I not trying hard enough? Now I am resolved to work even harder. Stay-see is my mate, and I must win her over.

"So what is your plan?" He does not look pleased, but he has not yet told me no. This is encouraging.

"There is a hunter cave near here. The big one." When he nods, I know we are both thinking of the same cave. "There is a cache there. I would like to take Stay-see there for a hand of days. It would give her time to rest and time for me to get to know her better."

"You are sleeping in her tent at night. How much better do you need to know her?"

I can feel my jaw clench. "Just because I share my warmth with her does not mean she shares her heart with me."

He seems to agree. "Go on."

"I do not know my mate. I would like to take time to get to know her, and with everyone busy with the journey, it is proving impossible. I would like to take Stay-see to the cave and give her time to rest and time for me to know her and my son."

"So you are taking her away, just like Hassen and Raahosh." His voice is flat.

He sees right through my plan. "My understanding was that they did not seek permission." I keep my voice guarded.

Vektal's stern expression cracks, and he gives me a rueful smile. "You are a sly one, my friend. I am glad to have you back. We all worried over you."

"I am not completely back," I tell him. "Not in all eyes."

He makes a grunt of acknowledgment and folds the tent up. I remain silent so he can think. He has a mate and a new kit. He will understand my struggle. After a moment, though, he shakes his head. "I cannot. Not with the brutal season so quick on our heels."

I fight back a stab of disappointment. "I spoke with Rokan. He says the brutal season will be delayed."

My chief looks up at the skies, gray and full of clouds. Snow is thick in the air. "Truly?"

"Truly," I agree. "He says after today's storm, we have until the next moon before the brutal season is truly upon us. That will be more than enough time." I give him a lazy smile to make it seem like I am less eager. "You know Rokan and his weather-sense are never wrong."

Vektal narrows his eyes. "You speak the truth?"

"I do. I have nothing to gain by lying to my chief."

"Don't you?"

I grin wider. "If I wished to lie, would it not be easier to just steal my mate away and then tell you I have forgotten where we are going?"

He stares at me for a long moment, and then a hearty laugh erupts from him. He claps me on the back. "If you did that, I would truly throttle you, my friend. I prefer you with your memory intact."

"I prefer myself that way, too." The ache returns to my breast. "This is important to me."

"I understand." He rubs his jaw, thinking. His gaze scans the encampment, and I know he is looking for Rokan. He is a short distance away, gesturing to his small mate. The chief looks back at me. "You are healthy? No pains? No problems?"

"Only that I cannot remember anything that has happened in the last few seasons. All else is as it has ever been." Only. I make it sound like it is not an issue. It is a huge issue, but I do not want my chief to worry over my health and decide not to let me take my mate away.

Because I am going to—with or without his permission.

Vektal rubs his chin for a bit longer. He studies me, then sighs. "You will go to the hunter cave near here. The one with two chambers."

"Across the valley?" I gesture at the distant landscape. It is not more than a brief jaunt in the snow from where we are. An hour of travel, maybe less. I know of the "double" cave he speaks of. It is like two small caves connected, and one of the largest hunter caves in our territory.

"Across the valley," he agrees. "That cave and no other. I want to know exactly where to find you."

I swallow my excitement, though I cannot stop the relieved grin spreading across my face. "The cave near here. No other." I repeat his words precisely.

"And you know where we are going?"

I nod. Hassen has shared the details of the "new" place under our familiar grounds so many times that I know the exact spot we are heading to. "I will not get lost."

"No, I suppose you will not." Vektal seems amused by my claim. "You are one of my best hunters, Pashov. If that has not changed, you will have no problems finding the place. Still, we will leave a marker of some kind so you will know you are in the right valley. A spear sticking out of the ground, or a fur tossed in a tree, perhaps."

"A fur would work," I joke. "I have many of them that Pacy has made filthy over the last several days."

He snorts and gets down on hands and knees, rolling the leather tent into a tight bundle. "You think I do not have bags and bags of frozen dirty wraps from my daughter? Georgie wails that she needs to do lawn-dree desperately." He shakes his head and looks up at me. "I cannot talk you out of this, can I?"

"No, you cannot." I fight back my jubilation.

"You will be careful? This is near metlak territory. We do not know how they will act with so many sa-khui coming into their land."

"I can protect my mate and kit."

"I know you can. I would be a bad chief if I did not remind you to keep eyes and ears open, however. I do not like this, but if the weather is as Rokan says it is, and you are determined, then I cannot stop you. Stay-see has agreed to this?"

I . . . have not asked her. I will not ask her, because I suspect her answer will be no. I nod at my chief and ignore the sickly knot in my stomach. I do not like to lie to my chief . . . but for Stay-see? I will lie.

"You have four hands of days. Our hands, not human hands." He wiggles his three fingers and thumb at me, as if to remind me that we have one less digit than the small human hands.

"We are at least one hand of days away from the valley," I protest. "Maybe two. It is not enough time." That will only give me two hands of days to woo my mate.

"No more," Vektal says in a hard voice. "Or I do not let you go at all."

"Four hands," I agree. I will make use of every day I have with Stay-see, then. It must be enough.

"Find us in the new valley. Be there within four hands of days, or I will come for you." The look he gives me is narrow eyed. "You had better not make me come for you. I will not be pleased."

I laugh. "You will not have to come get me. We will rejoin the tribe before the brutal season arrives. This I promise."

He thinks for a moment, then adds, "If you are not back by the turning of the moons, I will send Bek after you."

I shrug. Bek is prickly but competent. I do not mind him.

"And Harrec."

I scowl at that. "We will be back."

I am bursting with excitement over my plan. Vektal and I speak to the hunters who watch over the back of our group, letting them know that I will be breaking off from the herd shortly. Several look worried, but Bek looks pleased that I am taking action. He gives me a solemn nod before turning to leave.

When I return to my tent, Stay-see is awake. She gives me a curious look at my good mood but says nothing, focusing on feeding and changing Pacy. I hurry to pack our things, noticing with mixed feelings that the snow is coming down faster. It will give weight to my story that I will tell my mate: that we were separated from the tribe due to the storm and must shelter at the cave. I only wish it would not be so cold, because already Stay-see shivers miserably. I take the cloak off my shoulders and offer it to her, but she shakes her head. "You must stay warm, too."

"I will be warm enough pulling the sled," I tell her, but she refuses.

I bundle her and my son up on the sled, taking care to pack the blankets tightly around her. Once our things are packed, I grab the sled handles and set off into the blinding snow.

Soon we will be alone together.

Then Stay-see will have no choice but to confess her worries to me, and we will heal. If I cannot have my old memories back, we will make new ones.

I am eager to begin.

CHAPTER SIX
Stacy

The weather today is horrible. No amount of lotion can stop the wind from hurting my face, and no number of furs can stop the bitter cold from cutting through the layers. It's miserable, and I think of the last brutal season, when the weather was so awful that even the sa-khui stayed bundled in the cave. It doesn't encourage me much. But we'll get through this, because we have no other choice.

Pashov has made a windbreak with several rolls of furs on the sled, and I huddle behind it, shielding Pacy with my body as our sled plows on through the blizzard. The snow is falling so heavily that the skies seem dark as night, even though I know it's midday. I can't see any of the sleds we normally follow. Actually, I can't see much of anything except for Pashov's big body a few feet ahead, tirelessly pulling the sled. I'm grateful to him. I can't imagine trying to walk in this.

And I feel guilty that I've been treating him so poorly lately. I'm being selfish. I think he's trying, but it's hard for me. My exhaustion doesn't help, and the snow doesn't help, and the sex we had the other day sure didn't help, because now I want to have sex again. My body doesn't seem to grasp that this Pashov isn't quite the same as the old Pashov. It still wants him and still wants the comfort and release of sex.

As I huddle under the blankets and hug Pacy close, I think of the last few days and feel a bit ashamed for how I've been acting. It's not his fault. None of this is, and I feel like I'm blaming him. I'm not proud of how I've been coping with everything. I just don't know what to do. I've been on the defensive ever since he woke up.

Because he can't remember me, I feel like I'm a problem. Like Pacy's a problem. Of course I'm defensive about being a problem. But Pashov hasn't indicated that we're the problem. I think I'm just taking my frustrations out on him, and every time he does something that doesn't feel like the "old" Pashov to me, I resent it. So he doesn't grab my butt like he used to. He's still a good, kind man. He's still the father of my son.

Maybe instead of resenting the changes, I need to remind myself that he's alive and healthy. I have a mate. He didn't die in the cave-in. Pacy will have a father. Surely I can be grateful for that.

A father that doesn't remember him, my horrible brain whispers. My brain is a jerk.

The wind howls, and I cringe under the blankets. Pacy's unbothered by the terrible weather, burbling happily to himself and playing with a carved bone toy in my lap. I can't help but worry, though. The air seems to get more frigid with every passing moment, and the snow thicker. I peek out at the stormy gray world, and it's so cold my skin feels seared. "Pashov?" I call out. I have to raise my voice to be heard over the howling wind.

My mate immediately sets down the sled and turns to me, tucking blankets tighter around me and Pacy. "Are you well enough to travel? Do you need more blankets?" He starts to shrug off his cloak, as if to give it to me.

"We're okay," I tell him quickly. "Keep your cloak. Is the weather getting worse?"

He nods. "We will stop soon."

"Soon?" I repeat, not sure I heard him correctly or if it's just the wind ripping at his words. When he nods, I feel a tinge of relief. "Do you think we'll have a fire?" I yell out.

"I will make you a fire," he promises, tying my cloak tighter around my chin. "Get under the blankets and stay warm."

"Are you all right?" I search his face to see if he's feeling the chill as much as I am. He gives me a boyish smile and a nod, and my heart flip-flops in my chest at the sight. He turns back to the front of the sled and picks up the handles again, but I'm still sitting here stunned. That smile was the same Pashov as ever, and part of me wants to leap from the sled and turn him around and make him smile at me again.

And even though it's cold, I feel a bit of hope.

Pashov's idea of "soon" is apparently very different than mine. It grows colder by the moment, until my breath is frosting even under the blankets, and my entire body shivers with the need for warmth. The wind grows louder, the snow thicker, until I feel almost as if we're in a snow tornado. Do such things exist? If so, we've found one. The snow is pouring from the sky so heavily that I have to shake my blankets off over and over again so we're not buried. All the while, Pashov plods ahead, as strong and grimly determined as ever. I can barely make out his form several feet away. If there are others near us, they're impossible to see.

I'm also starting to worry. Surely no tent is going to keep us warm enough in this weather. No fire is going to be able to withstand this wind. What are we going to do? The thought of going through the night as cold as I am now fills me with helpless despair. I've never been so cold. My only consolation is that Pacy seems unbothered. In this, he's more sa-khui than human, and I'm grateful.

The sled stops. I frown to myself under the blankets, concerned. Is Pashov all right? I wait for the inevitable jerk of the sled as it starts again, but nothing moves. What if . . . what if he's hurt again? Panic clutches at my throat, and I fling myself upright, fighting through the layers of blankets. "Pashov?" I cry out into the blizzard. "Pashov!"

"I am here," he says, and he touches my face.

Oh gosh, his fingers are so warm, and I'm so damn cold. I want to burrow against him and just bask in his warmth. Thank goodness he's all right. "Why—why did we stop?"

He hesitates for a moment, then reaches over me to pull Pacy into his arms. "Come. We must get you inside, both of you."

Inside? I squint into the driving snow, but I can't see anything. "Are we stopping? But it's not night—"

"We are done for the day," he says in a firm, calm voice. He offers me his free hand and helps me down from the sled, then flings his cloak over me, shielding me from the snowstorm. "Come. Hold on to me, and I will lead the way."

"Pacy—"

"I have him. Come."

I cling to his side and let him lead me forward. It's impossible to tell where we're going, and this feels a bit like those trust exercises they do at summer camp. Only I'm not falling backward into someone's arms. I'm stepping forward blindly into the snow in the hopes of safety and warmth.

A few steps later, and suddenly the wind seems to die away. I peek out from under Pashov's fur cloak, and it's dark, but I can barely make out the glowing blue eyes of my mate and my baby, and the faint outline of rock walls. My breathing sounds different, and the wind seems to be howling behind us. I turn in surprise, gazing back out as I realize where we are. "Is this a cave?"

"A hunter cave," Pashov confirms, handing Pacy to me. "Hold him, and I will start a fire."

I take my son, carefully rewrapping him in his blankets so he stays warm and dry. I feel soaked to the bone from all the snow, but the wind isn't nipping into me, so it's not so terrible. "Where are the others?" I ask as he moves around the cave. I hear the sound of rummaging and then a spark lights in the firepit, illuminating Pashov's face. "Are they staying in caves?"

There is silence for a long moment and then another spark. "We have been separated from them."

I suck in a breath. "What happened?"

This time, the spark catches, and Pashov leans over, blowing gently to make the fire grow. I wait impatiently as he feeds it tinder, all the while carefully blowing on the tiny flame. When the fire is in no danger of going out, he glances up at me. "The snow grew to be too much. We fell behind."

And our sled wasn't even the biggest. "Oh my god. Do you think the others—"

"They will be safe. I promise. Do not worry."

"How can I not worry? Georgie and Josie and the others are out there in the storm! What about your parents—Kemli? Borran? Or Farli and your brothers—"

"We will catch up to them," he says, his voice calm and even. "I brought you here because you are cold."

"But won't they worry about us—"

"Do not worry," he assures me. He gets up from the small fire and moves to my side, tugging me gently toward the flame.

He pulls one of my sodden layers off of my shoulders, and for a moment, I want to protest that I need the furs, but then he sits me in front of the fire. It's beginning to catch now, and it's so, so warm. I sigh at the feeling of heat, scooting closer.

"I'm worried, Pashov," I say as I hold Pacy close. My mind is racing with fear. "We can't lose the others—"

"We will not," he says quickly. "I know where they are going. We will meet them there. For now, it is most important that you rest, Stay-see. You and my son both." He reaches out and chucks Pacy under the chin, and the baby giggles. "Wait here," Pashov tells me. "I will bring in our gear."

I want to help, but Pacy must be watched and the fire kept going. So I nod, trembling as I wait by the fire. Pashov dashes out of the front of the cave again and disappears into the blinding white flurries, and the knot in my throat grows huge. The weather is so bad. How can we be separated from the others? What are we going to do?

I swallow my questions as Pashov appears again with several bundles of furs. He sets them at the cave entrance and disappears into the snow again. I make myself busy with Pacy, feeding him before he gets fussy and letting him play in my lap near the fire. The heat feels wonderful, but with it comes guilt. The others are out there in this cold. They're suffering, traveling on, because it's important that we all stay together.

As much as I would love to sit by this fire for the next few hours and roast myself into oblivion, we don't have the luxury. If we're going to catch up with the others, we need to get back on the trail soon.

The next time Pashov comes in, I stop him. "Don't unpack more," I say, getting to my feet. "We need to get back out there."

"No," he says, stubborn. "You are cold. Sit down and warm yourself."

"The others are still out there. We can catch up with them. I can't sit here by the fire while they're out looking for us."

"They will not be looking for us," Pashov says firmly, moving to my side. He presses a gentle hand to my shoulder. "Sit. You are tired. You are cold. Rest and warm yourself."

I watch him, skeptical. "You don't seem very nervous for someone who's just been lost in a blizzard."

"There is no need to be nervous." Pashov pulls the privacy screen over the cave entrance, leaving just enough room to let the smoke trickle out. "I will care for you and Pacy. I can hunt. There is a cache nearby if the weather is too foul. We have fuel and blankets. All will be well. Rest and recover, Stay-see."

He's very calm for someone that has been left behind with his mate and child in a snowstorm. Too calm. I study his face. Pashov has always been a terrible liar, and when he won't look me in the eye, my suspicions are confirmed. "This was intentional, wasn't it?"

"What do you mean?" He feeds a bit more fuel to the fire. "Relax, Stay-see. Would you like some tea? I can dig out your tea pouch."

"Uh-huh," I say warily. "You're offering me tea when we should be getting out there, catching up with the others."

"Too much distance between us," he says stubbornly.

A worrying thought occurs to me. He's had no trouble keeping up for the last few days. "Are you feeling all right? You're not too tired, are you?"

"I am fine."

"But you would tell me if you were struggling, right?" I can't help but be anxious over him. He's just recently recovered from a devastating injury. If we hadn't had the healer . . .

"Stay-see." Pashov moves to sit next to me. His hand falls on my shoulder, and he gives me a patient look. "All is well. Please do not worry."

"How can I help but worry? We're left behind—"

He sighs and rubs his forehead. "Stay-see, please."

"Pashov," I say, a warning tone in my voice. "Either tell me what is going on, or get back out there so we can catch up."

His mouth flattens, and his tail does that hoppy little flick at the end that tells me he's lying. I raise my brows at him, waiting. After a moment, he grimaces. "Very well. I admit . . . no one will come looking for us."

"Because . . . ?"

"Because I spoke with my chief and convinced him he should let us stay here in the cave for several days. We will catch up with them at the new homeplace."

I stare at him, horrified. "What? Why would you want us left behind?"

"Because you struggle in the cold, and it causes me great pain to see it." He pulls the wrap off his shoulders and dumps it over me, tucking it close like I'm a toddler. "Because I cannot watch my mate suffer in the ice and snow for one more day."

I'm warming, and it's not just because of the fire. It feels like something is thawing in my insides as well. Is this the first time he's referred to me as his mate since the accident? "Everyone is struggling," I murmur. "It is just something we must endure—"

"No, it is not," he says in a flat voice. "I do not care if the other humans struggle. I care if *you* struggle."

I blink, because I don't know what to say to that. I want to protest that of course he cares if the others struggle, because we're a tribe and a family, but . . . he has no memory of them, either. Why would he care? "You really, really want to be left alone in a cave with me for the next few days?"

"Of course."

"Why?" I spread my hands, perplexed. "Pashov, you and I haven't been on easy ground since the accident. I haven't been nice to you, and I know I haven't. So why trap yourself in a cave with no one but me for company?"

"You have not been nice because you have been hurting," Pashov says. He reaches out and gently traces a finger along my jaw, as if discovering it for the first time. Goose bumps prickle my skin in response to that small, tender touch. He watches me, fascinated. "I have foolishly pushed ahead thinking that my lack of memories did not matter. That you would accept me as your mate again and everything would be fine. But I am realizing that perhaps I can do more . . . and that traveling is not the time or place to do it." He leans back on his haunches and smiles at me. "So I asked Vektal if I could steal you away."

"But why?" The timing seems utterly terrible.

"I want us to get to know each other once more," Pashov says. "You have memories of me. Mine of you are gone. If I cannot have them back, I would like to make new ones. With you."

I melt a little more at that. "You would?"

He nods, pressing a hand to his chest. "I feel my khui resonate to you. Every morning when I awaken, it sings a song to yours. Every time you come close, it calls for you. It knows what I have forgotten. And it is time to stop ignoring what has happened. I am not whole. I am missing a vital part of who I am . . . because I am missing you, Stay-see. I want to get that back." His expression is solemn. "Will you help me?"

The knot in my throat feels huge. He's engineered all of this?

To be left behind in the middle of a difficult journey all because we're fighting and unable to get along? It seems like a terrible idea, and yet, does it matter if we get to the new home a week after the others? What do a few days matter in the scheme of things? I hesitate. I don't want to get my hopes up. "Will it be safe to travel if we stay here and rest for a few days?"

He nods at me. "Rokan says the weather will hold. After this storm, there will be no more until the next moon."

Well, I can't say I'm displeased about that. "So what do we do?"

Pashov's gaze is intense as he watches me. "We make new memories, Stay-see."

I feel weirdly shy as Pashov putters around the cave, setting it up for us to inhabit. As caves go, it's nice and spacious, with two chambers. The larger one is the main part of the cave, and the smaller chamber is used for storage, though there's not much currently to store. Most of the equipment that is normally kept for travelers is down to a bare minimum, the rest having been scavenged since the big earthquake. There are a few blankets, at least, and a basket full of dried bones of varying sizes, since the sa-khui waste nothing. I let Pacy dig through these as I tend the fire and surreptitiously watch my mate.

Despite the grueling trip and the bad weather, Pashov seems to be in a light mood. His steps are full of enthusiasm, and he hums to himself as he unpacks roll after roll of leathers and furs from our sled. Some of the gear is his mother's, which he carefully stores in the back cave. Once all the gear is in, the sled is dismantled and also stored so the wet and cold don't warp it. Then Pashov sweeps the snow and debris out of the cave with a whisk before setting the door screen at the front of the cave. He's not happy with the way it flutters in the heavy wind and then gets to work reinforcing it with another layer of leather.

Every now and then, he glances over at me and smiles. I can't decide if he's pleased with his little plan or is feeling bashful himself. We're here alone now, without the rest of the tribe to act as buffers. And while I know him well, he doesn't know me. This is probably going to be a little awkward for both of us.

Then again, can it be? We've had sex. Even if he doesn't remember the two years we've spent together, the other night has to be burned into his mind. You can't get much more intimate than mating with someone. The sa-khui are pretty loose with their sexuality, but I know Pashov was a virgin when we resonated.

I'd forgotten about that.

Looking back, I wince at how I reacted to our having sex. It must have been mind-blowing for him . . . and then I cried. It had to have hurt his feelings, and I feel guilty. I've been so wrapped up in my own wounded emotions that I haven't given much thought to him. What kind of mate am I?

One who needs to change, that's for sure.

Pacy makes a high-pitched baby shriek, his little tail flicking back and forth on the furs he's seated on. Pashov looks back, a grin lighting his face. "He is full of energy."

"He is," I agree, a smile coming to my face. Even if he doesn't remember Pacy, it's clear that he has affection for him. "That's all sa-khui. His human half would have run out of energy hours ago." Even now I'm feeling drained and sleepy.

"Are you tired? Do you wish to rest?" Pashov puts aside the awl and leather thong he's double-stitching the privacy screen with. "I can watch the kit if you need to sleep."

"I'm all right," I tell him. I probably wouldn't be able to relax anyhow. I'd just lie in the furs and stew about how things got so wrong between us.

He watches me for a moment longer, then turns back to the screen and begins to stitch again. I watch his muscles move as he works, and my heart aches with fierce longing. Even if he doesn't remember our relationship, he is a good man.

Maybe . . . maybe I can fix this.

Pacy digs in the basket, making a frustrated noise. I reach over and absently pull out the bone he's tugging on, which is too big for him to pull out. It's a pelvic bone, flat and wide, and reminds me a bit of a plate. I lost all of my cooking gear in the big cave-in, and I miss it. If I had it here, maybe I'd cook something for Pashov, to jog his memory . . .

I pause, then dig another bone out of the basket. This one's a femur of some kind, but it looks a bit like a ladle. It's like the universe is giving me a sign.

Maybe I should cook for my mate. What's stopping me? I have time, now that we're staying in the cave for the next few days. And I love to cook. Some people sew to soothe their nerves, or whittle, or even work on hides. I cook. I started cooking for the tribe when we first landed, because I couldn't stomach all the raw meat that was being passed around. Some of the other girls were too terrified to protest that they didn't enjoy the sa-khui food, so I took it upon myself to figure out how to fix things that were more palatable to humans. The sa-khui are happy to have a diet mostly of meat, but we humans get sick of that easily. We've found some plants that are edible, and one plant in particular that is almost like a potato. I've used that dang not-potato for a ton of dishes, and while they're not quite what we had on earth, everyone loves to try them out. I've gotten really good at potato cakes, stews, and I've even made a chalky sort of cake out of the not-potato and a variety of seeds. It's been kind of a fun adventure to test out my skills and see what I could make with what the wintry planet provides, and it makes me happy to cook for others and see their faces light up when they get a little taste of home.

I haven't cooked for anyone since the cave-in. I move my fingers over the smooth surface of the pelvic bone, thinking. I could make myself a few dishes with these bones. They wouldn't be perfect, but nothing ever is. And I can dig through the supplies of dried food we have and see what I can make without being wasteful. I could make some food for Pashov. My mate has always been a hungry one, and he's the only sa-khui that eats most of my dishes with enthusiasm. Everyone else takes a polite bite or two, but Pashov eats anything and everything.

Well, everything except the hraku cake. It's made from the toffee-like seeds of the hraku plant and mixed with not-potato and more or less fried in the skillet and frosted. It's more like a donut than a cake, and very sweet. The sa-khui don't like sweet, and the one time I got Pashov to eat it, he made such a face . . .

I smile to myself at the thought. I could make it again if there's hraku stored somewhere. See if he makes the same face now as he did when he was himself.

Maybe the memory of it will jog his brain. Maybe if I cook for him, that will help him remember.

For the first time in days, I'm excited and filled with hope.

Pashov

Stay-see seems . . . happy.

My insides are filled with warmth as I watch her by the fire, picking through the basket of bones and humming a little song to herself. Pacy bangs two leg bones together, and she smiles at him. Her smile fills my chest with such aching and longing. Did she smile like that for me? Did she look at me like she does our kit—full of love and gentleness? I want her to gaze upon me like that.

I want her to watch me with heat in her eyes, like she did the night we mated.

I think of that night, over and over again. Not the part where she cried, because it wounds me. But the way our bodies moved together, the way my cock sank so deep inside her, the noises she made when she was gripped with pleasure; all of these things are burned into my mind. Most of all, I think of how it felt to hold her smaller body against mine and feel . . . complete inside her. There is no other way to describe it.

I want that completeness again. I want her smiles to be for me.

I want to remember. We were happy before my accident; this I know. She would not be so devastated if we had quarreled like Asha and Hemalo. She would not look at me with such hurt and need in her eyes.

It is up to me to fix it. Somehow. This time together alone in the cave will help us mend. I will get to learn Stay-see, and she will see I am the same male I always have been. That nothing about me has changed.

As if she realizes she is in my thoughts, Stay-see looks over at me, a soft smile on her face. A warm flush moves through my body, and my cock stiffens in my breechcloth. "Are these supplies for our use?"

Her voice is so soft I do not realize she is asking a question at first. I am too entranced by her pink mouth and the smile there. "Eh? Oh. Yes. We must leave supplies for the next hunter to visit, but we can take what we need."

"I need some utensils," she tells me, running her fingers along the shaft of one long white bone.

The sight of that makes my sac tighten and my mouth go dry. I have to fight the urge to rush out of the cave and take myself in hand. I am going to see her stroking that bone in my dreams tonight. "I . . . see."

"Do you think you could help me?"

"Show me what you want and I shall do it for you."

"No. I mean . . ." She bites her lip and gives me a shy look. "I'd like to learn how to do some stuff myself. I figure I can work on making spoons and dishes while Pacy is playing or napping."

Is that what yoo-ten-sills are? I was not paying attention. I am still thinking of her stroking that bone. "Sometimes bone can be heated and bent, and sometimes it can be carved into what is needed. What would you like first?"

She takes a pelvic bone from Pacy. Before he can cry, she waves the long leg bone at him, and he grabs at it with little blue hands. A smile curves her mouth, and I decide that her smiles are even more need-inducing than when she strokes the bone. "I would like to make a plate out of this," she says. "It's too big here, and here. I want this flat section." Her fingers sweep over the surface. "Do you think we can do that?"

"Of course." Just as soon as I stop imagining her fingers moving over me like that. I force myself to focus and get out my bag of tools. Every hunter keeps a set of tools to repair his weapons, and I was given a replacement one by my father to make up for the one I lost in the cave-in. I have a sharpening stone, a knife made from flaked rock, and a few other small tools. I give her the sharpening stone. It is rough to the touch and will be perfect for what she needs. "Use this to smooth the edges down."

She takes the stone awkwardly and holds the pelvic bone, trying to juggle the two. After a moment of consideration, she rubs the stone against one side. "Like this?"

Pacy reaches forward, clearly fascinated by his mother's new possession, and tries to grab the stone.

I chuckle and take the stone back, along with the bone. "I will do this one for you and show you how to proceed. You can do the next."

"Seems fair," Stay-see says, and pulls Pacy into her lap. He immediately grabs her braid and begins to play with it. "I appreciate the help."

"Of course. I am your mate. It is my duty to help you."

She looks displeased at my words. "I don't like the thought of being a duty."

"It may be duty, but that does not mean it is not a pleasure."

"Oh." Her cheeks flush. "I'm sorry. I'm not trying to pick a fight. I just . . ."

"You feel I am different," I say slowly. I take the pelvic bone and the rock in hand and spread a skin over my lap to catch the fragments. I rub the rock vigorously along one side of the bone, shaving it down. Once I have made the plate the shape and size she wants, I can use a less gnarled rock to sand it down to smoothness.

She watches me closely, my son nestled in her arms. "I don't mean to," she says after a moment. "I think I just resent the changes."

"I do as well."

"I know, and I keep forgetting that part." She makes a small grimace. "It's unfair of me. Forgive me?"

"There is nothing to forgive. It is a big change for both of us. We are both learning."

"I have been so wrapped up in myself," she confesses, her voice soft, "that I forget that you have woken up to find that you have a strange alien mate and a child. I imagine that is not easy, either."

"That is no difficulty," I say, turning the bone in my hand as I work. I keep my gaze on it, because I do not want to scare her with the intensity of my feelings. "I consider myself lucky. I wake up and all of my dreams have come true."

She sucks in a breath.

I look up. Her eyes are shining with emotion, and as I watch, she blinks rapidly. "I do not mean to make you weep, Stay-see."

"It's all right," she whispers. "I'm just a blubbery nightmare lately. I . . . did you mean that? About me and Pacy?"

I frown. "Why would I say something I do not mean?"

"To be nice?"

"Is this how you remember me? As a male that spits false words to be polite?" I am distressed by the thought.

"Not at all." She hugs our son closer, ignoring the fact that he is yanking happily on her brown braid. "I just . . . I can't imagine what it would be like to wake up and hear that you are tied to a stranger. One who doesn't even look like you." Her smile of acknowledgment is small, unsure.

"I did think your face was strange at first," I admit, moving the stone carefully around the edges of the pelvic bone. "Very flat, and your features are small. But I do not think it is strange any longer. I enjoy the differences . . . though I am not quite used to the fact that you have no tail." The horns I do not notice so much, but the lack of tail is noticeable and strange to me.

Stay-see goes still.

I worry I have offended her. "I am sure it does not affect your balance or your ability to sit," I tell her. "I did not mean it to be—"

"It's fine," she says softly, interrupting me. "I just . . . you sounded like yourself for a minute there." She waves a hand in the air. "Listen to me. Of course you sound like yourself. I only meant . . . that was one of the things we always joked about," Stay-see says. "Me not having a tail. Do you remember that?"

I shake my head. "I wish I did."

She looks sad, but manages a brave smile. Her eyes are shiny again, and I hate that I have disappointed her. I must think of some way to make her happy again. I work furiously on the plate, sending bone dust and chips into the air. Silence falls between us, and I want to hear her speak more. I want her smiles.

So I ask, "Will you tell me what it was like when we resonated?"

Stay-see looks surprised at my request. "You want me to tell you what happened?"

I nod. "Perhaps it will help me remember to hear about it." I press my hand to my chest, feeling the low thrum of my khui as it sings to her nearness. "This remembers you, even if I do not."

"All right," she murmurs. "I'm not much of a storyteller, though. I'm better at cooking."

"You can cook for me," I say eagerly. "I would love to eat what you make."

Her smile broadens. "Maybe tomorrow. I need dishes first." She gently retrieves her braid from Pacy's grasping hands and tilts her head, thinking. "Our resonance. All right. What do you want to know?"

"Everything," I tell her. "Spare no detail." I want to experience it through her words since I cannot remember it.

"All right." Stay-see presses her fingers to her mouth, thinking. "Well, I think it happened when I woke up out of the tube."

"Tube?"

She absently pulls a tuft of fur from Pacy's hand and gives him a bone. He immediately begins to gnaw on it. Her smile widens, and she looks over at me. "I should explain. When we first arrived, some of the girls were awake, and some of us were asleep in the wall of the ship. In stasis. It was like we were asleep, but unable to wake. The aliens were keeping us stored like . . ." She gestures at the bone Pacy is drooling on. "Like you keep the bones here. Waiting to be useful."

People were being treated like this? I frown to myself. "Go on."

"When Georgie and the others were rescued, they freed us from our sleep. One by one, we were pulled free from the wall and woken up. We didn't have much to wear, so each person was given a fur cloak to wrap around them. I don't remember who I saw when I first woke up, but I know it wasn't you." Her smile is indulgent.

"Why not?"

"You told me you were guarding the entrance. You were so excited and worried that all of the girls were going to resonate and there wouldn't be a mate for you. And then Vektal sent you away to dispose of the trackers we had in our arms." She rubs her upper arm in memory. "You were to dump them into a metlak cave, and you told me you resented every step of the journey."

I do not know what the trackers are that she speaks of, but the story she tells me is intriguing. "I did not wish to do my chief's bidding?"

"I don't think that was the part you had a problem with," Stay-see tells me, a smile on her face. "You were afraid you'd come back and all of the females would already be mated and you'd miss out. Someone else was already resonating, and Vektal had resonated to Georgie, and that only left ten women for the rest of the hunters. You told me you raced as fast as you could to finish your task and returned back to the hunting party because you wanted to be there just in case any of the females resonated to you."

"Any females . . . not you?" I frown at this thought. "I was not immediately drawn to you?"

"Oh, I doubt it." She tucks a strand of her mane behind one small, round ear. "I believe I spent most of those early days hiding under as many furs as I could wear and weeping copiously." Her brows go down, and she looks unhappy with herself. "Jeez, I guess I cry a lot."

"You were scared," I say, feeling the need to defend her. "I understand this."

The look she sends my way is pleased. "We were all scared. Some of us just handled it better than others. I was one of the blubbery weepers instead of one of the strong ones. I'm fine with that. People have different strengths, you know? Mine isn't bravery." As I watch, she picks up our son and pulls him close to her, hugging him. "I think I'm a better mom than I am a warrior. I'm definitely more of a nurturer than a fighter."

"I see no problem with that."

"Good," she says with a chuckle. "Because I don't think I can change. Georgie, though, she's strong. And brave. Liz, too. And Kira. They were our leaders when the rest of us didn't know what was going on." She shrugs her shoulders and presses a kiss to Pacy's forehead, even as he wriggles out of her grasp, reaching for the bones he was playing with. She lets him crawl out of her lap and looks over at me, her expression full of warmth and affection. "At any rate, I was busy hiding from everyone. You were all very scary-looking to me. Between the horns and tails, the glowing eyes and the blue skin, you all looked very fierce. When anyone tried to talk to me, I hid behind Kira and waited for them to go away." She raises her brows at me. "Not very brave, I admit."

I still see no fault in this. I try to imagine myself in her place, full of fear and surrounded by strangers. I think she is very brave, no matter her thoughts.

"You caught up with our group just as we made it back to the tribal cave. You walked up with this big dead animal slung over your shoulder like some sort of caveman and dropped it at Vektal's feet, looking all proud of yourself. You looked over at the girls like we should be impressed by your skills."

"And were you?"

"I don't know if 'impressed' is the right word. I do remember it made Ariana cry because she'd never seen a whole dead animal before then."

I do not know which one is Air-ee-yawn-uh. "What did you think?"

Her eyes light up. "I remember thinking that you were clearly trying to act smooth for the ladies, and if that was your way to do it, you were failing."

I grin at that. "What should I have done to impress you?"

"Bring me a fur coat." She chuckles. "Or hot soup. In the world that I come from, the meat we eat is all prepackaged and in nice, tidy little containers. You don't have to kill the animal to have dinner. You just pull out a package of meat and cook it up."

I try to imagine this and fail. "I . . . do not understand."

"I know." Stay-see sounds amused. "I have told you about it a dozen times and you have never understood it. It's something you have to see to believe, I think. At any rate, that animal—it was a dvisti—brought us together."

"It did?"

Her smile grows broader, more delighted, and my body reacts to her pleasure. She looks so happy in this moment that it makes me ache with need. I want her this happy all the time. "Yes," she says, continuing her story. "So there you were with this big kill you were proud of, and all of us humans had just arrived at the cave. Everyone was rushing out to meet us, and it was very overwhelming. I remember people trying to welcome us and steer us toward the fire, but we humans were scared, so we wanted to stick together. Someone parked us near the fire and told you to bring the kill so we could roast it. I remember you were very upset at the thought of all that good raw meat being burned."

I grunt acknowledgment. Even now, I still have a hard time understanding why humans wish to burn their meat before they eat it. When I first realized it, I thought Harrec was teasing me. It turns out that while some of the humans eat their meat fresh, most prefer to scald it until the blood is burned away . . . along with all the flavor. I suppress a shudder.

"That look on your face," Stay-see says with a giggle. "That was the exact expression you wore. You're no good at hiding your feelings, Pashov. Never have been."

I rub my jaw, feeling a bit foolish. "I do not understand why you wish to eat it burned. I am sure it is fine."

Her smile grows broader, and my khui begins to sing low in my chest at the sight of her delight. When she is happy like this, her eyes shine and her round face grows wide with her smile. Did I think humans had odd faces? Stay-see's is lovely in the firelight, for all its strangeness.

"You brought the dvisti over," she continues, her voice low and smooth and almost hypnotic. "And you started to carve it up right in front of us. I think you told me later on that you meant to pick out the best parts for the humans to impress us, but we thought you were being mean by butchering it right in our faces. I was sitting nearest to you, and you opened the thing's mouth and . . ." She makes a slashing gesture with her hand. "Wham, you cut the tongue out of it. Then you turned around and offered it to me."

I nod slowly. "The tongue is most delicious."

She makes a face. "At any rate, you were holding this big, drippy, bloody tongue out to me, and I thought it was some sort of weird come-on."

"A come-on?" I am not familiar with the human term.

"Like you were flirting with me in a gross sort of guy way."

With a dvisti tongue? When her cheeks turn redder, I realize what she means. Tongue. Ah. I think of the other night, when I buried my tongue in her cunt. Nothing has tasted good since. My mouth waters even now, thinking of it. I want to taste her again soon. I must be patient, though. "I would not do such a thing."

"I know that now. You were just being polite. And I didn't know what to do, so we just kind of stared at each other for several minutes. Then your expression changed. I couldn't figure out what was wrong with you until I felt it, too." Her hands press to her breast, and my khui thrums even louder in my chest. "We were resonating. It was the weirdest and most beautiful moment in my life."

I feel an ache in my throat. "What was it like?" I can feel the low, soft song of the khui in my chest, but it does not feel how I imagined resonance would. I have been told that it is all-consuming and maddening in its intensity. This is just pleasantness, like Stay-see's smiles or when Pacy giggles. It makes me feel good, that is all. I like it, but I wonder what the other side of it is like . . . the hunger. I am sad I have no memories of this. I want them, as much as I want memories of Stay-see and Pacy.

Her eyes close, and her face is even more beautiful. "It is like nothing I've ever felt before. You feel this . . . thunder in your chest. It comes up out of nowhere and just builds and builds, and it's so strong that you feel a bit like your entire body is quaking with the force of it. And as you look at your mate, the world seems to narrow in on just the two of you. It's like nothing else exists but you and the person you are resonating to. And there's this . . ." Her cheeks grow red. "Um, well, there's an overwhelming feeling of desire. You instantly need that person, and you want to mate."

She opens her eyes, but her gaze won't meet mine. She is shy about this.

"Tell me more?" I ask her. I am full of yearning. I want to know what she experienced. What I experienced. I hate that I cannot remember this. It is the moment every hunter dreams of, and mine is gone from my mind completely.

Stay-see licks her lips, and I am fascinated by the flick of her pink tongue against her mouth. "Well . . . I don't know if I can go into too much detail on that. Not comfortably." She presses the back of one hand to her flushed cheek. "I hope that's all right."

"Of course." I am disappointed, but I understand. Stay-see is not ready to speak of mating to me, despite the fact that we have mated in the past. I am sad. She still thinks of me as a stranger. I must get us past this. "So then we made a cave together?"

She shakes her head, and the amusement returns to her face. "Oh, not right away. I was pretty terrified of what was happening. I made you wait."

"You did?" I am surprised.

Stay-see gives a solemn nod. "A whole day."

I am startled. A day?

She laughs, pleasure making her eyes sparkle. "Right? I didn't hold out for long. It was . . . inevitable, I guess. It felt very right to me, though. I never second-guessed a single moment. You took me aside and talked to me, just talked, like we had all the time in the world, and I thought you were the sweetest blue-skinned, horned alien I'd ever met. So I jumped you."

It is this I wish to remember, more than the initial feeling of resonance. I want to know what it was like to see the fire in Stay-see's eyes when she looked at me. I want to know what it felt like to touch her that first time.

She shrugs to herself, continuing, "After that moment, we were pretty inseparable. I'm sure some of it is the resonance, but . . ." She spreads her hands. "We just kind of got along really well. You were so funny and sweet and protective, and I loved being with you. I don't think we've been apart since we resonated, except for a few extended hunting trips you had to go on." Her lower lip quivers. "I think that's why I took your . . . injury hard. I lost my mate and my best friend at the same time."

I absorb her words. She still feels like she has lost me. It is going to take more than a conversation to convince her that I am the same person. "I will get my memories back," I vow to her. "Just give me time."

She nods. "It's just hard."

"I am trying."

Her expression grows soft, and she reaches over to touch my bone-dust-covered hand. "I know. I'm trying, too. But I am going to try harder. I promise."

CHAPTER SEVEN

Stacy

We sleep apart at my suggestion. I'm not ready to have a bedmate, not when I'm all mixed up inside. I want to get back to where we were, but I also don't want to jump into things again and hurt both of us. I know that my rejection of him after sex the other day hurt, so I'm being more careful—with him and with myself.

If my request bothers him, he makes no sign of it. He hugs Pacy before I put him to bed, and gives me a brief smile before I retire to the back chamber of the cave. He will sleep in the front chamber to guard the entrance and watch the fire. The back cave is still warm, and sheltered from errant breezes that cut through the edges of the privacy screen, and I go to sleep easily.

When I wake up, there are three of the small bone plates waiting for me.

I touch the first one, feeling warm in my belly at the sight of it. The surface is completely smooth and polished, so pretty that you wouldn't think it's made of bone but instead of ivory. Each plate is slightly different in size, and I realize he's probably spent hours at work on these while I slept. It's . . . sweet.

Pashov is by the fire even now, feeding it small bits. He looks up as I enter, a pleased look on his face. "You are awake. Good. I need to go to the cache nearby and get fresh meat. Will you be all right here by yourself for a time?"

"Of course." I'm a little disappointed he's going to run out the door the moment I wake up, but we do need food. I pull Pacy into my lap and open my tunic to feed him to keep myself busy.

Pashov watches us for a moment and then unfolds his long legs, getting to his feet. "I put tea on the fire," he says, gesturing at the tripod with the hanging pouch set up over the flames. "It should be warm soon."

"Thank you," I tell him politely, though I'm not a big fan of the sa-khui tea flavors. It's nice of him to try, though, and I'll drink it just because he put in the effort. "And thank you for the plates. They're lovely."

He watches me with burning eyes. "Anything you wish for, Stay-see, you ask and I will bring it to you."

His expression is so intense, so earnest, that I feel my entire body flush in response. I murmur my thanks and concentrate on feeding my baby, wishing I wasn't being such an awkward dweeb about things. He's seen my breasts plenty of times. He's seen the baby nurse plenty of times. I shouldn't be weird about it.

But of course, I'm thinking about the story I told him yesterday of our resonance, and the intense longing on his face the entire time I spoke. It makes me hyperaware of his reactions to me, and even exposing a tiny bit of skin feels like a subtle tease. Which is stupid—breastfeeding is natural, and the way he's looking at me isn't sexual. It's longing. He wants to be included in the family.

And I said I was going to try harder, and I mean that. As he leaves, I hold Pacy close and look at the three little plates that

Pashov must have spent hours whittling down for me. Funny how I've been telling myself he can't care for us like he used to, and then he goes and does something as small yet meaningful as that.

I can do something similar, then.

Back before his accident, Pashov loved my cooking. He's never been completely fond of plain old roasted meat, but some of the concoctions I've come up with he's loved. He likes my soups, the little cakes I make from not-potato, and he especially loves the spicy little meat pies I make by combining seeds and ground up not-potato to form a type of crumbly dough. I was going to make him some of those the day of the cave-in, and the knot in my throat swells in remembrance. That time is gone, I remind myself. Look forward. Your mate is alive and healthy and wants to reconnect with you. Let it happen.

I should.

I let Pacy finish nursing. When he crawls out of my lap and heads for the basket of bones, I get up and grab a pack of the food supplies. Pashov's mother, Kemli, is our plant expert, and she's been in a gathering frenzy ever since the cave-in, trying to restock what we lost. As a result, I know we have a fair amount of herbs for flavoring. The herbs here on the ice planet are different than the ones at home—some are pine needle–like and stripped from small bushes. Some are a lichen that grows on rock, and there are a few types of strong, peppery seeds in a leather pouch. I dig through the supplies in the cave and find a couple of dried roots, but no not-potatoes. I'm disappointed, because I really want to make the meat pies for Pashov. I want to see if food can jog his memory. Didn't I see that in a movie once? If anything would bring his memory back, it'd be those pies.

I make a noise of frustration, staring down at the dried,

twisted roots in my hand. These are good for stew, but not for the pies.

While I'm frowning down at the roots, the privacy screen is pulled back and Pashov enters. He has a snowy, frozen carcass in hand, and his mane and shoulders are covered in snow. More drifts in as he steps inside, carefully replacing the screen.

"How's the weather?" I ask, putting the roots down.

"Warmer than yesterday," he tells me, shaking off the snow. "But still snowing."

"Do you think the others are all right?" I feel a little guilty that we're the only ones who stopped on our journey.

"Of course. Why wouldn't they be?"

"Because it's a blizzard," I point out. But if he's not worried, I guess I shouldn't be.

"The humans will not freeze. Their mates will keep them warm."

I don't know how to take that comment. Is he implying that I won't let my mate keep me warm? Is that why we stopped? Or is it an innocent remark and I'm picking it apart? Probably the latter.

Pashov removes his cloak and sets the carcass down by the stones of the fire. He gestures at the roots that Pacy's currently trying to pull from my hands. "Are you hungry? I can thaw a chunk of this—"

"I'm fine," I tell him. "There are trail rations to eat. I actually wanted to cook you something. A surprise."

The look of astonished pleasure on his face is painful to see. "You would make food . . . for me?"

"Of course. You loved my cooking before." My heart aches, and I feel guilty all over again. Have I truly been this awful to be around? "I thought you might like it if I cooked something for you today."

"Nothing would please me more."

"Nothing?" I can't help but tease.

The look he sends my way is playful. "Perhaps one thing would. But I enjoy cooking as well."

I giggle. "Cooking is all you are going to get today."

"Today," he agrees. "Tomorrow is a new day."

And I can't stop laughing, because this teasing side? This is my Pashov, for sure. My heart suddenly feels lighter than it has in weeks. "I can make stew and a few other tasty bits, but I really wanted to make you meat pies. I need not-potatoes, though. Do you think you can find me one?"

"Not-potato?" He nods and grabs one of the scattered bones to use as a digging stick. "I will be back very soon with your root."

Pashov leaves the cave, and I move to the carcass. It's quill-beast, which has a fatty, delicate meat that will be perfect for cooking. I pull out my belt knife and begin to skin it, thinking about all the tasty things I'll be able to make for Pashov. Quill-beasts have a layer of blubbery fat that will go great with some shredded not-potato to make my "dough" for my meat pies and . . .

And . . . wait.

I glance back at the entrance, thoughtful. The not-potatoes were discovered after the humans arrived here on the ice planet we jokingly refer to as Not-Hoth. Prior to our arrival, the roots of the pink trees were just thought to be that—roots. The sa-khui are happy to eat raw meat, but we humans like a bit of variety. I don't remember who it was that dug up the first not-potato, but I remember how excited we were.

If Pashov can't remember anything about the last two years, how does he know what a not-potato is? I ponder this as I work on skinning the quill-beast and cutting the meat into chunks. I'm distracted, and not only by the fact that Pacy is trying to put whatever he can grab off the carcass into his mouth. I'm thinking about Pashov and trying not to hope. Does this mean his memory is coming back?

Don't get too excited, I warn myself. Maybe he knew what it was before we got here. His mother's the plant expert. She might have mentioned it.

I can't help it, though; I'm practically quivering with anticipation of his return.

Pashov reenters the cave after what feels like forever. He's got one of the round, bulbous roots tucked under his arm and is covered in even more snow. He looks pleased with himself and brandishes the root proudly as he moves toward me. "Your not-potato."

I take it with reverent hands. "How did you know what I meant?"

He has his back turned to me, putting the screen back in place. When he turns around, his smile is bright but a little puzzled. "What do you mean?"

"I mean, how did you know this was what I meant? If your memories are gone?" I'm trying to keep my voice even to hide how excited I am. "How did you know where to find this?"

Pashov studies me, and then his gaze focuses on the rounded turnip-like root in my hands. He rubs his forehead, his fingers moving over the broken stump of his horn. "I . . . am not sure."

"Do you think you remembered something? Maybe if you concentrate, you can remember more?"

He nods and closes his eyes, concentrating. I bite my lip as I watch him, eager. After a moment, though, he opens his eyes and shakes his head. "I am sorry. I do not have answers." He rubs his forehead again.

"It's okay," I say quickly. That little touch to his forehead worries me. I bustle to his side and take the fur cloak from his shoulders. "You sit down by the fire and relax. I'll take care of you."

"Let me help—" he begins.

"Nope," I interrupt. "I'm good." I take the not-potato from him and move to the far side of the cave. "If you want to help me, watch Pacy and make sure he doesn't stick any organ meat into his mouth."

"The organ meat is the best part," Pashov says, but he sits by the fire and begins to play with his son.

I snort at that. "Says you." I get my favorite bone cup and fill it with tea from the fire, then push it into Pashov's hands. "Drink this." It smells like it's got intisar in it, and that's the closest thing that sa-khui have to aspirin.

He takes the cup and frowns, offering it to me. "I made this for you."

"And yes, I had some," I lie. I pat his shoulder again. "It would make me happy if you drank the rest."

He nods firmly and puts the cup to his lips, drinking deep. I watch him for a worried moment to make sure that his expression doesn't change and he's not in pain. When I see nothing seems to be wrong, I can relax a little and go back to my task of making food.

While Pashov watches the baby, I busy myself in a whirlwind of chopping, roasting, and seasoning. I'm disappointed that he doesn't remember anything, but at the same time, I'm hopeful. The knowledge of the not-potato had to come from somewhere.

Maybe other small things will bubble up to the surface given time. All I can do is encourage them along the way . . . provided it doesn't hurt his mind to do so.

I think I would rather have a happy, healthy Pashov with blanks in his mind than one that is in pain but has his memories.

The organ meat goes into the stewpot—well, stew pouch—along with a generous serving of chopped roots, a bit of not-potato, lots of peppery spices, and a couple of bones added in for brothy flavor. While that's working, I chop up more of the not-potato and grind it using a bone as a pestle. With a bit of water and fat, it makes a doughlike substance, and I'm going to use this for my meat pies. I watch Pashov and the baby as I work, and every time Pacy giggles at something Pashov does, my heart grows a little warmer.

When we're alone like this, it feels like we're a family again. I can't stop smiling.

Before long, the stew is bubbling and filling the cave with delicious scents. Pashov sniffs the air appreciatively and gives me an impressed look. "It smells good."

"Of course it does," I say, a teasing note in my voice as I pat little circles of "dough" together. "I know what you like."

He looks thoughtful as Pacy crawls into his lap and begins to tug on his long black braids. "Of course you do." He pauses, then continues. "Will you tell me more . . . about us? About what happened after we resonated?"

For some reason, I feel like blushing. I roll one of the dough circles into a ball and paint it with a bit of rendered fat before flattening it. "What do you want to know?"

"Everything."

I look up, and our eyes meet, and it's strangely intense and erotic. My cootie responds to him, and I feel a little flutter of excitement. Slow it down, Stacy, I remind myself. You're not good at moving slow, but try to do it right this time. Even if I'm feeling aroused and happy right now, I can't sleep with him again until I know for sure I'm not going to weep through it. That's not fair to him. "Well," I say, thinking as I work. "First, we had to have a cave of our own. You were still living with all the hunters, and I couldn't exactly squeeze in there . . ."

It's a lovely day. One of the best I've had in a long, long time. We stay in the little cave, happy around the fire, and just talk. We talk endlessly. I do most of the talking, telling him all about the early days after we resonated, and how strange everything was, and how he'd tried to teach me how to hunt without realizing that I was perfectly happy being a homemaker. I tell him of the first time I tried raw meat, of accidentally insulting his mother's efforts to have a resonance feast for us, of how our little cave was set up before we lost it in the earthquake. I tell him of everything I can think of, and I make food as we talk.

The soup turns out lovely—thick and meaty and full of broth. Pashov eats two bowls of it and looks hungrily at the leftovers, and I feel a sweet ache of happiness as he steals a bite from my cup when I'm not looking. This is like how it was before, I think. My mate dearly loves to eat, and I love to feed him. The meat pies are less successful—I don't have some of the seed meal I normally use, and I don't have my frying pan. I use the smallest of the little plates and end up scorching the heck out of the underside. I can't get them hot enough to crisp the outsides, but Pashov doesn't seem to care. He devours each one the moment it's off the fire, his eyes shining with pleasure. He declares them his second-favorite thing he has ever tasted, but won't tell me what the first one is.

I suspect it's dirty.

It kind of makes me want to jump him.

But I can't. I need to slow it down. I have to be sure that I'm totally fine with Pashov 2.0 before I jump in with him again.

It's still a wonderful day, though, and it gives me hope for the future.

Pashov

"Do you have more of those little pies?" I ask, licking my fingers as I finish the last of the soup. "I think they would go very well with the weather today."

Stay-see gives me an exasperated, affectionate look. "You ate all of them before they cooled yesterday. There is not a single one left."

"Could you make more today?"

Her laugh is sweet and happy and fills me with warmth. "I can if you take over my sewing." She holds out the small tunic she is making for Pacy. "I have to do what I can while he's asleep. Time is precious, you know."

Stay-see's words are stern, but her voice is all teasing and light. "I will get you a not-potato and sew, and you can make more of the delicious pies for me." I rub my belly and give her my most pleading look. "And then you can tell me more stories about us."

"All right," she says, her expression shy. "What would you like to hear about today?"

I glance over at my small son, sleeping in a basket in the next room. His eyes are closed and he sucks on his fist, fat and happy and content. "Tell me about Pacy," I decide.

"And how you wanted to name him Shovy?" Her brows go up. "Which makes me think of anchovy?"

I frown, because I do not see what is wrong with that name. A memory stirs of her making the same sour face, standing near a fire, her belly big and rounded with kit. In my memory, she turns and I am fascinated by the round curves of her tailless bottom. It is bigger now that she is with child, and I like it very much.

But then the thought is gone as quickly as it came, and I am hit with a stab of disappointment. "I will return soon," I tell her, and throw on my cape, heading out of the cave.

Once outside, I breathe deeply of the crisp air. It is cool today, but there is no snow. The landscape is white and undisturbed, nothing but rolling hills of fresh snow covering the scrubby trees that struggle toward the sunlight. I should be pleased that I have had a memory of Stay-see. I am pleased, but I am also worried at how quickly it disappeared from my mind again. Even now, I try to recall what it was, but my mind is blank. What if I do not remember it ever again?

Worse . . . what if I continue to forget things? What if the memories that Stay-see is telling me about do not stick? What if I do not remember this day, either? What if my mind is permanently like a woven container with a hole at the bottom? The thought makes me sick at heart. Stay-see deserves a mate with a whole mind, not one like a leaky basket.

Troubled, I jog out to the distant trees. I will get Stay-see a new not-potato, and she will make me more tasty treats and smile and tell me stories. I will not think about my mind or baskets. Not today. I am going to enjoy today.

As I head to the trees, I see tracks in the snow, and my steps slow. I pull out my hunting knife and carry it at the ready, but there is no movement; whatever was here before is long gone. I examine the tracks left behind; the snow is so deep that they are little more than drag marks, so it is impossible to tell what creature made them. Dvisti, perhaps. Or a large snow-cat. When I get to the trees, though, I see even more tracks. They circle around the copse of trees and then head off over a ridge.

I rub my jaw, frowning at the sight.

This is where the cache of frozen meat is kept. The cache is at the base of one of the thin pink trees, and several notches are in the slick, spongy bark. The notches tell the hunters how many kills are left inside the cache, and a notch is marked through again if something is taken from the cache. It is so a starving hunter does not waste his time digging for meat that is not there. I run my hand over the tree, ignoring the sticky feel of it. Notches run down the length of the bark, but most of them are double-notched, indicating that the cache is nearly empty. I count the notches at the top that indicate meat—four of them. A good cache has twenty or more.

But the snow here is thickly churned.

I do not like this.

I sniff the air, but there is no scent of bad meat or any other animal. No one would know this cache is here except for another hunter. I look around, turning, but there is no one to be seen. I run my fingers over the bark again, and the last notch is one that I made yesterday, sticky and fresh. If a hunter was here, he did not take food from the cache.

Just a wandering animal, then. All the same, I dig up a frozen dvisti and mark it off on the tree. It is the largest kill in the cache, and far more than Stay-see and I can eat by ourselves, but the thought of leaving the meat makes me uneasy. We will smoke the extra and store it, I decide.

When I return to the cave, Stay-see looks surprised at the amount of meat I have brought, but does not complain. We move the fire to the front of the cave, remove the screen, and proceed to smoke haunch after haunch. We work as a team, and Stay-see tells me stories of when Pacy was in her belly. The time passes pleasurably, and Stay-see even manages to make me a few of the meat pies before Pacy wakes up and demands her attention.

By the time the suns go down, the meat has been smoked but is not dry enough to serve as trail rations. I will smoke it again in the morning to dry it out so it can be stored easily. We move the fire back to the pit, return the privacy screen to its spot, and settle in for the night.

Stay-see sniffs her braid and wrinkles her nose. "I smell like smoke and sweat."

She does. I do as well. I do not mind her scent, though. I could happily bury my nose in her cunt and inhale her muskiness for days on end. "Do you want to bathe? I can get snow and we can melt some."

Her eyes light up. "I would love a bath. Pacy needs one, too."

"Then we will all bathe," I tell her. "There is enough snow for all of us." I dig through one of the packs and produce a small pouch of soapberries. "My mother's store. We will have to bring her more when we return."

"Soap, too? I'm in heaven," Stay-see exclaims, taking the pouch from me. "This is wonderful."

I am pleased such a small thing makes her so happy. I set up the tripod over the fire and hang the pouch and go out and scoop snow. I repeat this until the pouch is full of fresh water. While the water warms, she strips Pacy out of his clothing, and my son crawls around the cave, naked, his little tail flicking as he tries to grab everything possible—my spear, the plates, the meat hanging on the smoking racks, everything. His small face scrunches up with anger when Stay-see pulls things out of his grip, and he looks over at me each time as if asking me to give it back. I feel my heart melt when he looks to me, like ice left out in the sun for too long. I hold my hands out to him, and when he laughs and crawls toward me, my heart feels whole. I hold my son close, his small, naked body against my chest, and feel true happiness.

Until he pisses on my chest, that is. I hold him away from me, giving Stay-see a troubled look. "He is wetting himself."

"I noticed," she says, entertained by my shocked expression. "Though it is more like he is wetting you." She plucks the kit from my hands and holds him close, kissing his cheek as if he has done something to be proud of.

Amused, I wipe my chest off with a scrap of leather, watching as my son's little legs jiggle and dance in the air. "He likes being naked."

"Takes after his father," she says, and her cheeks grow red.

Her reaction is interesting. "Do I wander around naked, then? In front of you?"

"You have in the past." Her lips twitch. "You are very proud of your, ahem, assets."

"My cock?" I ask, unsure what she means by ass-etts. "It is a healthy one. And I have a large sac."

"I am not having this discussion." Her voice is prim, but her expression is one of embarrassed amusement, and I know she is not offended. I wonder if I can make her cheeks red again. She splashes a hand in the water and squeezes a few soapberries into the pouch. "All right. Bath time for my little man."

"And then bath time for your big one?" I ask hopefully.

Her cheeks turn bright red, and I feel pleased. "You can bathe yourself."

"I can, but I imagine it is more fun if you do it." I rub my chest idly, thinking about her small hands on my skin. I like this idea a lot.

"You're very flirty tonight," she comments as she dips the bit of leather into the pouch and begins to wash Pacy's wriggling body.

I watch them both, fascinated by my mate's graceful movements and my son's joyous ones. "Am I?" Perhaps I am. Being here with her, spending time together alone, it fills me with a great sense of pleasure. Together like this, with little Pacy between us, it does feel as if we are a family.

It makes me . . . happy.

She finishes washing Pacy, rubbing the tufts of his mane with the cloth to clean it, then swaddles him in a fresh, warm fur to dry off and hands him over to me. My son gives a screech of delight when I pick him up, and it makes me grin. "If only my mate made the same noise when she saw me," I tell him.

Stay-see just chuckles. "I'm making that noise on the inside. Promise."

I play with my son for a time, and when he gets sleepy, I hold him and rock him against my chest while Stay-see tidies up the cave. Pacy's plump little face is so small and trusting, and it makes me feel both powerful and vulnerable to look down at him as he drowses.

This is my son. A kit made from my body and Stay-see's. It is incredible to behold. He is the same color as me, and his face looks similar to my brother Zennek's, and to Farli's, which means Pacy must look like me as well. I could stare at him for hours, memorizing his small features, and never grow tired.

Stay-see moves back to my side, and there's a soft look in her eyes as she kneels next to me. "Do you want to hold him for a while longer, or should I put him to bed?"

I do want to continue holding him while he is sleepy and quiet and not tearing the cave apart with his curiosity. But Stay-see will need more water if she is to bathe, and I will need to wash as well. Reluctantly, I get to my feet. "I can put him to bed."

"I'll do it," she tells me, though she looks pleased that I offered. "Can you get more snow for washing?"

I hand over my son and watch as she takes him to the back chamber of the cave, settling him into his basket next to her fur bedding. Her hips sway with the movements, and I watch her bottom flex as she bends over. I am fascinated by that round behind. Did I caress it when we mated? I cannot remember, and I feel I should have done this. It looks as if it needs caressing, and a lot of it.

My cock is reacting to my scrutiny of her backside, however, and I do not want to make her uncomfortable. So I get up to retrieve more snow. By the time the water level is replenished, my body is back under control. I sit back down by the fire and pick up my sharpening stone. There are more bones I can carve into cooking plates for her. Her pleasure at the sight of the three plates was so great that I wish I could carve her twenty. But I will make what I can, and hope that a larger creature stumbles nearer to the cave so I can make her more. I pick up a long leg bone with a knobby end and run my fingers over it. Perhaps I can make this into a round ball for my son. He would like that. Aehako is the best carver in the cave and normally makes playthings for the kits, but I can manage something simple. My son should have gifts that make him smile . . . because then his mother will smile at me as well.

Stay-see moves to the side of the fire and dips a finger into the water. "It's warm enough again."

I nod. "You bathe. I will take my turn last." I will get her more water if she needs it, too. Washing out of a pouch is not nearly as nice as the hot pool we had in the caves, and I feel a pang of loss for our old cave. I think of my parents, my sister, and my brother and his mate, and the rest of the tribe. Are they at the new home now? Are they happy? Am I doing the right thing by keeping Stay-see behind for a few days?

I am lost in thought, studying how best to carve the bone to keep the round shape, when I notice she is not moving. I look up, and her cheeks are bright red with charming embarrassment, but I can see no reason why. "Is something wrong?"

She clasps her hands in front of her and paces on the far side of the fire. "I just realized how small this stupid cave is."

I glance around. This is a large, spacious cave. Small? "Is it?"

"It is when you're supposed to bathe in front of someone."

I . . . do not understand. "Do humans not bathe?" Stay-see has always smelled nice. She must bathe.

"Oh, they bathe," she says, fidgeting nervously. "It's just that . . . you don't remember me."

Oh. It is me she does not like bathing in front of. Strange. "But you bare your teats to feed Pacy in front of me."

"That's different."

"Did you not bathe in front of me in the past?"

"That's also different."

"Because I had my memories? But we have mated. I have had my face between your legs—"

She raises her hands in the air. "I know. I'm being silly. I know we've mated recently, but that was in the dark. And I know you've seen naked people before, but this is just you and me, and it feels a little more . . . intimate." She licks her lips and shoves her mane behind her ears. "It's just . . . okay. Here's my thing. I had a baby, right? And everything's not as tight and small as it used to be. I hate that your only memory of my body is going to be post-pregnancy." Her jaw sets in a stubborn line.

"You think I would have a problem with your body?" I am shocked. Does she not realize how much I need her? How even her slightest movements set my khui to singing?

"Maybe?" She puts her head in her hands. "Okay, you know what? I'm being silly. I'm just going to do it. Fuck it. It doesn't matter. It's just a body, and you've touched it, so it's not like you're going to be shocked if my ass is big."

Mystified, I watch as Stay-see gets to her feet. She begins to strip off her leathers with great determination, her jaw clenched. She will not meet my eyes, her focus entirely on getting naked. And I am . . . fascinated. I want to see what it is she is so worried about.

She steps out of her leggings and tosses aside her tunic, leaving her body bare. Her skin prickles in response to the cold, her pink little nipples hardening. My mouth goes dry at the sight of her body. She is all pale softness and curves, her breasts large and full with milk. Her hips flare out, her cunt covered by a tuft of dark hair. Her belly is soft and rounded, with darker pink marks reaching up the sides like fingers. Her legs are long and graceful, and as she turns her back to me, I see her smooth, soft shoulders and the fragile line of her spine. She is lovely.

She is . . . trembling. Her fingers shake as she undoes her braid, and this makes my heart hurt. My khui hums a gentle song, and I get to my feet.

I clasp her hands in mine. "Why do you shake?"

"I just . . . don't want your only memories of my body to be like this, you know?" She gestures at her belly and breasts. Her eyes are shining with tears. "Believe it or not, I used to have a tight belly and a nice ass. Now I just have too much ass and too much belly."

"But this is the belly that carried my son," I tell her, releasing her hands and putting my fingers on her stomach. "And it is round and smooth and soft and sweet, like my mate."

Her laugh is choked and she gives a little sniffle. "And my ass?"

"It did not carry my son," I tease, "but I do not think there is too much of it. I like how much there is."

"You're being too nice," Stay-see says with a watery smile and pulls my hands off her, squeezing them to let me know she's all right. "I really wanted my body to bounce back after Pacy was born, but it's not really 'bouncing' as much as it is kind of limping back."

Her words are nonsense, but I do not point this out. "I like your body. I would mate with you right now if you would let me. I would put my mouth between your legs and lick your cunt until the fire dies—"

Stay-see's fingers press to my mouth to shush me, and her cheeks are the delightful pink I so enjoy. "I . . . I'm not sure I'm ready to jump back into bed with you yet."

I nod. "I understand." I caress her lovely pale shoulder and run my fingers along her jaw. "But I do not like it when you cry over your body. You are my mate. If these are the only memories I have of your body, I have no complaints."

"Even though nothing is tight?"

"I like soft," I tell her. Even now I cannot stop touching her skin. "Soft and smooth and warm and all Stay-see. I like you soft. I would like you hard and sinewy like an old dvisti, if that is what you want." At her giggle, I feel relief. "I would like you as round and plump as a quill-beast in the brutal season." Actually, I like that idea a lot. Her bottom large and fleshy, teats bouncing, and her belly full of my kit? It is an idea that appeals to me very much. "I would even like you if you never bathed again."

Her brows go up. "Never, huh?"

"I would spend less time licking your cunt, perhaps—"

She laughs and gives my shoulder a little punch. "You are terrible." But her eyes are shining and she is no longer nervous.

I smile and touch her cheek again. "Take your bath."

CHAPTER EIGHT
Stacy

I don't know why I worry about these things.

I'm still feeling the warm fuzzies from his sweet, thoughtful words about my body. Having Pacy did a number on my flat stomach, and it's still poochy and lined with stretch marks. My thighs are bigger than they used to be, and my butt . . . Well, it's not my favorite body part. I just didn't want Pashov's only memories of me to be of a post-pregnancy body. But the things he said to me just now? I feel beautiful and like I'm glowing from inside out. I'm smiling as I crush more soapberries into the water and begin to bathe.

I just wish he'd grabbed my butt like he used to. Maybe made a joke about my lack of a tail.

Guess a girl can't have everything.

I wash quickly, getting the worst of the smoky scent off of my skin and cleaning away a few days of grime. I scrub at my skin and there seems to be more dirt than I thought, so I swipe over my body a second time, acutely aware that this isn't the sexiest bath I've ever had. Pashov's not watching me, though—I think he realizes it'd just make me nervous to see him eyeing me as I scrub at my skin.

Maybe when we get to the new home, there will be time for me to have a sexy bath for him. I'm not sure I'm ready for it just yet, though. Maybe when I stop being such a blubbery baby about everything. I hate that I'm constantly crying and emotional. I just . . .

I don't want him to be disappointed in who he's mated to. I don't want him to be disappointed in my body. In our son. In me.

It's hard not to be nervous about that sort of thing. I'm not tall and statuesque like Liz. I'm not beautiful like Ariana or dainty like Josie. I'm just average, and before, it didn't matter because we had resonance bonding us. With resonance, he'd want me even if I looked like a hag. And by the time it had worn off, we were so in love with each other, nothing else mattered.

I worry that it matters now. Then again, I worry about a lot of stupid stuff.

It's just . . . what if his memories aren't the only thing that's gone? What if his love for me disappears, too? What if, now that he no longer has our memories of resonance, he doesn't feel anything for me anymore? And this is just a sense of duty rather than affection? I'm so full of self-doubt that I can't think straight.

I finish the quickest, unsexiest bath ever and toss my spare tunic on. I braid my wet hair tightly and bind it with a tie, trying not to watch him as he adds more snow to the pouch so he can bathe. Maybe I should go to bed and leave him to his bath. The last thing he needs is me staring at him like a creepy, sex-starved mommy. Which is what I am, but hey.

I linger around the fire because I can't quite bring myself to get up and leave. I tuck my legs under me and pull out a pair of leggings that I've been sewing. The leather is thicker and tougher than usual because we haven't had time to cure it properly, but we need more winter clothing, and thick, hard leather is still leather. Beggars can't be choosers, and I want Pashov to have enough warm clothing to last the brutal season. He doesn't have much in the way of gear since the cave-in, and I want him to be prepared for the weather to turn. I can't hunt, and I'm not much of a provider, but I can cook and sew at least.

"Have you finished your bathing?" Pashov asks, dumping another scoop of snow into the pouch to melt.

I look up at him and gesture at the sewing in my hands. "I'm done. I'm just going to work on this."

"Do you mind if I bathe?"

"Not at all." I get to my feet. Of course he's going to ask me to leave. Since I was weird about my own bathing, maybe he's taking that as a cue that he needs to have privacy for his own wash.

"Wait," he says before I can leave. "Would you . . . help me?"

Help him? I can feel my body tingling in response to the question. "Of course." I've washed him in the past, though it usually led to sex. It feels like a bold move, and I'm both fascinated and a little nervous at him asking me to do something so intimate for him. My fingers itch to run all over his skin, to feel the heat of his body against mine.

So when he hands me his sharpening stone, I'm more than a little confused.

"Um?" I ask, frowning down at it.

Pashov gestures at his broken horn. "Can you smooth this out for me?"

Oh. Of course. I'm a little disappointed I'm obviously the only one thinking dirty thoughts. He has no mirror, so of course he needs my help to file down his broken horn. I grip the rock tight, wondering how I'm going to do this. He's a great deal taller than me—almost two feet, really. Even as I consider this, I'm still a little shocked when he kneels in front of me, his face upturned to mine. There's something curiously intimate about him on his knees before me.

Either that or my brain is just in the gutter. Permanently.

Also entirely possible.

From this angle, I get a good look at the stump of his horn. The edges are rough and jagged, but there's a smooth stump of bone underneath that looks untouched. I can't help but touch it. "Does it hurt?"

"It does not." His voice sounds thick. When I glance over at him, his eyes are closed, his expression tight. "If you can, grind down the hard edges, please."

"Will it help it grow back?"

"No, but I worry I will accidentally stab you or Pacy with the edges."

"Not much of a chance of that happening," I murmur, though it's sweet of him to think of us. "You're two feet taller than I am."

"When we lie in bed together, we are the same height."

Is he thinking about lying in bed with me, then? I feel a warm flush of pleasure. "I see." I hold the grinding stone against the remnants of his horn and hesitate. "This won't hurt you?"

"I will feel nothing, I promise."

I lean in, and his hands go to my waist. He's just steadying me, of course, but as I put the stone against his horn again, I realize that his face is level with my breasts. And now that I've thought about his proximity, I can't stop thinking about it. I rub the stone against one jagged break, and my breasts sway in response to the movements. Oh boy.

He doesn't grab my tits, though. Nor does he even comment on the fact that they're shaking in his face like maracas as I saw down the hard, broken points of his horn. He just kneels, utterly still, as I work on his horn. And I'm a little disappointed. Doesn't having my breasts in his face do anything for him?

I finish smoothing down the hard edges and study my work. Now instead of all splintered, it's smooth and a little sad looking. "Did you say the healer could fix this for you?"

"She cannot fix it, but she can encourage it to regrow," he tells me as I hand him the stone. "I will not be like Raahosh forever. Does it bother you?"

I think of Raahosh, his face scarred and his horns broken and twisted. He's not the most attractive alien. Would I still be in love with Pashov if he was as frightening looking as the fierce Raahosh? I study him and decide that I would. It's not the broken horn that turns me off, it's what it represents. It reminds me that I nearly lost him, and I hate the sight of it. "It's fine. How long will it take to grow back?"

He shrugs. "When Pacy is grown, it should return to its full size."

Oh my goodness. That long?

I must show my surprise, because he gets to his feet and pats my shoulder. "I am sorry."

Why is he sorry? It's not his fault. I was the one who sent him back into the storage cave to get spices that day. If his injury is anyone's fault, it's mine. "Don't apologize."

He smiles crookedly at me. "I do not want you to have a mate that is unpleasant to look at."

I'm shocked at this. Why would he think that?

I stare at him as he dusts the fine grains of ground-up horn off his shoulders. Then again, why wouldn't he think that? The few times he's touched me, I've cried. I've given him nothing to indicate that I'm attracted to him, and he doesn't remember our past together. And the horns . . . maybe those are a pride thing with sa-khui men. I never thought about it before, but everyone always talks about Raahosh's horns like they're shockingly terrible. Maybe because I don't have horns, I've never thought about it.

But I'm thinking about it now.

Pashov finishes shaking himself off and strips down to his loincloth. Once his leather leggings are off, he tosses them aside and then reaches for the washcloth I've left drying by the fire. He dunks it in the water and begins to scrub his bare chest, all vigorous movements and determination.

I suddenly realize that I've been going about this all wrong.

I've been pushing my mate away and treating him like he's a stranger. He's the same person. He's the same sweet, funny, flirty man I fell in love with. He's just missing a patch of his memory. And yet I'm acting like he's someone completely new, a stranger wearing my lover's face.

It's the same person.

And I'm an idiot, because my actions have been pushing us further apart when I should have been working to pull us together.

"Here," I say. "Let me help." And I step forward and take the cloth from his hand.

Pashov looks surprised and then delighted. His simple pleasure breaks my heart and makes me want to do more. I want to have that silly look of joy on his face all the time. To think that such a small thing—washing his chest for him—can make him so happy.

I can do a lot more than just wash his chest to bring him pleasure.

I take the berries from his hand and squeeze them over the water, making my movements slow and sensual because I know he's watching me. I make sure to lean over, thrusting my ass out as I do so, and dip the cloth into the pouch. When it's wet and sudsy, I straighten and turn back around to him.

He's watching me with eyes that burn like coals, and I know I've got his full attention. My skin prickles with awareness, and I gently drag the wet cloth over his chest. "Do you remember the times I used to do this for you?"

I watch as his throat works, and he swallows hard. "No."

I nod, because I expected that. It's all right that he doesn't remember. We can make new memories. I'm suddenly excited at the thought of teasing my mate. This is all new for him. For Pashov, this is the first time his mate has given him a sexy bath. He doesn't remember all of the playful things we used to do together, and he sure doesn't remember his first blow job. I shiver, because this is going to be fun. So fun.

But I'll start out slow. "Is there any part of you that is particularly dirty?" I ask, my voice all innocence.

He watches me hotly for a moment, and realizes I'm waiting for an answer. "Dirty?" he echoes.

"Anything in particular you'd like for me to clean?"

That scorching look flares in his eyes again. He thrusts out an arm.

Not the answer I was expecting, but a good place to start. I smile as I rub the soapy cloth up and down his muscular arm. I've missed touching him. The feel of his skin against mine is wonderful, and he's warm and sweaty-smoky-smelling, but I don't mind that at all. I love the scent of him almost as much as I love touching him.

Pashov extends his other arm, and I obediently move to that side, dragging the cloth up one bicep and then down his forearm. I think about telling him another story of us—maybe of Pacy's birth—but this moment feels so intense that I don't want to distract from it. He's silent, the only sound his harsh breathing and the flicking, distracted whisk of his tail against the floor.

And the rumble of his khui, of course. I can hear it, just as I can feel my own humming in my chest at my arousal. I slide the cloth over his shoulder and move it slowly over one pectoral. I should probably rewet it, but I'm not all that interested in the water aspect of this bath at the moment. I'm far more interested in his reaction to my touch, because Pashov has never been very good at hiding how he feels. I don't have to look in his eyes to know that his gaze is intent on my face. I can feel them, burning. I'm utterly aware of everything he's doing, the little movements of his body as he shifts on his feet, the unceasing flicking of his tail, the pounding of his heart making a rhythm against the song of his khui. His hands clench at his sides, and I suspect he wants to touch me but is trying very hard not to in case he scares me off.

I'm not going anywhere.

I trail the cloth down his hard abdomen. His stomach is all rock-hard muscle, without an ounce of fat. I love tracing the lines between each muscle, counting the six-pack that's so clearly defined. The thick protective plating on the center of his chest ends near his navel, and then it's nothing but soft blue skin. I swipe my cloth there, too, because I know he'll be able to feel it even more down here. I peek down, and his massive erection is straining hard against the breechcloth he's sporting.

My mouth goes dry at the sight. How long has it been since we had sex? A few days at least. I made a promise to myself that I wouldn't have sex with Pashov again until I was centered and I was sure I wouldn't cry. I definitely don't feel like crying right now. It doesn't have to be sex, though. It can be touching, just for the pure pleasure of caressing my mate and seeing his reaction.

There's so much I need to teach him again.

"Do you remember me touching you?" I ask him, the cloth hovering at his navel.

He groans heavily. "I wish."

"Then you don't remember all the times I touched you . . . like this?" I drag my free hand along the length of his cock.

The breath hisses between his teeth. "Keep going. I will see if it stirs my memory."

I chuckle, amused. My sweet Pashov. So funny and flirty, even in moments like this. I gaze up at him, and he's watching me with hooded eyes, arousal stamped clearly on his strong face. I stroke my hand up and down his cock again, through the leather, and watch his mouth tighten imperceptibly.

His tail flicks hard against my leg.

"Shall I stop?" I ask lightly.

"Never."

"Thought that might be the answer." I tilt my head and pretend to study him. "Should I take off your loincloth?"

His slow, intense nod is delicious.

Tomorrow, I decide, I'm going to teach him how to kiss again. Not right now, because I don't want to distract from what I'm doing and the fact that tonight is going to be all about me pleasuring him. Tomorrow, I'll show him how to kiss again—long, slow kisses and short, passionate ones and all the kisses in between. Tomorrow, I'll make a game of it.

Today, though, I'm in the mood to tease. And so I'm not stopping what I'm doing. I toss the wet cloth aside, all pretense of washing him gone. After I'm done with him, he can scrub himself as much as he wants. I don't think he's going to mind where this is going. I tug on one side of his breechcloth, and the ties come apart in my hand. The leather slides away and falls down his leg and his cock is exposed, thrusting into the open air, so thick and eager for my touch that it's practically rubbing against his spur.

I sigh happily at the sight. I wasn't a virgin when I landed here, and I knew my way around a guy's junk, but I can safely say that my mate has the biggest, juiciest cock I've ever put my hands on. He's thick and girthy exactly where he should be, the head prominent, and the ridges along the length of him are perfection. I wrap my fingers around him and sink to my knees in front of Pashov. "You tell me if you want me to slow down," I whisper.

He groans. "If you go any slower, I might die."

And here I thought I was already moving fast. Guess there's always room for improvement. Amused, I trace his length with my fingertips, pleased with just how intensely he's watching me. He's waiting, his entire body practically vibrating with tension, for me to take him in my mouth.

I'd hate to disappoint him, especially after he's been trying so hard to please me. I grip his shaft and skim my lips along the side of his cock, pressing hot kisses along his length. I can feel a tremor rock through his body at the first touch of my mouth, and his hands fist again. He's determined not to distract me.

Which means I need to be that much more distracting. I want to see him lose his control. If he's got no memories of our fumbling early attempts, I want to give him a memory that'll blow his mind into next week. So I use all of my skills on him. I move to the head of his cock and lick it like it's a melting Popsicle. Great, exaggerated licks that get my lips glossy and involve dragging my tongue over the head repeatedly. He's leaking pre-cum, and I lap it up with my tongue, making soft little noises of pleasure as I do.

"My mate," he groans. "My sweet mate." His hands flex at his sides, over and over again.

"You can touch me," I say between flicks of my tongue. "I won't break."

He hesitates, and then his hand goes carefully to my hair. I increase the intensity, taking him deep into my mouth and sucking. He chokes on his breath, and his hand tightens in my hair. I can feel his hips jerk, as if trying to fuck my mouth, and I feel a quiver of excited pleasure.

That's what I want. I want him to lose himself in the moment. I want to make him wild. My cootie's purring loudly in my chest, singing to him, and he groans again as I suck hard, taking him deep. He whispers my name, pumping slowly into my mouth. I make a sound of pleasure, letting him know that I want this, too, and his movements increase in their rapidity and his hand tightens on my head even more, until he's holding me by the hair and fucking my mouth, and I love every moment of it. When he comes, it's with an explosion, and he coats my tongue with his release, jets of cum filling my mouth. I drink it down, enjoying the choke of his breath as he struggles for control. I love that this is going to be one of his memories, this sexy wild moment we've stolen for ourselves.

I lick my lips clean and wrap my arms around his thigh,

pressing my cheek there. His hand moves over my hair, stroking it. "My Stay-see," he breathes, still panting hard. "You are . . . wondrous."

"Was it good?" I ask softly, tracing my fingers up and down his inner thigh, just because I love feeling the shivers that move through him when I do so.

"I . . . I cannot . . ." He stumbles over his words.

I glance up at him. "You cannot what?"

Pashov rubs a hand over his face. "I cannot believe I have forgotten that."

His tone of horrified wonder makes me burst into giggles.

Pashov

I wake from sleep in a cold sweat, vague flashes running through my mind of rocks falling and the sensation of being crushed. It takes me several moments to realize that I am safe, that my mate is safe, that our kit sleeps peacefully in his basket.

After that, however, I do not sleep. I stare at the ceiling of the cave, my mind filled with visions of it collapsing on top of me.

Even though it is early, I decide to start the day's work. There is always more to be done and, with just me and Stay-see here, never enough hands to do it all. I rouse from my bed and dress, stoking the coals of the fire. In the next chamber, Stay-see sleeps peacefully, and Pacy is quiet in his basket. I can put on tea, then, and heat up some of the stew from yesterday before she wakes up. I picture her smile widening at the sight of a meal ready as she wakes up, and am pleased. I want to make her happy. I want to see her smile.

I want her mouth on me again.

I am wrapped up in thoughts of Stay-see as I move the privacy screen aside and step out into the snow to relieve myself. No new snow has fallen overnight, and trails of footprints lead to the front of the cave and then away again. I frown to myself, squatting by one. It is a smaller foot than my own. Did Stay-see leave the cave yesterday and I was not aware of it? I try to recall, but my mind is fixed on the image of Stay-see kneeling before me, her tongue flicking over my cock.

I am easily distracted this day, it seems.

Perhaps my memory is messed up again. I decide to follow the tracks for a bit, checking for spoor. It is entirely possible that a creature wandered near our cave and the snow melted just enough for the tracks to look human-sized. I follow the trail for a time, but when they eventually disappear, I have seen nothing to alarm me, and I am getting far from the cave and my mate. I am just uneasy, it seems. Time to go back before the fire dies down.

Stay-see sleeps late, and when Pacy begins to stir, I take him out of his basket and let him play in the main chamber while she dozes. She gives me a grateful smile when she wakes up, stretching with a sensual motion that makes me itch to touch her again.

I set up the meat to smoke for a second day, and she sews by the fire, and we spend the day talking. I ask her to tell me as many memories as she can, and she does. She tells me of the hawl-ee-deh with gifts and games. She tells me of the time that I played a joke on her, replacing all of her sweet hraku seeds with the peppery seeds my people love so much, and how mad she was. She tells me how she sewed all the cuffs in my leggings shut in revenge, and how I ripped two pairs before I figured it out. She tells me of lazy days spent by the fire, and of the sleepless nights after the kit was born. She tells me of Pacy's birth and how he came out squalling at the top of his lungs and I dashed around the cave and shoved him under the noses of everyone in the tribe, so very proud of my son. They are all good memories, and I soak them up, eager for more.

The day passes quickly, and all too soon, the meat is dried and ready to be put away. The leggings Stay-see works on are completed, and Pacy finishes nursing for the last time before sleep and begins to yawn against his mother's teats. Stay-see looks content but not overly tired, and I hope she will continue to talk after Pacy is put in his bed. I am hungry for her company, and even a day of idle chatter and shared memories is not enough. It will never be enough. With Stay-see, I am always thirsty for more of her time, her sweetness, her smiles.

She gets up to put Pacy to sleep, and I watch her eagerly, the sway of her hips, the swing of her brown braid as she leans over, the curve of her tailless bottom. She straightens and returns to my side at the fire, and I feel a surge of joy that she will choose to spend more time with me. I cast about, trying to think of something new to speak of, something that will make her bright smile light up her face. Perhaps food. "Are you still hungry?"

Stay-see raises a hand in the air and shakes her head. "I've had all the smoked meat I can stomach for now, thank you."

I know how she feels. While smoked meat is not my favorite, fresh meat is harder to come by in the brutal season. We will be eating smoked meat for many, many days on end while the snows whip through the land. "I wish I had something else to offer you."

She sits down next to me and pats my knee. "It's fine. I'm just glad we have plenty of food to eat. We don't have the luxury of being picky."

Even so, I am already mentally planning to dig up a few more of the not-potatoes for her tomorrow. "What did you eat back in your human land?"

Her eyes widen. "Oh, wow. Gosh, a little bit of everything, I suppose. Noodles, rice, burgers, pizza. All kinds of stuff. So many different types of food." She gives me a little smile. "You know what I miss the most, though? Breakfast."

"Break-fast?" This sounds familiar, and then I realize what she speaks of. "Ah, the morning meal?"

"Yes! I would kill right now for a big batch of scrambled eggs." She clasps her hands in front of her heart. "Maybe some pancakes and toast with butter, but definitely eggs."

"Eggs?" The thought makes me queasy. "You eat eggs?"

"God, yes." Stay-see closes her eyes in bliss at the thought. "A big, steaming pile of scrambled eggs was my favorite."

And humans think we are strange. "Did you eat the shell?"

"What? No." She opens her eyes and laughs, giving me a puzzled look. "With all the weird stuff you guys eat, don't tell me you don't eat eggs?" Her brows go down. "Though, come to think of it, I haven't seen you eat any eggs. What's up with that?"

"They are unborn young."

"You sound so shocked. I'm pretty sure we've eaten young dvisti before."

"Hunters try to take the kills that will not affect the herd overall. I would not rob a mother of nursing young, nor would I steal an egg. What if there are fewer animals to hunt in the next year if I do so?"

She laughs again, clearly amused by my reluctance. "That's kind of sweet, I suppose. But no, we have animals—chickens, mostly—that are kept just to lay eggs. They lay an egg every day and people go and gather them."

I am shocked. "You keep the animal captive and steal its young every day?"

"It's not as bad as it sounds, truly." Stay-see giggles again and reaches over and pinches my cheek as if I am a kit. "It's cute that this is your line in the sand. You eat your meat raw and you eat everything on the animal. Why is an egg different?"

"Because it is," I say stubbornly. It just feels . . . wrong. Especially now that I have a kit of my own.

"Well, I am going to find an egg layer or two on this planet at some point and then we are going to have scrambled eggs out the wazoo." She tucks her head against my shoulder and puts her arms around my waist, snuggling close. I am so surprised by this that I do not move for fear that she will get up and leave. "There are creatures that lay eggs here, aren't there?"

"Sky-claws," I say, gently placing my hand on her shoulder. "And scythe-beaks. And some of the creatures that live in the great salt lake."

"Well, shoot. I don't want to see any sky-claws. And we're not going near the ocean. What about scythe-beak nests? Where do they make their homes?"

"On the sides of cliffs." She's so warm as she curls against me. Her hand rests on my belly, and I want it to go lower. Now I am thinking of what she did last night when she pulled off my loincloth and caressed me with her hands and mouth.

"Mmm. I guess it's too much to hope for a few eggs, then." She sighs. "It was nice to think about, though."

"I will get you eggs the next time I go hunting," I vow. "Once you and Pacy are settled in the new cave-home."

"No." Stay-see pats my stomach. "I don't want you to do that. If they're up on cliffs, it could be dangerous. We'll just skip it."

"Shall I get you other kits to eat for your early meal?"

She giggles. "You make it sound like I'm a monster devouring the young." She raises her hand and makes a mock claw. "Rawr. Though I don't know why I'm the fearsome one. You're the one with fangs." She reaches up and pokes one of them with a fingertip.

I do not move. I do not breathe. Her hand is too close to my mouth, and she feels warm and soft and lovely against me. I want to stay like this forever.

She studies me, and her fingers move from my teeth to my lips. She traces them gently and then licks her own lips. "You don't remember kissing, do you?"

I shake my head. "What is it?"

"Mouth on mouth?"

Ah. I have seen the others push their mouths against their human mates and thought it was a strange gesture. "Do you want to do that?"

"You don't sound all that interested." She seems amused.

"I would rather put my mouth on your cunt and—"

Her fingers press over my lips, and her expression is shy. "You go from zero to a hundred, don't you? There's no ramp-up for you."

Ramp-up? "If we are talking about places to put our mouths, I am telling you my favorite."

"But you might like kissing, too."

I shrug. "I will kiss if you wish to. I will do anything you wish to do, Stay-see. My greatest desire is to please you."

"Then we start with kissing," she says, stroking my cheek with her soft fingers. "And we move on to the other stuff when I'm ready again."

I nod. "Then let us do kissing." We can start there. I want her to be comfortable with me. I want her to crave my touch like I crave hers.

She shifts and sits up, watching me. "Why don't I take the lead?"

Is she worried I will do it wrong? "Did I do kissing before?"

"Oh, yes." Stay-see gives a dreamy sigh. "You were a great kisser."

"Tell me more about that."

Her mouth curves in a smile. "I'm not sure there's a lot to tell. I just liked kissing you. You didn't know how to do it at first, of course. It's not a sa-khui thing . . . much like eating eggs." Her lips twitch as she gets on her knees and slides one leg over my thighs. A moment later, she settles onto my lap and puts her arms around my neck. "But you learned it really fast, and then you got really, really good at it." The look on her face is dreamy as she scoots closer.

My hands go to her hips, and I fight the urge to push her down on my cock, already hard and aching in response to her nearness. But I want her to stay where she is—I love the feel of her straddling me. "Then I will learn to be good at it again."

"You will," she says softly. Her fingers play with my mane, and she strokes my jaw again. "Or you'll remember."

"I want to remember," I say, and my voice is thick with need. "I want it more than anything."

"I know. Maybe this will jog your memory, then." She leans in and presses her mouth to mine.

Her lips brush over mine, and the feeling I get is one of overwhelming sweetness. My Stay-see is all that is kind, and soft, and sweet in this world. I feel a possessive surge as I hold her close, letting her press her small lips against mine. If this is what she wants to do, then I will gladly go along with it.

Then she licks me.

I am so startled by this that I jerk back, staring at her.

"What? What is it?" Her mouth is wet and shiny, and fascinating.

"Are you supposed to do that?"

She smiles at me. "We can do anything we want to each other, silly, as long as it feels good. Did you not like it?" Stay-see looks concerned.

"I was just . . . surprised. Let us do it again." I want to taste her little tongue once more.

She slides a little closer to me, her cunt resting directly atop my rock-hard cock, and there's a smile curving her mouth. "Still want me to lead?"

I nod. I am too fascinated by how she is acting to protest. I like it when she takes control. It is such a different side of her . . . and it is exciting. I put my hands on her hips, determined not to disturb her.

Stay-see leans in again and brushes her lips over mine, like she did before. I can feel her excitement, the hot scent of her arousal perfuming the air. Her khui hums a low song, and mine responds in kind. As she leans forward, her teats brush against my chest, and her little nipples are hard. It makes my cock jerk in response because I want nothing more than to throw her down on the floor and bury my face in her cunt, devouring her until she's crying out my name. My hands clench into fists, and I close my eyes, determined to remain in control. I do not want to frighten her with the intensity of my need.

But last night, when she put her mouth on my cock? She has

only made my need worse. Now I cannot think of anything but her.

Her tongue flicks against the seam of my mouth again, and I part my lips, curious to see where this goes. Her little shiver of response fascinates me, as does the sensation of her tongue sliding against mine. She is licking me again . . . and it feels indescribable. I groan as she begins to tease me, her tongue traveling lightly against mine, coaxing me to participate. Then she thrusts into my mouth, and I gasp because it reminds me of . . . mating with her. Is that what this is? Mating with mouths?

I think I am going to like kissing. A lot.

I brush my tongue against hers, and she makes a breathless little moan when I do. Her response rocks through me, and I can no longer sit back and concentrate. I must participate, and I hold her tightly as my tongue battles with hers, slicking and stroking against one another. Her mouth is wet and hot, like her cunt must be right now, and when I thrust my tongue into her mouth, it is like I am promising her a mating, teasing her with what my cock will do to her.

And she clings to me and pants, excited by my kisses.

Over and over, our mouths mate and come together, tongues melding. My hands roam over her back, pressing her smaller form against me. She is perfection, my mate, all curves and soft skin, and I grip her backside, fascinated by how round and plush it is. Sa-khui women are lean and muscular, but my Stay-see is nothing like that, and I love her body.

She moans against my mouth and her hips rock against my cock, eliciting another groan from me. I think of last night, when she knelt before me and pleasured me with her mouth. She did not cry out her pleasure like she did when we mated. She has had no release—and I want to give her one. I slide a hand up her front, cupping her full teats. "Stay-see," I rasp between kisses. "Let me kiss your cunt. I want to lick it like you lick my mouth."

My mate shudders against me, her breathing harsh. "You don't have to—it's not about being reciprocal—"

"I want to." I tug at her tunic. "I want nothing more than this."

She pulls back and gazes at me with eyes full of need. "Are you sure?"

I growl at her. "Female. Your scent has been tempting me all day. I am hungry for it. Let me taste you."

Stay-see shivers again, and she licks her lips. "Pashov—"

I kiss her to silence her excuses. I do not know how I was in the furs before my memory loss, but I do not think it is something I disliked in the past. Even now, the scent of her makes my mouth water, and I think of our brief mating from before. I only got to taste her for a moment.

I want more. Always more.

I lift her off my lap, still kissing her, and roll our bodies onto the floor until she is underneath me. My furs are nearby, and I tug them forward so she can have something soft to lie upon. She clings to me, her nails digging into my skin in a way that is exciting and oddly fierce.

"Tell me if you want me to stop," I murmur to her as I begin to press my mouth down the fragile column of her throat.

She laughs breathlessly. "I don't think that is going to be a problem."

"Did I do this for you often in the past?"

"Oh, yes."

I am glad to hear it. "And was I good at it? Did I make you cry out?"

She shivers again on the furs. "Oh, yes."

This pleases me. I find the tie to the front of her tunic and pull it loose, and the leather falls away. Her teats are plump and heavy, the nipples hard and each beaded with a drop of milk. I am fascinated by the sight of my mate, her body lush from feeding our kit. I lean down and kiss each droplet of milk off of her skin, and she whimpers in response. More milk rises to take the place of the other drops, and I lap them up as well.

Stay-see gives a little sigh. "As much as I like your mouth on my breasts, you're going to be there forever if you wait for them to stop leaking." Her smile is shy. "And we should probably save the milk for Pacy."

I nod, kissing lower. "I will put my mouth on other things, then."

"I'm not objecting to that." She chuckles.

Her laughter makes me feel warm. The only thing better than tasting Stay-see's skin is making her smile, and I am pleased to do both. I put my mouth on her soft stomach and then tug on her leggings. They are tied at the sides, and I want nothing more than to rip at the cords and yank the clothing off of her, but I think of the long hours she spends sewing. I do not wish to create more work for her. She already has much to do. So I carefully pry the knots apart and pull the leggings down. Patient. I am being patient.

The sight of her is a gift. Her little thatch of fur between her thighs calls to me, her scent more powerful than before. "I love this," I tell her, brushing my fingers over the bit of fur. "Are all humans like this, or am I the luckiest male?"

Her laugh is breathless. "All humans have hair there to an extent. But you can still think of yourself as lucky."

"I do," I tell her, and press a kiss there. "Because this is mine."

"It's attached to me," she says, amused.

"Yes, and you are mine, too. But this is especially mine," I say, and cup her cunt with my hand. Even here she is small, but her skin is scorching hot. I can feel the thrum of her khui through her body, responding to my touch. "It is wet and hot and delicious and all mine."

She laughs again, shivering slightly. "I don't know if this is dirty talk or I'm just really turned on at the moment."

"Are you nervous?" To me, she seems nervous.

Her nod is silent.

"But why?" I press a kiss to her mound again. "I have done this many times before. I have kissed all of your body. You have borne my kit. Why are you nervous now?"

"Because it's important." Her voice is a mere whisper. "Because I've missed you so much."

"I am here," I tell her. I take her hand in mine, and she squeezes my fingers tightly. "Let me pleasure you, my mate." When she gives me a tight nod, I bend my head and kiss her mound again. I will lick her until she screams . . . but I will never let go of her.

I settle between her legs and place my free hand on the inside of one creamy thigh. I cannot stop a groan of need from escaping my throat at the sight of her pink folds, gleaming wet. I have been waiting days to taste her again. Her fingers squeeze mine once more, as if letting me know that she wants this, too. I waste no more time; I lean in and give her a long, slow lick.

Her breath shudders.

The taste of Stay-see on my tongue is delicious. I lap at her again, so juicy and sweet here. She tastes better than I remembered, and I cannot help but lick her over and over, fascinated at the softness against my tongue and the taste of her musk. She moans, and her hips rock in time with my tongue, pushing up against me. She is enjoying this, but I want to make her insane with need, like she did to me.

So I begin to explore her with my mouth, learning every fold and curve. I slick my tongue over the bump at the top of her cunt that resembles a nipple. I drag my mouth down to the entrance of her core, where she is hottest and slickest. I want to lick her even lower, but when she arches her hips so sweetly as I tongue her core, I decide to focus my attention there. I push the tip of my tongue inside her, and she moans, her grip tight on my hand. I use my tongue like my cock, pushing in and out of her. My own need is raging through me, but I ignore it. This is all about Staysee and her need, not mine.

"Touch my clit," she whispers.

I lift my head, surprised. It is the first noise she has made that was not a moan or a cry. "Your clit?" I do not know the word. "Show me."

"Here," she says. Her free hand slides between her thighs, and she parts her folds. Her fingers skim over her slickness, and then she circles the little nipple at the top of her cunt.

I am fascinated by the sight of her touching herself . . . and jealous. She is mine to touch. Mine to pleasure. But I will take what she shows me, and learn. I watch her as she slowly traces around the nipple—her clit—and her breathing quickens. She likes soft touches here, then.

I push her hand aside and bury my face between her legs again, finding her clit with my tongue. I can hear her gasp when I find it, and I set to copying her motions, tracing the tip of my tongue around it in a circle like she did. Her entire body trembles in response, and she releases a small cry.

Encouraged, I redouble my efforts, licking, nibbling, and

sucking on that small bit of flesh. If she wants me to tease her clit, I will. If she wants me to lick it for hours, I will. I watch her movements and pay attention to the grip of her hand in mine. I learn which things she likes—like the quick swipe of my tongue over her clit—and which do not move her. Over and over, I pleasure her with my mouth, and the taste of her fills my senses. I want to spend hours here between her thighs, feeling her quiver.

One of her legs twitches, and I push my free hand down on it, forcing her legs to spread wider. "Mine," I growl hungrily between licks.

She whimpers, and her hand goes to my mane. Her fingers knot in my hair and she cries out softly, her hips arching. "I'm so close," she pants. "Don't stop."

"Never," I vow, and lap at her with newfound determination. She grips my hand tightly as I continue to work her clit, over and over. Her hips rise higher with every lap of my tongue until she is pushing against my mouth, a little keening noise escaping her throat.

Then she comes in a rush of wetness, her entire body trembling. She gasps loudly and quakes, and I grip her hand tightly and continue to pleasure her with my mouth. I do not let up until she pushes me aside some moments later. "You're going to kill me if you keep that up," she tells me, all breathless wonder.

"I am pleasuring my mate," I tell her, ready to do more.

"I've definitely been pleasured," she says, panting. "I . . . wow."

"I did well?"

"Better than well. Amazing." She squeezes my hand again. "Thank you."

"Why do you thank me?"

"Because you didn't have to do that."

"I have been dreaming of that for days." I press a kiss to the inside of her thigh and enjoy her little quiver of response. "There is no greater pleasure than tasting you on my lips, and watching you come apart."

She smiles and pats the furs. "Come snuggle with me for a bit?"

"Snuh-gul?"

Stay-see nods and, as I move beside her, puts her arms around my waist and presses her cheek to my chest. She tucks her body against me and twines her legs with mine. "Snuggling. Cuddling. Holding each other."

"I would be happy to." I put my arms around her and feel content. Happy. My khui sings a song of contentment. My cock aches, and my need is fierce, but I do not need more in this moment. I have my mate in my arms, her taste on my lips, and her well-pleasured body resting against me.

It is more than enough for now.

CHAPTER NINE

Stacy

"You're sure the weather will hold?" I ask Pashov as I peer out of the cave at the clear skies the next day. The weather is lovely—for Not-Hoth. It's sunny and there are only a few fat flakes drifting on the breeze. Instead of Antarctic winter, it's more like . . . Canadian winter. Still chilly, but not nearly as miserable. "As much as I like being here with you, I also worry we're going to lose our window for travel. Maybe we should be traveling while the weather is good?"

"Rokan says the brutal season will wait a bit longer," my mate says stubbornly from his place by the fire. He holds Pacy by the hands and is trying to get the baby to walk instead of crawl. Pashov looks over at me, a touch of hurt on his broad face. "Do you not wish to be here with me?"

"That's not it at all. I love being with you." I pull the privacy screen back over the entrance and move toward him. "Being here together has helped us reconnect," I say, and touch his arm. "It's been wonderful to have private time. I would love to stay in this cave for months on end if we could." The little cave is big enough that we're not tripping over each other, and just small enough to be cozy. It's a little smoky at times, but I could be happy here. "I just worry about the travel. It hasn't exactly been easy. I don't want us to get stuck in the storms when they do come in."

"Rokan is never wrong," Pashov tells me. "He says it will be clear for longer, and my chief has given us four hands of days before they will come searching for us."

"But you said it would take at least five days to get to the valley, right? Maybe six if we travel slow. That means ten days here, and we've already been here four. I don't want to cut it too close." I stroke his arm. "I just worry."

He gives me a knowing look. "You do not wish to cut it close, or you wish to see your new home?"

I laugh and feign lightness. "Am I obvious?"

Pashov smiles at me. "You like to keep a tidy cave, and this one is a mess."

I glance around at the crowded little cave. Our gear is piled up in one corner, along with a lot of Kemli and Borran's gear. We haven't unpacked much, because I am acutely aware that we're going to have to gather it all up again and cram it onto the sled. Because of that, we tend to have to step over rolls of furs and baskets of dried meat while we move around the cave.

That isn't what's bothering me, though.

Last night, after the oral sex–athon, I fell asleep curled up in Pashov's arms, content and happy and feeling like my mate was back. That things were starting to get back to rights in my world.

I woke up to the sound of his nightmares.

Sometime while I was sleeping, Pashov had moved me back to my own furs, and I'm not sure how I feel about that. Part of me thinks it's sweet that he remembered to put me back, and part of me is disappointed that he didn't hold me all night. I know he's just following my wishes, though, so I can't be mad. Pashov was asleep in the next room in his own blankets, and thrashed wildly.

Pashov has always been a heavy sleeper, and he's never struggled with nightmares. Not since I've known him. Last night, though, he flailed and moaned in a nightmare until I woke him up. He sat bolt upright, eyes wide with terror, his skin beaded with sweat. When I asked him what was the matter, he murmured something about the cave falling in on him.

Then he promptly fell back to sleep.

After that, however, I couldn't sleep. The restlessness isn't like him.

I worry he needs the healer after all. His memories haven't come back, and with the nightmares, I'm scared he's hiding a deeper brain injury. Or what if he has PTSD after the ceiling fell in on him? It's possible, and I feel ill-equipped to help him through something like that.

I also worry that we're vulnerable alone out here in a cave by ourselves. What would happen if there was another earthquake and something should happen to Pashov? It would be beyond devastating to lose my mate after such a near miss recently, but even more awful . . . what would I do to keep Pacy safe? I can't just think about myself; I have to think of our child. I'd have to somehow hunt and survive and find the others.

Our existence is so fragile here.

But I don't want to stress Pashov. I also don't want him to feel like he's not enough for me. If it was safe? If there were no worries? I'd miss the others, but I'd be perfectly happy spending the entire brutal season curled up in the cave with my mate.

There's too much to worry over, though. I nearly lost my

mate once. I don't want to lose him again. So I smile and shrug and decide to pretend I'm excited about the new living quarters. "It'd be nice to see what the new little houses are going to be like. And Georgie said there would be toilets. I admit, I'm looking forward to toilets."

Pashov turns his face up for a kiss. "You will have more than enough time to set up your new nest, my mate. Let us enjoy our time together, yes?"

"All right," I say, and press my mouth to his with affection. Maybe I'm being paranoid. Nightmares don't mean a brain injury. The healer would have seen it already. And we're safe here. Pashov wouldn't take me and his son somewhere like this if he thought we were in even the slightest bit of danger.

I'm just overthinking.

I pull out one of the big hides from a recent kill. We've scraped it clean of all meat and fat, and it's dried out. Now it's stiff and ready to be worked, and I consider it, trying to figure out what to make. Extra boots would probably be wise, even though it's not waterproofed. But Pacy needs more diapers, or as the sa-khui refer to them, loincloths. This particular hide is too tough, but I could get out a scraper and work it over to soften it up. Pashov needs winter tunics, I need a couple of ponchos to go over my winter tunics, and there's just so much stuff to make that I get a little stressed thinking about it all. I wish we could hop in the car to the nearest Walmart and buy supplies, but it's all on us. Sometimes it's a little overwhelming.

So I focus and try to think about what is most urgently needed. Boots are probably the smartest idea for now, because one pair only means that my feet turn into blocks of ice by the end of a day of travel, and the boots take longer than one evening to dry out. My current ones can be reinforced with more padding to make them warmer, and I can use the hard leather to make a spare pair. Extra diapers are nice to have, but I can just use a bit more arm muscle and scrub the ones I have. The good thing about frozen leather is that you can just scrape off the gross bits and wrap the skins in herbs to freshen them. It's not quite the same as having disposable diapers, but beggars can't be choosers. I should make Pashov a new tunic, but the leather's poor quality, and I don't know how soft or comfortable I can make it, even with scraping. It would need days and days of scraping to be supple. That might be wasted effort. I spread the skin and look at Pashov. "Boots for me or a tunic for you, do you think?"

"Boots," he says without looking over at the leather. "You need to keep warm. I am not as bothered by the weather."

"Yes, but you're out in it more than I am," I fret. "It's just that the leather's so hard and unpleasant for a tunic. You need something soft." I look over at him. "Are you going to hunt anything with a better hide that I could use for you?"

"I do not like the thought of leaving you and Pacy here alone while I hunt," he tells me, taking Pacy's small hands and helping him wobble a few steps forward. He has a delighted smile on his face at the baby's progress, and reluctantly looks over at me. "But I can check my traps, and if they are empty, I can see what else is frozen in the cache, but it means smoking more meat."

"I'm fine with that," I tell him. "Better too much meat than not enough."

He picks Pacy up and gives him a noisy kiss on the baby's round cheek. "Then I shall go and do as you ask. Will you be all right alone with this fierce little one for a short time?"

I chuckle, and not just because Pacy is so clearly delighted with his father's playfulness. "I'll feed him and put him down for a nap." He's been playing with the baby for a good while, and I'm hoping Pacy will be tired enough to sleep. That'll give me free time to work on the skins without having to fish things out of Pacy's small, grabby hands. This cave isn't exactly baby-proof.

My mate nods and gets to his feet, swinging Pacy into his arms as he does. "I will try not to be gone for long." He moves to my side and gently hands my son down to me.

"Are you feeling okay?" I ask, since I can't help but worry.

Pashov gives me a curious look. "Of course. Why would I not?"

"No reason," I say brightly, figuring now is a bad time to ask about the nightmares. "Just be careful when you go out."

"Always," he tells me, and kneels in front of me. He cups my face and, while my arms are full of wiggling child, leans in and gives me a deep, delicious kiss full of tongue and promise. "Perhaps if he sleeps when I return, you will let me lick your cunt until you whimper again."

I can feel my face get scorching red. "All right," I say, and I sound as fluttery as I feel. That was a bold statement if ever there was one. And it's not like I'm going to protest that statement. I'm down with another round of pussy-licking. I'm thinking my mate is back to his old self more and more every day, and it makes me so happy.

If only I could stop worrying.

Pashov takes his spear and puts his knives in his belt, then heads out of the cave. "Back soon, my mate."

"I'll be here," I call back after him wryly.

A few moments pass, and the cave starts to feel very empty. I begin to worry. What if his playful mood from today is an act? I can't stop thinking about the nightmares, or the fact that it's been weeks and his memories still haven't come back.

He won't be gone for long, I remind myself. Hunters go out all the damn time. I need to stop being such a worrywart. I can't help it, though. I nearly lost my mate recently. Of course I'm going to worry about him.

I occupy myself with feeding Pacy. He's fussy and doesn't want to settle down, but with a belly full of milk, he starts to get drowsy and even crankier. I let him cry himself to sleep, though I'm starting to feel like I need a nap myself. Eventually, though, he's quiet and drifts off, and I get up to put him in his basket in the next room. Finally, I can get some work done.

I hear the screen move in the other room and relief shoots through me. Pashov's back already? I tuck Pacy in one last time and head back to the main cave.

It's . . . not Pashov.

At first, I don't know what it is. I've spent my time on the ice planet sheltered in the tribal cave, and so I'm not familiar with some of the creatures that live here. All I see is dirty white fur and long arms and legs as something sneaks into the cave. Then the stench hits me. Like wet, filthy dog, it permeates every inch of the small cave and makes my eyes water. I must make a sound of some kind, because it turns to look at me. That's when I see the big, rounded eyes, the small owllike mouth, and the flat face.

This has to be a metlak.

The creature is hunched over on the far side of the cave, away from the fire. It hisses at me, and I feel a bolt of alarm. My little Pacy is asleep in the next room. I have to keep him safe—but my knife is near the metlak, and Pashov is away from the cave. I don't know what to do. Frozen with fear, I stare at the creature, waiting.

It crawls along the side of the cave, as if trying to get as far away from the fire as possible. It heads toward the packed baskets we have stacked along the back of the cave, and sniffs the air. It opens one, finds a packet of herbs, and shoves a handful into its mouth.

Is it . . . hungry?

Pashov told me that these lands were close to metlak territory. I didn't give it much thought, considering that they, like the dvisti, aren't much of an issue in the safety of the tribal cave. Out here alone, though, I stare at the creature and try not to panic.

How do I get it out of here? They're known to be wildly unpredictable and fierce when cornered. Being in my cave probably counts as cornered.

It spits out the handful of herbs and swipes at its tongue with its long fingers, then makes a high-pitched whistling sound before yanking down another basket and digging through its contents. As it moves, I can see ribs showing through the dirty, matted fur.

It's starving.

And I feel a twinge of guilt over this creature. It's clearly struggling to survive. I'm still scared of it, but maybe I can feed it and get it out the door before anything bad happens.

"Are you hungry?" I ask in a low, soft voice.

The creature hisses at me again, and I remember what Lila told me—that she had found one that understood hand signals. Well, to a certain extent. Maybe this one does, too? I gesture at my mouth, miming chewing.

The thing pauses, watching me with avid eyes.

Okay, yeah. It definitely is interested now. My skin crawls, but I force myself to move forward.

It stops hissing and growls low in its throat instead. It's a warning to me, but I need to show it where the food is before it destroys all of the things we've worked so hard to replace since the cave-in. I pick up one of the baskets of dried meat and pull out a dried slab, offering it up.

The creature grabs it from my hand, sniffs it, and then flings it aside.

"All right," I murmur. "You're clearly not a meat eater." I try to remember what Lila said about these things, but all I can think about is that my little Pacy is sleeping in the next room, and I don't want this creature to know he's there. I need a weapon. Actually, scratch that. I need this thing gone.

It grabs at another basket, and I wince, because it's another one full of smoked meat. The creature grabs a handful—a dirty handful—and then casts it aside like it's garbage. It's ruining all of our food, and that's something we can't afford. I need to do something.

I push the metlak aside, reaching for one of the large, basketball-sized not-potato roots that my mate brought back yesterday. I was going to dry it and save it for later, but if it gets this thing away, I'm game.

The metlak hisses at me again, and it bats at my arm, its claws leaving raised welts. I bite back my yelp of shock, recoiling. "I'm trying to help you, asshole," I whisper. I have to keep my voice low so I don't wake up Pacy. He's a sound sleeper like his daddy, but he's also still a baby and easily startled.

The creature clutches at its side, and for a moment I think it's wounded. But then the fur wiggles and moves—

—And I realize this starving creature has a baby. It's a she and it's a mom, like me. I'm suddenly flooded with sympathy. The metlak is clearly scared of the fire, and probably scared of me, too, but she's desperate to eat. I'm guessing her milk is close to running dry if she's starving, and it's fear for her baby that's making her be so bold as to come into an occupied cave after food.

"Here," I say softly. I offer her the bulbous root and make the miming gesture for eating again. "Eat."

She snatches it from me and begins to sniff it. The furry bundle on her chest makes a peeping noise, not unlike a baby chick. With another wary look at me, she takes a bite directly out of the not-potato. Her eyes widen, and she begins to devour it with frantic, enormous bites.

And I notice for the first time that despite the fact that she's a vegetarian, she's got some impressive fangs . . .

Pashov

Maybe we will spend the brutal season alone, Stay-see and I.

I muse this as I head back to our cave, a freshly slain dvisti slung over one shoulder. One of the many herds happened to be passing through the nearby valley, and so I followed the trails over and picked off a shaggy elder. There are many kits with the herd, and I watch them run past as the herd races away, frightened.

I do not think I can kill the young anymore. Not with my own son so helpless and small.

But now I have even more meat and a new hide for Stay-see to fuss over. We will have much smoked meat, and the cache is still half-full. If the weather holds for a few more hands of days like Rokan said, that will give me plenty of time to fill the cache and to dig up several of the not-potatoes that Stay-see makes delicious things out of. With only two mouths to feed, it would be no problem for Stay-see and me to ride out the brutal season alone, even if the snows last longer than usual.

And it will give us more time to bond.

I know my chief wants us to return sooner, but I worry it will not be enough time. I do not have my memories back yet. The ones that return are fleeting and disappear as quickly as they flicker through my mind, leaving me only with the knowledge that I did remember something. Each time it happens, it fills me with a sense of loss and frustration, like I am failing both myself and my mate.

She worries, too, I think. There are questions in Stay-see's eyes when she looks at me. She has concerns, and I think they are not just over my health. She has not yet invited me to sleep in her furs again. I am trying to be patient, but it is difficult.

I think of Rukh, the newcomer, and his mate, Har-loh. Out of all of the tribe, they seem the most tightly bonded. He hovers over her obsessively, and she seems to need him as much. Harrec told me they spent the last brutal season in a cave down by the great salt lake. It makes sense that they are so close. After moons and moons of time alone together, of course they are intertwined like roots.

I am jealous, though. Did I have that with Stay-see before? I want it back. And if it takes spending the brutal season alone with her, I am willing to do so. It will be lonely without my family and tribe nearby, but I crave closeness with my mate more than I crave my mother's herbal teas or the company of other hunters.

I have not told Stay-see of my plans yet. She will not like them, I suspect. She will want to return to the tribe for fear that I am still too injured to hunt. I feel fine, though. I am fit and capable. There is nothing wrong with my body, and I can only hope my memories will return in time. Until then, I must be patient.

The only problem with this plan that I can see is that my chief will not be happy. Vektal said he would send a hunter out to bring us back if we did not show up at the scheduled time. I can talk a hunter into seeing the reason behind my decision, though. He will have to go back empty-handed, and by the time that happens, the brutal season will be upon us and the weather will be too bad for others to venture after us.

Stay-see will be mine and mine alone throughout the cold months. I like that thought. I can hold her in my arms by the fire, and she can tell me of more memories until my mind is so full that I cannot help but be the male I once was.

Even though I am occupied by these thoughts, I am so attuned to my mate that when I hear her voice drift outside of the cave, I stiffen.

"Are you done eating?" I hear her murmur. "Leaving soon, I hope?"

A bolt of jealous anger surges through me. Is one of the hunters here? Did Vektal lie to me and send someone after us sooner than he said? Is it Harrec? Is he flirting with my mate even now?

I'm so occupied by this that I don't notice the smell emanating from the cave. I fling the dvisti down on the ground outside the cave and stalk inside. It barely registers in my mind that the privacy screen is pushed aside until I enter.

And then I see the creature.

It crouches near Stay-see, my mate strategically blocking the entrance to the next chamber of the cave with her body. The cave is a mess, baskets of food strewn about, and as I watch, the metlak shoves a mouthful of not-potato into its maw. Crumbs and filth litter the thing's coat, and it turns to look at me, hissing its anger as I enter.

All I can see is that it is too close to my mate. My precious, fragile mate.

I growl at the sight. I am both shocked and full of fear that a metlak would dare to enter my cave and approach my mate. It is bigger than Stay-see, for all that it is thin with hunger. The look in its eyes is dangerous, and I pull out my knife.

"No," Stay-see calls to me, raising her hands. "Don't! Pashov, it has a baby."

The metlak hoots angrily, slapping Stay-see's arms aside. I surge forward at that, determined to protect my mate. I will kill it for touching her.

It scrambles over her, a sharp cry of surprise escaping Stay-see as the thing climbs over her lap and then scurries past me and the fire, rushing out the door of the cave. The smell of singed fur chokes the cave, and I realize it must have burned itself as it ran.

I turn and chase after it, just long enough to make sure it does not come back. My heart is pounding in my breast, and all I can see in my mind is the creature hissing at Stay-see. Clawing at Stay-see.

My mate was in danger and I was not here.

What if I had stayed out longer? The image of the metlak striking Stay-see goes through my mind again, and my body goes cold with fear. What if it had harmed her? Or my son?

The creature races through the snow frantically, darting away from the cave. I watch it go, my knife held in my sweaty hand. I want to chase it down and ensure it does not return . . . but I do not want to leave Stay-see unprotected again.

I turn and head back to the cave, my stomach churning with unease.

Inside, I do not see my mate, just the destruction of the cave. Baskets are torn apart, their contents spilled. They will have to be discarded, the meat thrown away, because metlaks are filthy creatures. It is a waste, but I do not care. All I care about is my mate.

I enter the second chamber of the cave, and Stay-see is there, clutching Pacy tightly to her chest. My son hiccups and begins to cry, and Stay-see's cheeks are wet with tears, her eyes closed.

"My mate," I say, voice hoarse as I stalk toward her.

"I'm okay," she chokes out. "Really. I just need a moment to recover." Her fingers smooth over the kit's mane, and I see her hand is trembling.

I wrap my arms around her, the kit squeezed between us. "It did not hurt you?"

"Just a few scratches," Stay-see tells me, shaky. "Nothing big. I think it was just hungry. It had a baby, Pashov." She hugs Pacy to her even tighter. "Oh god. I kept feeling sorry for it, and yet I was terrified it would see Pacy in his basket and hurt him."

I smooth a hand down her hair. "I am here. You are safe."

She nods jerkily, pressing another kiss to Pacy's cheek as he wails in her ear. "We're lucky," she says after a moment. "Lucky all it wanted was food."

I continue to stroke her hair, though I feel helpless and frustrated. "They fear fire. I do not understand why this one approached—"

"She had a baby," Stay-see says with a shake of her head. "She was scared of the fire, but she still came inside looking for something to eat. Maybe her tribe or her mate didn't survive the earthquake? She was starving." She focuses on me, eyes wide. "You don't think it'll be back, do you?"

I want to reassure her, but the truth is, I do not know if it will be back. If a metlak is brave enough to storm inside a cave with both fire and sa-khui scent, I cannot predict if it will stay away. Metlaks are cowardly creatures for all their viciousness, and usually the sight of fire or the scent of a hunter will keep them at bay. They rarely disturb hunter caves.

But this one was hungry enough to confront my mate. I hold her close against me again, feeling her soft, trembling warmth.

So fragile. Her and my son both.

"I will make a big fire tonight," I tell her. "And we leave in the morning to rejoin the tribe."

Stay-see does not protest this. She nods and kisses Pacy's cheek again.

I cannot endanger my family. We cannot stay here alone through the brutal season after all. I will need to hunt, and after today, I will live in fear of the thought of more metlaks returning. What if that one has gone to get its tribe and they will return tonight to steal more of our food?

I wish I had killed it. Mother or not, it has put my family in danger. This place is not safe. We will rejoin the tribe because it will be safe for Stay-see and Pacy there.

I will simply have to woo my mate while we are with the tribe. I want the closeness with her that we once had . . . but not at the risk of her life, or that of my son.

Their safety comes first. I press my mouth to Stay-see's hair and try to calm her trembling. "Tomorrow morning," I promise her. "We will repack the sled and leave at dawn."

"What about tonight?"

"I will not sleep tonight," I vow grimly. "I will watch the fire."

CHAPTER TEN
Stacy

FIVE DAYS LATER

"Are we there yet?" I tease from my spot on the sled.

"We are close." Pashov's voice floats back to me. He glances over his shoulder, casting a smile in my direction. "Not too much farther."

I can't say I'm sorry to hear that. While we haven't had any issues with traveling, I'm more than ready to be done and settle into our new home. It's been a long week, and my face still feels windburned and frozen, no matter how much cream I put on it. I'm cold, tired, hungry, and physically exhausted to my bones. I feel like I could sleep for a week . . . except that wouldn't be fair to Pashov, who is probably just as tired and is doing all the work.

My mate seems tireless, though. Over ridge and valley, through waist-high snow or across rocky plateaus, he moves forward with sure feet and endless, bountiful strength. I'm both incredibly grateful for his stamina and a little worried at how vulnerable Pacy and I are. If anything should happen to him, we're screwed. It's just another reason why I'm so glad we're heading back to rejoin the tribe. There's safety in numbers, and as much as I enjoyed our time at the little cave, I'm ready to rejoin the tribe.

I just don't know if Pashov agrees.

He's been distant while we've traveled. Not in an unpleasant way, but it's clear he's holding me at arm's length. At night, we huddle together for warmth, but it never goes beyond him stroking my hair.

Which, okay, I'm a little too tired to get wild with him, but at the same time, I wouldn't turn it down. I'm hungry for the closeness we used to have, but it's pretty apparent to me that I'm the only one. But I can't blame him. He pulls the sled all day long, and I'm not sure that he's sleeping at night. He's obsessed with keeping the fire built high, if nothing else to protect us from wandering metlaks.

I worry that he's going to collapse out of exhaustion, but he seems to be handling things well. Maybe it's just me who's tired and my head's spinning with worry. Pacy's fussy, too, but I can't blame him. After a week of sitting around, he wants to stretch his legs. He's been good so far, but he's ready to play and get free from my arms.

And after a week of holding him? I'm ready for him to be free from my arms, too. Maybe when we reunite with the tribe, Kemli can watch Pacy for a night or two, and that will give Pashov and me some time together. We'd have to work out feeding times, but it's doable, and I could a steal a few hours alone with Pashov after we relax and recover a bit. I like the thought of that.

Of course, we have to get there first. I gaze around the wide-open canyon we're traveling through. The rocky walls are high but distant. There's snow on the ground, but it's not as thick as it has been in other areas. In the distance, there are copses of the thin pink trees, and overhead I see a few scythe-beaks flying past, cawing at each other. At the far end of the valley there's a large dark mass moving along the snow. Dvisti. This area has a little bit of everything. Too bad we can't stay here.

"You're sure that we're close?" I ask Pashov. I don't see any signs of the tribe. Surely we'd see signs of them if we were close, wouldn't we?

"There was a mark on one of the trees at the entrance to the valley," he tells me. "It was made by a knife. We are close."

"Mmm." I'm ready to be done, but I don't say that out loud. I don't want to seem like I'm griping when he's the one doing all the heavy work. I shift on the sled. "How are you holding up, Pashov? Do you need to rest?"

"No resting here," he tells me. "This is metlak territory. Best to keep moving until we find the tribe. We are close, I promise."

I'm not sure if he's trying to convince me or himself. Still, if this is metlak territory, it's wise to keep going. I pull the blankets close around my body and hug Pacy tight. It's been days, but I still keep thinking about the metlak mother that invaded the cave. Did she survive? Did she come back? Or did she and her baby starve to death? I suppose I won't ever know, but it makes me hold my own child a little tighter. I wish I could have done more for her, even though I was terrified of her. Maybe we should have stayed to try and help her out.

Then again, what if she had come back with her entire tribe? They would have killed us without a flash of remorse, and stolen our food. If I have to choose between feeding them and feeding Pacy and Pashov, I'm going to choose my men, of course.

The sled stops, interrupting my endless worrying thoughts. I immediately tense. "What is it?"

"I see it," he says in a low voice, and he sounds awed.

I crane my neck, because I don't see anything at all. Just snow and more snow. No cluster of houses, which is what I was led to expect. "Where?"

Pashov points ahead, and I squint, wondering if I'm missing something. Then I see it a moment later. It's a gaping dark line next to one of the cliffs. I thought it was a shadow, but I realize a moment later that the sun is facing in the wrong direction for there to be a shadow there. It's a gorge . . . in the ground.

Maddie had said that, hadn't she? I guess I'd conveniently forgotten that we're going to be living in a valley . . . in another valley. I shiver at the thought, holding Pacy tighter. "In the hole?"

"Is it a hole?" Pashov chuckles. "I guess it is." The look he casts in my direction is boyish with excitement. "Let us go see it, yes?"

Like we have a choice. I smile, though I'm not sure I'm excited about this. That "hole" looks ominous. And deep. And it's triggering my fear of heights like crazy. But it's not like there's anywhere else to go, is there?

It'll be fine, Stace. Pashov is here.

I take a deep breath and keep smiling until I relax a little. It can't be as bad as it looks.

Pashov begins to pull the sled again, his steps quicker, as if the sight of our destination has rejuvenated him. I settle back in my seat, tucking the blankets back around Pacy. It's grown colder every day, even though the weather is clear, and that means we don't have much longer until the brutal season rains down endless tons of snow on us. It's good that we're arriving now, because I don't have the same trust in Rokan's weather-sense that the others do. I'm worried about getting caught in a blizzard.

If it's this nasty when the weather's "nice," it's going to be truly awful when it turns. Before, it wasn't so bad because we were tucked away in a safe, warm cave with a heated pool and enough room for everyone. This time . . . I shudder, looking at that dark shadow ahead.

This time, the brutal season's going to be very, very different.

"Someone is coming," Pashov calls out.

I look ahead, trying to see around his big shoulders. It takes me a moment to focus in on the small, dark blue object that seems to emerge from the ground. It's startling to see, and even more startling when I realize just how tiny that blue blob is compared to the gorge.

It's . . . huge.

My stomach gives a queasy little flip.

"Harrec," my mate says in a curiously flat voice. "Of course."

We're still a fair distance away, and I can barely squint to make out features. Maybe it's Harrec, maybe not. Pashov's vision is better than mine if he can tell at this distance. "You think he heard us coming?"

"No. It is probably just luck." He doesn't sound pleased, either. A moment later, a second figure emerges, and Pashov adds, "Bek, too. They are likely leaving to hunt." He raises a hand in the air. "Ho!"

I wince as my mate's loud voice booms over the valley. Pacy gives a startled cry and begins to whine, and I hug him close, tucking him under my tunic in case he wants to comfort nurse.

"Ho!" one of the distant figures calls back, raising a tiny hand in the air.

A few minutes later, Bek and Harrec both jog up to our sled. Harrec's grinning broadly, but Bek is as solemn as ever. He rarely smiles, and today doesn't seem like it's going to be one of those days, even though he gives Pashov a friendly clap on the shoulder. "It is good to see you again, my friend."

"And you," Pashov says. "It has been a long journey. How is the new home?"

"Different," Harrec chimes in. "But good. It is a strange place, but there is plenty of room and we are sheltered from the winds." He moves around to my side. "Stay-see. How are you faring?"

"Hi, Harrec. I'm good."

"And your little one?"

Pacy's currently latched to my breast, and I don't pull him out to show Harrec, even though I know he enjoys playing with the babies of the tribe. "He's been very patient with all the travel." I smile. "It's good to see more people again. How is everyone?" It suddenly feels like we've been gone forever, not less than two weeks.

"Everyone is settling in," Harrec says, even as Bek moves to the handles of the sled and begins to pull it, giving my mate a rest. Harrec steps in next to the sled, chatting with me. "The biggest problem was figuring out who would live where," the hunter tells me with an amused look. "Everyone wants to be closest to the big bathing pool in the center of the vee-lage."

"Vee-lage?" I ask. As I say the word aloud, I realize what it is. "Oh. Village."

"Yes," Harrec says. "The humans say we should call it Crow-ah-to-an. It was Leezh's idea."

I sound the word out in my head. Croatoan? Oh, Jesus. It takes me a moment to realize where I've heard that word before—the lost colony of Roanoke. When the ships had returned to bring supplies to the colony, they found it deserted, and the only clue to where they had gone was the word "Croatoan" carved into a tree. "Liz sure is morbid."

"Shorshie did not like it, either, but it is the name we are using." He shrugs. "It is bad?"

"It's fine," I lie, though I'm a little creeped out by the name. I'm more concerned with my mate. He's silent, just like Bek. And while that's pretty normal for Bek, Pashov's normally a more laughing, friendly sort. He doesn't seem to be pleased right now, and I wonder if he's worried about our new home, too. "Why does everyone want to be closest to the bathing pool?" I ask absently.

"The floors are warm there." Harrec gives me a smug nod. "It feels good on the feet."

"Oh, wow." I've heard of such things back home, but having a thermal floor here seems like a ridiculous luxury. "I can see why everyone was fighting over it."

"Do not worry," Harrec says. "Shorshie has made sure you will have a good howse." He says the word strangely, like it fits funny in his mouth. I guess it does, considering everyone has lived in caves up until now. Harrec looks over at Pashov and elbows him. "You can bunk with us hunters, eh?"

I wait for Pashov to protest. To say that he's going to stay with me.

Pashov only nods. "Good."

And just like that, I'm hurt. Beyond hurt. In front of his friends, he's basically pushing me aside? What the heck happened? I thought we were reconnecting. And all he can say about not staying with me is *good*?

I'm silent for the rest of the journey. The talk turns to metlaks, and Pashov tells the others how the starving one invaded our cave. Bek and Harrec make concerned noises, as this is clearly unheard of. Harrec tells us that despite this being metlak territory, they have not been seen since we arrived. Bek speculates that they have left this area for another, but it is too early yet to tell. The hunting is good in this area, with many dvisti herds and lots of scythe-beaks. The next valley over is full of not-potato trees, and the chief is quite pleased with the new home.

And I listen with only half an ear, because in my head, all I hear is Pashov's voice.

Good.

You are staying with the hunters. Good.

Why is that good? I don't understand.

"Here we are," Harrec declares as Bek stops the sled. Harrec holds a hand out to me to help me down.

Pashov pushes him aside, growling. "Leave Stay-see alone."

The hunter merely laughs and shrugs, ignoring the dark looks that both Bek and Pashov give him. I'm mystified by this reaction—Harrec has always been a close friend of Pashov's. Why the sudden dislike for him now?

Is something else going on that I'm unaware of? Has he forgotten his friendship with Harrec? Cold sinks into my belly at the thought. Is this why Pashov is distant? He's forgetting more and more?

It is a good thing you are back, then, I tell myself, trying not to panic. The healer is here. She will know what to do.

I hope.

Pashov takes Pacy from me and helps me down off the sled. It feels good to stretch my legs, but I can't help but stare at the gorge, the edge of which we are standing far too close to.

Did they say this thing was a valley? It looks more like the ice-age version of the Grand Canyon. I shiver at the sight of it and move closer to my mate. "And this appeared out of nowhere? After the earthquake?"

Bek grunts. "Someone says it may have been covered with thick ice and that the ice broke during the earthquake."

That must have been some damn ice. "How . . . how deep is this?"

"Oh, many, many hands deep," Harrec says cheerfully. "The metlaks and snow-cats do not dare come down here because they will not be able to get back up!"

That . . . doesn't make me feel much better. "How do we get down?"

"Rope," Harrec declares, gesturing at a spot on the edge. There's a rock jutting up near the lip of the canyon, and I can see a loop of rope around it, leading down. I take a step closer to the edge—

—And immediately get dizzy. It's deep. Oh god. Really deep. I whimper and jerk backward, flinging myself into Pashov's embrace.

"Shhh," he murmurs, stroking my hair.

"What is it?" Harrec asks.

I can't speak. I'm panting, terrified. My heart is hammering in my chest, and my entire body tingles with fear. I can't do it. I can't. It's too far to fall.

"It is nothing," Pashov says. "Can you unload the sled while I speak to my mate?"

They get to work, and Pashov steers me gently away from them—and the edge. "Be calm, my mate."

I press my hand to my mouth, only to feel my fingers trembling wildly. "Did I mention I'm scared of heights?" I say with a nervous laugh. "Because I am. Really, really afraid. Can't we walk down?"

"If there was a way to walk down, I do not think they would use the rope," Pashov says, his voice hinting at amusement. "It will be all right, I promise. And you will only have to do this once." He strokes my cheek. "After that, you will be safe, and you will be home."

Oh sure, easy for him to say. I shiver, trying to erase the mental image of the yawning gorge out of my brain. I can't stay up here. I have to go down. Have to. At the bottom is the village, and people, and safety. I just have to get there. "I don't think I can climb and carry Pacy at the same time," I tell him.

"I will carry him," Pashov says easily. He continues to stroke my cheek, doing his best to soothe my panic. "Will that make you feel better?"

"An elevator would make me feel better," I say with a watery, nervous laugh. I'm trying not to lose my cool, but it's hard. All I want to do is turn around and run . . . which is stupid. We've traveled so far and there's nothing to go back to. I try to look over at the canyon again, and the sick feeling clenches in my belly once more. "I think I need a minute to prepare."

He nods and presses a kiss to my forehead. "I will help them unload. Can you hold Pacy until we are ready?"

I take my baby back and hug him close, ignoring his little cry of protest at my tight squeezing. The wind picks up and whips my leather tunic around my body, and I shiver, imagining the earth underneath my feet moving like it did in the earthquake. It feels very fragile and unstable here on the edge of the cliff . . . but that just might be my imagination. I feel like if I lean too far over to one side, I will tip over the edge and tumble into the ravine. Which is crazy, considering I'm standing about twenty feet away from the side, but I can't help the way I feel.

I watch as the three hunters unload the sled, casually tossing bundle after bundle of furs down to the bottom of the gorge. They fling things over with abandon, and then Bek grabs the rope and climbs down after. Harrec helps Pashov dismantle the sled, and they toss down the long bones, which will be reused for other things, because the sa-khui waste nothing. Harrec then disappears over the ledge, and then it's just me and Pashov and Pacy up here.

Pashov turns to me. "You go first. I do not like the thought of you up here alone while I am down below." He holds his arms out for the baby. "Let us put my son in his carrier on my back, and I will climb down after you."

I nod, trying to hold back my nervousness, even though the urge to throw up is growing stronger by the moment. I don't like this. I don't like the thought of Pacy going down the gorge, either, but I know that's just my anxiety speaking. He's going to be perfectly safe on Pashov's back because Pashov won't let anything happen to him. I tuck Pacy into the carrier and triple-check the straps. The baby's in a good mood, waving his little fists in the air and babbling happily to himself. I wish I could be so carefree. I check the straps one more time, and realize I'm stalling.

There's nothing I can do now except go down the rope. I suck in a deep breath.

Pashov turns to me and cups my cheeks in his warm, warm hands. "You will be fine." When I give a slow nod, he continues. "Take off your mittens so you can grip the rope tightly. Move as slowly as you need to. Brace your feet on the wall to help you move."

"Got it," I breathe.

I move forward to the edge of the cliff and grab the rope. There are knots tied every few feet, so it makes it easier to climb up and down, but my hands are shaking so badly and my palms are so sweaty that I nearly drop the rope.

"Stay-see—"

"I'm fine," I tell him. "Really. I can do this."

I grip the rope again and then peer over the edge. There's a scatter of bundles down on the snowy ground below, and Harrec and Bek are walking away, burdened with our things. I can't stop staring at the ground, though. It's at least twenty or thirty feet down, and my brain gets a little woozy at the sight. Twenty feet might as well be a hundred. It's also a completely sheer drop. I wiggle one foot closer to the edge and try to figure out how to get my feet braced on the wall, like Pashov said.

My hands slip and my foot does, too. My body skids backward. Suddenly I'm flat on my stomach on the ledge, my legs dangling in midair over the lip of the canyon. A terrified whimper escapes me.

"No!" Pashov cries out. "No, Stay-see. Stop!" His hands grip my upper arms, and he hauls me back over the ledge. "Stop," he tells me again. "There must be another way."

"I'm sorry," I say, trembling. I cling to his neck, burying my face against his chest as he holds me tight. "I'm trying."

"I know." He strokes my hair. "I know. Let me think."

I cling to him. "I wish I wasn't so afraid of heights."

"You are who you are. Make no apologies for it." He presses a kiss to my forehead. "I would change nothing about you."

He always knows what to say to make me feel better. I burrow against him, clinging to his big strong body. He might not want to change anything, but I do wish I wasn't such a coward.

"Hold still," he tells me after a moment, and I feel his hands go around my waist. He pulls at the wide leather belt I wear and tugs it off. Surviving on the ice planet (for humans, anyhow) is all about layers, and I tend to wear several furs and then belt them tightly around my waist, going over it twice. That way the furs catch no wind and don't let a cold breeze in.

He takes my belt and ties my waist to his, cinching the length of leather through the bone circle so we are roped together.

Pashov takes my hand and puts it on his shoulder. "Arms around my neck and hold me tightly."

"What are we doing—"

"You are holding on to me," he says. "And I am going to get us both down."

But he's already got Pacy. I'm going to be a deadweight on his front, and that's going to make it hard for him to climb. "Pashov, I don't know—"

"I do. Hold on to me," he says, and hitches me up a few feet off the ground, so now my feet are dangling.

I give a little whimper of fear and cling to his neck. He's not leaving me with much choice.

"Keep your eyes closed."

"Pashov!" I cry out when I feel his body shift. "I'm scared!"

"Do not open your eyes, then," he tells me. "I have you."

"Don't let me fall!"

"Never. Trust in me, Stay-see." I feel his big body flex as he moves. Oh god. Is he climbing down already? I fling my legs around his waist and cling to him with all my might. I try to focus on everything but the fact that I can feel his body sway, or that I can feel him grunt with exertion. That I can feel the muscles in his arms straining. Pacy babbles happily to himself, the burbling nonsense syllables sounding loud and uneven as they echo off the canyon walls.

Then . . . Pashov's body thumps hard, and I feel the impact of it move through my body as well. I swallow a nervous little scream.

He pats my back. "We are down, my mate."

"W-we are?" My eyes are still tightly squeezed shut.

"Yes. You can stand on your own now." To his credit, he sounds very patient and not annoyed with me at all. I dare to open one eye and glance around. I see nothing but ice and shadow, and I look down. Sure enough, Pashov's big furry boots are planted firmly on the snow. I slide one leg down off of him and feel solid ground beneath my feet.

I burst into tears.

"Come now," my mate soothes, cupping my face. "It is not so bad as that, is it?"

"I'm just relieved," I tell him between tears. All the frantic, nervous energy being sapped right out of me through my tear ducts. I feel drained. I rest my face against his chest, sniffling. "I'm sorry I'm such a mess."

"You are not a mess. We all have fears."

I want to ask what he's afraid of, but I know the answer. I think of his nightmares, always about cave-ins. Well, that particular fear is justified. I can't blame him for that.

His hands slide to my butt, and he cups it. "Besides," he teases. "I got to enjoy your legs around my waist, and now I get to put my hands on this round bottom of yours." He pats it, teasing. "No tail. So strange."

I hold my breath. That . . . that's our old joke. He always grabs my butt and makes cracks about my lack of a tail. I wait, hoping he's going to say something else. That he'll remember more.

But he just gives my butt one final pat. "Come. Let us get to the new homeplace and see what your howse will look like."

My house. Not his. Not ours. Mine.

I don't know what to think. Man, talk about mixed signals.

Pashov

This place is nothing like I had imagined. I have lived my entire life in the sheltering walls of the tribal cave, and even though I have been told what this vee-lage should look like, my mind pictured it differently. I could not envision a place where so much rock is so neatly set together. The path under our feet locks together like fat fingers, dusted by snow. It feels hard on the boots, and I wonder why anyone would set stone in the ground like this with such regularity.

"Cobblestones," Stay-see murmurs as she comes to my side. "Nice."

Is it? It feels strange under my feet. "What are they for?"

"Um?" Stay-see gives me a strange look. "To make roads. Floors. To keep the ground even. So it doesn't get slushy or muddy. And it's good for wheels." She nudges me. "I don't think you guys are up to wheels yet."

"But you have seen this before?"

"Oh yeah. Mostly in older cities. But I've seen it." She seems relaxed and comfortable at the sight. "I wonder what the houses will look like."

I am curious about this as well. I gaze around us. The crevasse walls grow higher as we walk forward, and they block out a lot of the sunlight. The shadows make it colder down here, and I worry my mate will suffer. I hold my worries back, though, because Stay-see seems excited. After the trouble getting down here, I do not want to take her back out of the valley. Not if there are metlaks up there. She will be safest with the tribe.

The crevasse winds around and splits. We turn a corner, and there ahead, I see the vee-lage. It is so . . . strange. Squat piles of rocks form regular, small caves neatly lined up in a way that looks unnatural and makes my mind hurt to see. Some are topped by leather suspended by poles until it forms a high triangle of sorts that points up at the sky. Smoke rises from a few different leather triangles, and I see people walking between the little stand-alone caves.

"Oh wow," Stay-see breathes at my side, clutching my arm. "Check it out. They look like teepees on top of walls. I wonder who thought to do that."

"I will ask," I tell her. If it is important, I will find out for her.

"I'm sure we'll find out." She continues to hold on to me as we walk forward. Her eyes are wide, and she can't stop staring. "It looks like everyone's setting up in the small houses. I wonder what the big one is for." She gestures, and at the far end of the rows of howses, there is a larger stone building, still with no top to it. "Maddie said there was a pool there, right?"

"I believe so—"

"Stacy!" An excited squeal erupts from one of the tee-pee howses as we pass it. It is Jo-see, the chattery one. She springs out, practically dancing with excitement. "You guys are here! That's wonderful! I'm so excited to see you!"

"Josie," Stay-see calls out, extending her arms. The smaller one flings herself at my mate, and the two women hug. "How was the trip here? Did everyone make it all right?"

"We did! It was great." Jo-see beams at me. "Making our way down was a little hairy, but Harlow's talking about setting up a pulley and a lift of some kind. I haven't seen her this motivated since the earthquake."

My mate gives Jo-see a gentle smile. "It's been hard for her—the ship was her baby."

"Where is the chief?" I interrupt. "He will want to know we have arrived."

"I think he's out hunting with a few of the others. Gotta get in the last-minute brutal season supplies and all that." She shrugs.

"We'll find Georgie and let her know you guys are here, though, and she can pass it on." Jo-see snaps her fingers and then waves her hands in the air, all excitement. "Oh wait! You guys need to see your house!"

"Our house? Someone picked one out for us?" Stay-see looks at me.

I am crestfallen when I realize she must be waiting for me to correct Jo-see. "I will be staying with the hunters," I volunteer.

Both women stare at me.

"What?" I ask.

Stay-see gives a little shake of her head and turns back to Jo-see. "Will you show us where the house is? I'd love to see it."

"Of course!" She links her arm with Stay-see's and leads her forward. "It's over here in the center of town. You guys weren't here, and the floors are warmer closer to the main lodge—that's the big building on the end there—and so we thought it'd only be fair if we drew numbers out of a basket to see who got to pick first. You ended up being number three, and Georgie picked for you guys." She beams at my mate. "You got a fantastic house! Mine's on the outskirts, but I don't really mind, because Haeden says it means I'm that much closer to him when he comes home from hunting, and you know how much I miss him when he goes out." She sighs.

I stop listening as Jo-see starts to go on and on about how impressive and wonderful her mate is. The female chatters like she will run out of air if she stops, but Stay-see does not seem to mind. She glances back at me every now and then, but seems content to let Jo-see lead her forward. I gaze around the vee-lage. To the back of the cluster of dwellings, I see Hemalo helping my brother Zennek and his mate set up their tee-pee atop their cave. Two human females are walking to the big lodge, holding a conversation, with their kits on their hips. I can hear the murmur of voices and the sounds of hammering. Somewhere in the maze of stone that is now our home, a kit cries.

It feels very strange to be in this place and realize this is home.

"So, Croatoan? For real? That's what we're calling this place?" my mate says, and I am drawn back to the conversation and her sweet voice. "Liz came up with that?"

"Who else?" Jo-see gives a little snort. "But you have to admit, it does fit. The whole abandoned village and mystery thing."

"I guess. I still think it's spooky. Do we know who was here before us, then? Did they leave any clues?"

"A few," Jo-see says. "I'll show you when we get to your house. Come on. We're almost there. You're going to be next to Maddie and Hassen."

"I like them," Stay-see says in a quiet voice.

"Psh. You like everyone."

It is true. My mate does not have an unkind bone in her body. I am pleased that Jo-see leads us up through the main section of the cave—I will always somehow think of our home as a cave, even if it is not—and am doubly pleased to see that the howses here are firm and steady. The stones are neatly stacked in their little rows as they make up the walls, and Jo-see points out Mah-dee and Hassen's dwelling, which is already covered with a large hide that seems to be sa-kohtsk and a few dvisti hides sewn to it. A small plume of smoke rises from their dwelling, and I watch a curl of it rise, only to be carried away by the wind. Smoke in my eyes is one thing I will not miss about the cave. But with no protection from the weather, I do not see how this will be safe for my Stay-see and my son.

"Here we go," Jo-see calls out. "Home sweet home." She

gestures at the doorway of the howse next to Mah-dee and Hassen's dwelling. "Georgie picked you out a good one."

"I'll have to tell her thank you," my mate says, letting go of Jo-see's arm and wandering into her new home. She touches the wall. "The bricks are tight together."

"Mortared," Jo-see says. "No cracks to let the wind in. You might have to plug a few, but otherwise it's pretty snug, which is a relief."

"It is."

"The stone helps keep the heat from the fire in, too. It's pretty spiff."

Stay-see brightens. "That seems nice." Her hand caresses the bricks again, and I realize both she and Jo-see seem very small next to the wall. This is not a human-sized dwelling, then.

"Was this made by sa-khui?" I ask.

"I don't think so," Jo-see says, stepping farther into the howse. "You guys crashed here, like, three hundred years ago, right? This is way older than that. It's so old that the roofs rotted off." She gestures at the open air. "Ariana said she was studying archaeology in college and that a lot of the ruins would look like this. The roof was made out of something that rotted away and all we have left is the stonework."

Curious. I follow them in and notice the stones on the floor are even and hard here, too. The walls are all covered with a thin layer of ice, which will make things slippery and cold. "This ice will have to be removed."

"Yeah, it's not on the floors because they stay warm. If you take your shoes off, you'll notice it. Well, I don't know if you'll want to take them off right now. Kinda needs sweeping in here. But in general." Jo-see gestures at the wall, stepping over to one side. "But let me show you this."

Stay-see glances at me and then follows Jo-see over. "What is it?"

"Carvings," Jo-see says. "All of the houses have a few. Some of them are more detailed than others. You can just barely make them out under the ice." She slides a hand over the ice, as if trying to wipe it away.

Stay-see leans in and squints. I move to my mate's side, curious if they look anything like Aehako's carvings. Aehako likes to carve swirls and soft shapes into bone. These carvings are nothing like his—hard and angular, they seem to be made of all sharp edges just like this vee-lage. I do not realize what I am looking at until Stay-see gasps. "Is that a person?"

I lean in and stare at the carving a bit closer. It does not look like a person. It looks like blocky lines. Blocky lines leading to more blocky lines. "Where?"

"Here," Stay-see says. "It's pretty stylized, but I guess these are legs, and the head, and . . ." She gestures at four of the lines. "I guess these are arms? Four arms?"

"Unless they're two tails," Jo-see says, amused. "And they grow out of shoulders. It's hard to say, considering it's little more than a stick figure, but it's kinda cool, huh?"

"Weird." Stay-see runs her hand along the ice, peering at the wall. "These down here aren't people, though. They almost look like trees. Human trees."

"Yeah," Jo-see says, and there's a wistful note in her voice. "We've been talking about that. There's a couple of critters that no one's ever seen drawn on another wall. Big, round, roly-poly things with long noses. Which kind of made us speculate if we're in the middle of an ice age here. Maybe these people lived here in warmer times and left when it got too cold."

"But where did they go?"

She shrugs. "Your guess is as good as mine."

None of this conversation makes sense to me. Ice has always been here. "There is no place anyone can go that does not have ice," I point out.

"I believe you," Stay-see says. She turns to Jo-see and clasps her hands. "All right. Show me the toilet."

Stay-see seems very pleased with the howse. She exclaims happily over the toy-let, the small area in the back with a lip of stone she says will be perfect for a kit-chen, and does not seem to mind that there is no top to her cave yet. Hemalo comes by to speak to us, and we discuss the number of hides needed and the bones that must be used to support the dwelling's lid.

Then, suddenly, it seems as if the entire tribe stops by to say hello. People stream in, hugging Stay-see and me, and my mother takes little Pacy, declaring that we need time to unpack and relax and she will take care of him. She does not realize that I will not be staying with Stay-see.

Even though things are no longer uneasy between us, my mate still has not asked me to come and live with her. She has not invited me to her bed. She has not accepted me as her mate once more. Until that time, I must wait patiently, and if it means living with the unmated hunters for now, so be it.

But I will make sure my mate has everything she needs to be comfortable. I will not neglect her again.

CHAPTER ELEVEN
Stacy

The wind howls high above the canyon. One of the strange things about living here at Croatoan is that the wind whistles and hums all day long. It's an endless white noise and takes some getting used to after the quiet of the cave. I like it, though. It drowns out the small noises of living in a tribe.

Like the sex. Jesus, Maddie and Hassen are *loud*. I can hear them in my house, over and over again. Several times a night. Every night. On days like that, I hope for high wind, because our little huts are awfully close together, and hearing that sort of thing makes me feel awkward . . . and lonely.

I miss Pashov. I miss him so much.

For the last few days, he's been staying with the hunters at night. He shows up every morning for breakfast, and I feed him and pamper him, and we talk, and it's wonderful. It's almost like we're mates again. He talks to me about his day, plays with Pacy, then kisses me senseless until he has to go out hunting. He returns at night, and we share a dinner together, more kisses and cuddles . . .

And then he leaves to go stay with the other hunters.

I won't lie, it's really messing with my mind. I don't know what to do. Should I complain? Is there something else going on that he doesn't want me to know about? Is it his nightmares? I worry about him. I worry about him and I miss him fiercely when he's gone. Even though I like the hut I'm now in, it doesn't quite feel like home when he's not here.

Other than that, though, Croatoan is really dang nice. Despite the abandoned city's initial creepiness, I'm getting used to the place. I like the stone walls because they keep the heat in. I like the teepee top of the house because it lets the smoke out. I love the little kitchen area that makes it easier to prepare food. There's no dishwasher or fridge, of course, but there's a long stone counter and a basin I can use as a sink, and those are awesome. Most of all, I love my toilet and the cushionless stool that Pashov rigged over it so I don't have to squat. It's the small things that make a house a home, and I never thought I'd be so dang happy over a toilet, but I am.

It's a little odd being in a stand-alone house after living in a central cave system with the others for so long, but the lodge roof is coming along nicely, and we've taken to gathering there during the daytime. There's a pump near the pool that's been repaired thanks to Harlow's ingenuity, and now we can pump fresh, warm water instead of melting snow. The pool itself feels warmer than the old one in our cave, but it also seems to be fed by a current of some kind, which makes it easy to do laundry at one end of the pool and not muddy the waters for the bathers at the other end. There's room enough for a fire and gatherings, and Pacy's had several playdates with Nora's twins and Ariana's fussy little Analay. Even Asha's been showing up to hang out and play with the babies, and I don't mind her babysitting because it lets me do a bit of housework without having to watch Pacy constantly.

Really, everything is great. Sort of.

It's just me and Pashov that can't seem to get it together. Have I somehow offended him? Or is he tired of being around us constantly? Does he not want to be a father and a mate to me and he's trying to let us off the hook slowly? Maybe . . . maybe he just doesn't want me anymore. Maybe he's no longer feeling the connection between us and is trying to extricate himself.

I don't know, and it's driving me crazy.

I climb out of my furs and pad over to Pacy's basket. The floors are deliciously warm and I can actually go around barefoot in my own house. It's nice. I pick the baby up and give him a kiss. "Good morning, little man."

Someone coughs on the other side of the privacy screen over my doorway.

Is it Pashov? A flicker of annoyance moves through me—why won't he enter? It's his home, too, even if he doesn't want to be here. Holding Pacy close, I move to the entrance and peer out. The brief patch of skin I can see through the cracks near the door tells me it's not Pashov, and I'm still in my sleep tunic. Eep. "Who is it?"

"Harrec. May I come in?"

Pashov's friend? I hurry back over to my pallet of furs to dress, setting Pacy down on the blankets. "Is something wrong?" I call out. While it hasn't been unusual in the past for Harrec to come by and visit, it's early. Is there something wrong with Pashov? My heart beats a little faster.

"I wanted to see if you had some of those tasty little not-potato cakes you used to make at the fire. I am tired of eating dried meat."

I exhale with relief. It's not a problem . . . he's just hungry and a bachelor. Harrec has no family to feed him. "Give me two minutes to dress." I bind my leaky breasts and fling on my favorite tunic and leggings. Pacy seems restless, but not so irritated that I can't start breakfast for someone else. I head over to the screen and pull it back, inviting him in. "Come inside. I need to stoke the fire."

Harrec pats his flat belly and beams a smile at me. He's wearing a fur wrap over his shoulders, and his long hair is tied into one thick braid, which bounces against his arm as he moves inside. "You are a good female, Stay-see."

"Thanks," I say drily. "Keep an eye on Pacy, will you? I'll get food started." I don't mind cooking for him or any of the other hunters that show up. I enjoy feeding people.

He bounds over to my furs, where Pacy is crawling around, and scoops the baby up. I hear Pacy's delighted giggle and smile to myself as I stoke the fire. Harrec is one of the quirkier tribesmates. He's a hunter, but at the sight of his own blood? Faints dead away. He's got a weird sense of humor, but he's also got a kind heart and likes kids. "This little one has a messy loincloth," Harrec announces. "Shall I change him?"

"You would be my hero if you did," I say. Once the fire is blazing again, I spear my last clod of dvisti dung and toss it on to keep things blazing, then head over to my little kitchen. I pull out a small not-potato from my basket of roots and chop it with my bone knife. I can't stop thinking about Pashov, though. A bolt of longing shoots through me, and I decide that I'll make double the breakfast cakes for when he shows up. If he shows up. Gosh, I really hope he shows up. I glance over at Harrec and he's changing the baby, making silly faces for him as he does. "Where's Pashov this morning?"

Man, that did not sound casual at *all*. So much for keeping my cool.

"Oh, I am sure he will come when he learns that I am here."

I glance over. That's a weird thing to say. "Why's that?"

"Because I am trying to make him jealous, of course." He grins at me and swings Pacy into his arms. "What better way than to come and flirt with his mate and play with his kit?"

I chop a little faster, irritated. Is that what this is about? He's come to flirt? "Hate to break it to you, but I am not interested."

"Oh, I know this." Harrec laughs, playing with Pacy some more. "You are my friend's mate and I would never do such a thing. But he does not know this."

What on earth is he talking about? He's such an odd duck. I frown as I grab a bit of dried meat and mince it, but he says nothing else, just plays with Pacy. Maybe I misheard him.

I move toward the fire and put the little cakes on my scorched bone plate. It's not holding up well against the repeated use in the fire, but without my skillet, I don't have another option. No sooner does it start to sizzle than Pashov peeks in through the doorway. "I smell cakes?" he asks, a delighted look on his face.

That delight changes to a thunderous frown when he sees Harrec.

"Good morning to you," Harrec calls out, bouncing Pacy on his knee. "Enjoying our fine weather?"

Pashov enters and moves near the fire, his eyes narrow. "The weather is poor."

"Is it?" I ask. "It's so hard to tell here in the canyon." The little city is insulated from the worst of the snows, and apparently they have been raging pretty hard lately. All we get is the occasional sprinkle of drifting snow and the incessant howling above.

Pashov nods, moving to sit next to the fire. I don't miss that he's sitting between me and Harrec. I'm a little surprised—and irritated—by that. Does he truly think I would show any interest in his friend? All I want is him.

The first cake is ready, and I plate it, then offer it to Pashov. He looks surprised but gives me a grateful smile, then scarfs it down. Between bites, he glances over at Harrec. "Are you hunting today?"

"Of course." Harrec blows a raspberry on Pacy's belly. "I just wanted to get fed first."

Pashov grunts and then looks over at me. "It is good. Thank you."

I nod and feel like blushing a little, but I get to work on the next cake, slathering it with a bit of fat so it'll cook up tasty. They discuss the game in the area and the fact that no one has seen a metlak since we arrived. I don't mind if the metlaks are completely gone, and say so, though I do think about the mother with her little baby every now and then.

Eventually all the cakes are made and both hunters fed. Pacy starts to get fussy, and so I hand the last cake over to Pashov and put the baby to my breast.

Pashov sets his little plate down, watching me.

"Not hungry?" Harrec asks, reaching for the plate. "I will take that—"

Pashov slaps his hand away. "This is for Stay-see. She has not eaten."

"Hmph," Harrec says, an amused smile on his face.

I'm surprised—and a little touched—that Pashov would save one of his cakes for me. He loves them fiercely and can eat them by the dozen. "You go ahead," I tell him. "I'm fine with a bit of dried meat."

Pashov shakes his head, stubborn. "It is for you." He nudges the plate closer to me. "What will you do today?"

"Me?" I shrug. "Some more sewing, I think. Pacy's growing so big that his tunics barely fit, and I need to line them with fur since it's getting colder."

"Do you have enough leather?"

"I can bring you some skins if you like," Harrec volunteers.

Pashov shoots him another irritated look, and I'm mystified. These two used to be good friends. Why does Harrec seem obsessed with needling him?

"I'm good," I tell Harrec. "Thank you." I turn to Pashov. "But I could use some more dung chips for the fire. I'm burning the last one right now."

"I will gather you some," Pashov says, leaning in and putting his hand on my knee. There's a hint of a smile on his face as he glances down at Pacy, nursing at my breast.

"No need," Harrec interrupts, surging to his feet. "There is an entire wall of dirtbeaks on the far side of the canyon. We've been harvesting their nests. There are so many of them that the birds do not notice, and one good-sized nest can burn all day long."

"Dirtbeaks?" I ask. "What the heck are those?"

"Bad eating," Pashov says, making a face. "You do not want to taste one."

"No one is going to eat the dirtbeaks," Harrec says, amused. "We just want their nests. Shall I show you both? It is not so far from here."

"Is it dangerous?" I ask. I am not a fan of the thought of being so close to an entire "wall" of bird nests, but it surely can't be dangerous or someone would have said something earlier, right? If it's not dangerous, well, I'm curious to see these harvestable nests that will make good fuel.

Also, I have to admit I'm curious what a "dirtbeak" looks like.

"Dirtbeaks?" Harrec snorts. "Dangerous? Not likely."

I look at Pashov. He shrugs, indicating that it's my choice. "I wouldn't mind seeing them," I say. "Let me finish feeding Pacy, then I can see if Asha can watch him for a bit."

"I can take him to her while you get your boots and cloak." Pashov leans in and traces a finger down Pacy's chubby cheek. His hand is so close, I half expect him to touch my breast, but he doesn't. And then, of course, I'm disappointed.

What I wouldn't give to be groped.

Asha is all too happy to watch my son, and I set off with the two hunters. We are joined by Farli, who is walking her pet, Chompy. She jogs to Pashov's side and gives her brother an adoring look. He hugs her and rumples her hair, and my mood lightens at the sight of their affection.

It's not a bad walk. We wander through the twisting, narrow valley of the canyon, and I marvel at just how deep it is and how the wind howls above but we're barely touched by it down here. It's definitely colder and the weather looks dreary above, but it's not uncomfortable. Maybe this brutal season won't be too bad, not if we're shielded from the snow and there's an easy fuel source to grab nearby. The canyon winds away from Croatoan, snaking in a few different directions. "Stay to the left," Harrec instructs as we walk. "If you get separated, just turn around, put your right hand on the wall, and follow it back to the vee-lage."

"Got it," I say, and pick up the pace. I don't intend on getting separated. No one is leaving my sight. Not even Chompy.

After about fifteen minutes of walking, I start to hear . . . birds. Not just one or two, but dozens. Hundreds. It sounds like the birdhouse at the zoo I last went to, caw after caw layering in on each other, so loud that even the wind howling above us can't drown it out.

I slide a little closer to Pashov and put my hand on his tunic. He encircles my waist with his arm and gives me a smile, and some of my tension eases.

Even though there's a ton of noise, I'm still not prepared for the sight of the dirtbeaks. When we enter the side canyon, it's like being hit by a wall of them. The stink of bird poop smacks you in the face, and the cawing and hooting get even louder. From floor to ceiling, they cover one of the icy walls of the canyon, fluffy white birds nesting in crevices and on shallow lips of rock. There have to be thousands of nests, all piled on top of one another, covering the wall. About a third of the nests are empty, and the ones that are occupied are inhabited by fat, adorable-looking balls of snowy white fluff with brown triangular beaks. Each bird squats over its nest, occasionally shaking its feathered wings and calling out to its neighbors.

"They're so damn cute," I tell the others. "How come we don't eat them?" I mean, I don't think I mind, because they're adorable, but it seems strange to me to have this many birds roosting and not want to toss a few of them into the stewpot.

Farli makes a face.

"Not good eating," Pashov says again. "Look closer at their nests."

I do, though I'm not sure what I'm supposed to be looking at. The nests look like they're made of mud and form perfect little cups on the side of the canyon wall. I'm about to ask what I should be searching for when a bird flutters in and arrives at her nest. She's got something big and round in her little beak, something far larger and flatter than she should be able to carry.

I realize a moment later that it's a dvisti dung patty. My jaw drops. I watch as the bird flies to its nest and begins to pick the patty apart with its little beak, reinforcing its nest with what can only be a mix of bird poop and dvisti poop.

Lovely. It's not a dirt nest at all. It's a shit nest.

"Well, that explains the smell," I say faintly.

"They are not good eating," Pashov tells me again. "They can be eaten if starving, although the meat tastes unpleasant. But the nests do burn for a long time."

"I see. I'd hate to take a nest that's occupied, though." I study the wall of calling, flapping birds. God, there really are so very many of them. "How come only some are in use?"

"Dirtbeaks mate for life," Harrec says. "The female will lay an egg and the male will cover it. The female feeds him."

"Poor female birds, always having to feed the men," I tease. "There's a good analogy for you." When all three of them stare blankly at me, I clear my throat. "Um. So what happens if there's no mate?"

Harrec shrugs. "The egg does not hatch."

Oooh. "So there could be a bunch of eggs up there in empty nests because the female doesn't have a mate?"

Pashov gives me a speculative look. "Do you want me to check for you?"

Oh god, do I ever. Eggs are my favorite food in the world. "Can we? I mean, if there's one in a nest that's been abandoned, it's probably frozen, but I could thaw it." And then scramble it. Or fry it. Or use it to cook up a potato and meat quiche . . . and now I'm drooling.

My mate nods firmly. "I shall get you an egg and a nest."

"The old nests are at the bottom," Farli chimes in. "You might have to look to the top."

Harrec snorts. "He cannot climb nearly as high as me. I will get an egg for you, Stay-see."

Pashov shoots him a black look. "You will not. She is my mate, and I will get her an egg." He points at Harrec. "From the top."

I glance up at the wall. "Guys? That's kind of high. I don't know if that's a great idea."

But the two men are ignoring me, locked in their own weird pissing war. They stare at each other, Harrec's expression challenging, and Pashov's angry.

"From the top?" Harrec repeats.

"All the way to the top," Pashov agrees, and storms forward.

I shoot an uneasy look at Farli, but she just rolls her eyes. If she's not worried, I guess I shouldn't be.

I watch as Pashov storms up to the wall of birds. I expect them to fly away, but they only squawk and flutter their wings at him. They're either going to give him a fight, or they're too lazy to retreat. Pashov grins over at me, and it's clear he thinks it's the latter. Maybe he's right and the birds are harmless. He would know.

I relax a little. Pashov loves to have fun, but he wouldn't let things go too far.

He begins to climb, each hand anchoring to rock, then he hauls his body up. He's surprisingly graceful for his size, and I watch his tail flick back and forth as he moves. Pashov is nimble and scales the cliff quickly, heading to the first nest, which is a few feet above what I could reach. It's empty, with no squatty, angry bird in it, and he pries it down off the wall, then tosses it to the ground. "No egg."

Farli trots forward to retrieve the nest, shying away at the angry calls of the birds as she approaches.

Harrec just cups his hands to his mouth. "Climb to the top, fool! That is where the newest nests are!"

Pashov's tail flicks harder with irritation, but he continues climbing. As I watch, one of his hands gets close to an occupied nest and the bird squawks angrily and pecks at his hand.

"Be careful," I call when he switches handholds. "Maybe this is a bad idea." I don't know if he can hear me from his position on the wall. I don't want to be a nag or a spoilsport, but at the same time, I'm watching my mate climb and my concern is growing. Perhaps it's just my fear of heights, but he's climbing . . . really high. And those birds are really pissy. Another snaps at him as he climbs near, and another looks like it wants to take a bite out of his tail. Those are just the ones in the nests, too. If some of the ones perching high on the lip of the canyon get an idea to come and attack, it could get ugly.

My mate is high off the ground now, at least twenty feet above us. The birds are riled, their angry cawing turning deafening. Some are starting to take to the air, and one swoops at Pashov's back, which elicits a laugh from Harrec and Farli, and a horrified gasp from me.

I suddenly don't want eggs anymore. This doesn't feel safe. I just want Pashov back on the ground so he can put his arm around my waist and I can touch him and smile at him. Nothing else matters.

"Higher!" Harrec calls. I want to smack him.

Pashov reaches the next empty nest, and his shoulders move a little. He holds something aloft in the air, and it's large, rounded, and a delicate speckled brown. An egg.

"Great, now just come down," I whisper. He has to be thirty feet up by now. I'm tired of this. I don't like it.

As I watch fearfully, Pashov tucks the egg into the front of his tunic. He pries the nest off the ridge and tosses it to Farli below. Instead of coming down, though, he moves his feet along a ridge of rock, climbing sideways. He's moving to a nearby empty nest. He reaches into it and then brandishes another egg high in the air with a flourish. My lips twitch with amusement at that. Show-off.

A bird swoops in from above. It attacks his upraised hand, knocking the egg away. I watch with slow-motion clarity as Pashov leans outward, trying to catch the egg . . .

. . . Only to lose his grip on the wall entirely.

Then he falls backward onto the canyon floor, and I'm screaming. This is my worst nightmare come to life, all over again.

I can't lose him again, can I? *Please, no.*

Farli, Harrec, and I all rush forward, but we won't be in time. Pashov lands on his back with a sickening crash and then lies still.

A sob escapes my throat, and I fling myself to his side. "Pashov! Pashov!" I run a hand over his face. His eyes are closed, his body still, and my world feels like it's ending all over again. I grab the front of his tunic and shake him, terrified. "Pashov!"

His eyes open.

Pashov gives me a slow smile and cups my face, pulling my mouth to his for a kiss.

What. The. *Fuck.*

I rear back, both relieved and shocked, even as Farli and Harrec break into laughter. Pashov grins, too. "It is not so big a fall," he tells me.

My fear gives way to blinding fury. He thinks this is fucking *funny*? I curl my fingers into a fist and punch him in the shoulder.

He shrugs it off, grinning. "Do not be mad, Stay-see—"

Not be mad? He just risked his fucking life for a fucking egg and I nearly lost my mate again and everyone's laughing and this is funny to them? I punch him again, and then I can't seem to stop hitting him. They're not hard hits—my hands are small and my strength is crap—but I need to get it out of my system before I start screaming and grab a knife and castrate him for being such a dick in this moment.

"Stay-see," Pashov soothes again. "It is all right."

"It is not fucking all right," I say, punctuating my words with slaps. "You're an asshole." I jerk to my feet and turn my accusing stare on Farli and Harrec, who are still laughing. "All of you are assholes!"

Chompy belches at me.

That does it. I am out of here. I feel frustrated and terrified and full of anxiety and I don't see the humor in this at all. I'm about to start crying, actually, and the last thing I want to do is get all blubbery in their faces. So I turn on my heel and leave.

"Remember to keep your fingers on the right-hand wall to find your way home," Harrec calls after me, amused.

I shoot him the bird and continue marching away.

"Stay-see?" Pashov jogs after me and grabs at my arm.

I shrug his touch away. "Leave me *alone*. I don't want to talk to you right now."

"You are mad?"

Oh, understatement of the year. "I am fucking furious."

Pashov

My mate has used the human curse word more times in the last few minutes than she ever has since I met her. I know this "fuck" word. It is a very angry one. She has only used it a few times in the past—once when she sliced open her finger while dicing roots, and once when Pacy was being born.

I . . . I remember that. Delighted, I jog after my mate. I want to share this with her.

But Stay-see is marching away, her little back stiff with anger. Her shoulders are shivering—no, wait. That is not shivering. She is crying. She is hurting.

I turn back to Harrec and Farli, who are equally mystified. "What did I do?"

Farli shrugs, the nests in her arms. "She is worried you hurt yourself."

"Pfft. Over that small drop?" It left me winded and made my ribs creak, but I have fallen from much worse. It is nothing to panic over . . .

And yet Stay-see is upset. Very upset. I have never seen her so furious. Mystified, I stare after her as she marches out of the canyon.

"Well?" my sister prompts.

I turn to look at her. "Well what?"

"Are you going to go apologize?" She juggles the two nests in her arms, twisting away before Chompy can grab at one with his teeth.

Am I? I pull the frozen egg out of my tunic. It is still whole, rock hard and frozen solid in the frigid weather. Stay-see will be pleased . . . I think. I got this for her. All I wanted to do was make my mate smile. Make her say, *Yes, Pashov, I want to be your mate again. Please come back to my furs.* But those were not the words she said.

I am fucking furious.

I do not want her upset. I want her smiling and hungry for my kisses.

Harrec scoops something off the ground and offers it to me. It is the other frozen egg. "Go after your mate," he tells me. "Quit being a fool."

"I am being a fool?" I echo, surprised.

"Are you not? You are here, talking to us, when you should be kissing your mate." He takes one of the nests from Farli's hands, drops the egg into it, then offers both to me with a grin. "Go and tell her that you miss her and wish to take her to your furs. Everyone in the hunter cave is tired of your snoring. You should return to your mate."

"If she will have me," I say, dubious.

Farli rolls her eyes. "Do not be stupid, brother. Stay-see is upset because she worries over you. If she did not care, she would not worry so much. Go chase after her." My sister thinks for a moment and quickly adds, "And tell her that she is pretty."

"Pretty?"

"A female likes to be told she is attractive," my sister lectures me as if she is the expert. "When was the last time you told Stay-see you thought she was pretty?"

I think . . . and I do not remember if I have told her that at all lately. I grunt acknowledgment; maybe Farli is right. I put the two frozen eggs in the nest and tuck it under my arm. "But what—"

Farli points at me. "You are thinking too much. Just go!"

I do. I turn and jog down the canyon after Stay-see. She is now out of sight, which means she is likely walking fast—storming—back to the vee-lage.

It takes a few moments, but eventually I can see her stiff back as she marches through the valley alone. She looks very small and lost, my mate. I feel a sense of unhappiness that she is so alone. I should be there at her side, comforting her. Stay-see is obviously scared and unhappy about something, and it is my fault.

I want to make her smile again.

She is also going in the wrong direction to get back to the vee-lage. The thought makes me smile, because my mate is so sheltered and protected that she cannot even find her way around in a canyon. In that moment, I vow that she will always be cared for enough that she will never have to worry about hunting, or hiking, or getting lost. I will protect her from the world.

But first, I must get her to stop crying.

I think for a minute, then begin to creep up behind her, my steps slow and silent. There is not much snow here in the gorge—strange, since most of the valleys in our land fill up quickly with snow. But this one is protected by the high lip that keeps the worst of the wind and snow out, and today I am thankful for it. The lack of snow on the rocky ground means that I can move silently without my footsteps crunching. I sneak up on her and watch her swaying backside as she moves.

And then I grab it.

Stay-see emits a shriek so loud that it echoes in the canyon. She jumps around and gives me an incredulous look. "What the *fuck*, Pashov!?"

Oh, the fuck word again. She is very angry. Perhaps that was a mistake. I shrug, trying to play my actions off. "I cannot help myself. I am fascinated by your lack of a tail."

Her expression changes, softening. She swipes angrily at her cheeks. "I'm very mad at you right now. Don't even try to be cute."

Am I being cute? She starts to walk away again, and I follow her. "Tell me why you are angry, Stay-see."

She ignores me, still trying to push past.

"Will you not speak to me?" I entreat again. "Tell me what I did wrong so I may fix it?"

"I don't want to talk right now," Stay-see says, a husky note in her throat, as if she is about to start crying again.

It tears at me, her unhappiness. It also frustrates me, because how can I know how to fix what I am doing wrong if she never tells me? Is she trying to push me away? To make me seek out another mate? So she can be with someone else . . .

Someone like Harrec?

Jealousy gnaws at me, hard and brutal in its intensity. "It will not work," I declare, suddenly furious. "I will wait for you."

She spins around again. "Wait for me? What are you talking about?"

"You will not invite me to your bed. You will not let me be your mate. You push me away. It does not matter." I make a slashing motion in the air with my hands. "You wait for my memories to come back, but they do not change who I *am*. They do not change that I am the mate that loves you. They do not change how I *feel* when I look at you."

Stay-see stares at me. "And how do you feel when you look at me?"

I move toward her. The urge to touch her is overwhelming. I want to caress her face, stroke her hair. My fingers twitch in response, and I clench my hand tight, pressing it over my heart. "Like I am not whole unless you smile. Like the suns rise when you move closer. Like there is nothing sweeter than touching you and hearing your moans of pleasure." At her hesitant smile, I continue. "I do not need memories to feel joy when I see you holding my son. I do not need memories to know that there is no greater feeling than sinking my cock deep inside you. I do not need anything in this world but your smile and your heart, Stay-see. And that is why I will wait until you invite me back. If it takes twenty seasons, I will wait."

She gives a small, confused shake of her head. "I don't understand you. If you love me as much as you say you do, why did you leave me and Pacy the moment we got to the village?"

"Because you told me to?" Now I am as confused as her. "You said you were not ready to take me back as your mate. Not until I had my memories back." I give a small shake of my head. "Stay-see, I would never push you into something you did not want. I can wait."

She presses her hand to her mouth. "Oh my god."

"What is it?"

"Nothing. I'm so stupid."

"You are not stupid. You are wonderful—"

She flings herself into my arms and clings to my neck. Her mouth seeks mine, and I toss aside the nest with the frozen eggs in it to grab my mate's rounded bottom. I haul her against me and hold her close as we kiss, our tongues melding together.

"Does this mean you will take me as your mate again?" I ask between fierce, nipping kisses.

She nods quickly and kisses me again, then bites at my lower lip in a way that makes my cock ache. "Thought you didn't want me. That was why you left."

I groan. "If I did not want you, why would it make me so crazy every time Harrec pays attention to you?" I tear at her tunic, at the knot under her breasts that holds it wrapped shut.

To my surprise, she laughs. "He said he was trying to make you jealous. I couldn't figure out why. I guess he wants us back together, too." She leans in and runs the tip of her tongue along my lower lip. "That's kind of sweet."

"As long as that is all he wants," I growl, feeling possessive. This is my female. My mate. And I've waited long enough to claim her again. I kiss her deeply even as I pull her tunic open.

She gasps against me, peeking around. "The others—someone will see us."

"You went the wrong way to get back to the vee-lage," I tell her, pressing my mouth to her neck. She is so soft here, so sweet. "Make enough noise and they will know to stay away."

Her shocked giggle tells me that she is not displeased with the thought. I slide my hand between the layers of clothing and find her breast, plump and delicious. She moans at my touch, and her kisses take on a more fevered edge.

I am going to make her mine, right here, right on the canyon floor.

I like the idea so much that I immediately drop to my knees. Stay-see squeaks in surprise but does not protest when I pull her down with me. I continue kissing her bared skin, feverishly undoing the ties on her leggings and then mine.

"Right here?" she asks softly.

"Right here," I agree. "I have waited endless days for you. I am hungry to be inside you. For us to become one again."

Her hand strokes my face. "Me, too."

My mouth is on hers in the next moment, my tongue slicking against her smooth, soft one. Everything about my mate is soft and gentle and it fills me with a fierce protectiveness as well as hunger.

In the next moment, her leggings are down, and her freed leg hooks around my hip. I sink into her warmth, marveling at how perfect, how incredible she feels.

Stay-see gasps, her eyes going wide. She feels tight around my cock, her cunt slick with heat and ready for me. "My mate," I growl fiercely. "My Stay-see."

"Yours." She trembles under me, tearing at my clothing as if desperate to touch my skin. "All yours!"

I thrust into her again, my cock buried deep inside her, my spur sliding along her folds. She cries out as I do, and I lean down to give her another claiming kiss. "I am going to take you hard, my mate," I tell her. "Hard and fast."

She nods, eager.

I stroke into her once more and begin to pump with quick, decisive movements. It is as if her permission has freed me; it has also stolen my control. Over and over, I pound into her, Stay-see's little cries fueling me. I claim her with swift ferocity, and when her cunt begins to clench hard around my cock, I feel a near brutal satisfaction as she cries out her pleasure.

Mine comes but moments later.

Afterward, she caresses my face with her small hands and cold fingers, as if marveling at what we have just done. A happy smile plays on her mouth, and I press a kiss to her bountiful breasts, feeling lazy and content. Her hands move to my mane and she plays with my hair, then touches my broken horn. "You're sure the fall earlier did not hurt you?"

"Not at all. I am sorry it frightened you, though."

"I just thought . . . I thought it was happening all over again." She shudders underneath me. "That I was going to lose you once more."

"Never. You will never be rid of me." I wrap my arms tightly around her torso. "Every day I will bury myself so deeply inside you that your khui will send its regards."

She chuckles, her fingertips grazing over my brows. "As long as you are in my furs every night, that is fine with me."

"Every night," I agree. I slide my hand under her bottom and stroke the pale curve of flesh. "No tail here," I murmur, patting her backside.

Stay-see stills under me. "You . . . did you remember?"

"Remember what?" I look up at her.

A flash of disappointment crosses her face, but is quickly gone. "Nothing. I guess it's not important after all."

"I did remember something earlier," I tell her. "That you used the word 'fuck' when Pacy was being born. And that you did not tell me of this when you shared the story of his birth."

Her smile widens. "It wasn't my most ladylike moment. You really remembered that?"

I nod. "I did. I think the memories will come back in time, if you are patient with me."

"Of course," she says, and touches my mouth with her soft little fingertips. "You and I are forever."

I like the sound of that very much. "I agree."

She gives a contented sigh. "And I wish we could stay right here, like this, forever."

I squeeze her bottom again. "I would wish that, too, my mate, except you need to make your mate and your son an egg."

"An egg?" Her brows draw together. Then she sits up so quickly that her head almost bangs into mine. "Oh my god. You saved the eggs?"

"They are frozen and the shells are hard," I tell her, rolling off of her soft body. I lie on my back and tie my breeches, tucking my cock back into my clothing. "I have two of them for you."

Her squeal of delight warms me down to my toes.

EPILOGUE
Stacy

TWO MONTHS LATER

"Da Da, Da Da!" Pacy bounces on his hands and knees, tail flicking. Across the room, my mate sits on the floor, cross-legged. He waves his fingers at his son, indicating he should come forward.

"You can do it, Pacy," Pashov calls out. "Come to Da Da." He uses the English word—or a bastardized version of it—since Pacy seems to be able to say that easier than the sa-khui word for "father," which has a lot of swallowed syllables.

The baby plants one foot on the ground, then the other, his bottom wiggling in the air. Then he stands upright. I stir my egg while it slow roasts on the fire. After endless experimenting, I've figured out the best way to cook the frozen dirtbeak eggs: crack open the top and let it scramble in its own shell, occasionally stirring it. It makes a mountain of perfect, delicious scrambled eggs that go amazingly well with a bit of not-potato and is my favorite go-to meal when I'm tired of dried meat. Pashov has taken to eating the eggs, too, but he prefers his as more of an omelet peppered with chunks of meat and roots. They've helped save my sanity so far in the brutal season, when there's plenty to eat, but most of it is dried, smoked meat. The hunters filled our storage coffers as much as possible before the weather got bad, and the women harvested a lot of not-potatoes, and now we're just riding out the blizzards above, snug in our little nook in the ground below. I have an entire storage area full of frozen eggs, and we're all being extremely careful to make them last. We should be good through the brutal season after all, and the men go out to hunt only on the days that it's not pouring snow. Since most days are so cold that it hurts to breathe and the skies are so dark they look like a bruise, the hunters stay home with us a lot of the time.

And while the food's a bit monotonous, I don't mind it because I enjoy having Pashov around all day. He gets to spend quality time with his son—like right now.

Pacy stretches out his little arms and wobbles forward on one foot, then the other.

I hold my breath. "Is he—"

"He has it," Pashov says proudly, and gestures for Pacy to come forward. "You can do it, little one."

"Da Da!" Pacy says, staggering forward. He only makes it a few steps before he falls into Pashov's arms, but my mate laughs and catches him, then tosses him into the air as if my son has made the greatest accomplishment ever.

"Did you see that?" Pashov asks me between Pacy's peals of laughter. "Three steps this time."

"He'll be running up and down the streets soon," I say with pride in my voice. My little son is so smart. I don't know a lot about babies, but it seems to me he's always just a little ahead of the other kits in the tribe. Or maybe that's just my mommy side speaking. Whatever it is, I'm proud of my clever little Pacy.

Pashov grins over at me and gently sets Pacy back down. The baby immediately tries to get on his feet again, reaching for his father.

"You'd better hurry up and eat," I admonish him as I use a pair of bone tongs to take the egg off the fire. "Josie will be here soon and she's been having pregnancy cravings for eggs."

"You can cook her up another," my mate says lazily, scooping up my son and shooting me a heated look that tells me breakfast isn't the only thing on his mind right now. He carries Pacy over to the playpen Hemalo recently made for him—a series of privacy screens interlocked together to make a safe area for him to play—and comes to my side. He nuzzles my neck and his hands slide over my ass.

"Frisky this morning," I tease, breathless. I'm feeling it, too.

"I am just imagining how my mate will react when she sees the gift I have for her," he teases, nipping at my ear and sending skitters of pleasure through my body.

"Gift? But the holiday's not until next month." We've already talked a bit about it as a tribe, and last year it broke up the brutal season so delightfully well that Claire's already planning out days and days of activities to keep things exciting through the long snowy weeks.

"I know. But I cannot wait any longer for you to have it."

"But your food—"

"It can wait."

My eyes go wide at that. It's not like my walking, talking stomach of a mate to push aside food. "This must be good, then."

"Oh, it is." He gives my butt one last caress and heads over to the far side of our little house, where the rolled-up furs are waiting for curing. Curious, I watch as he digs through the bundles and pulls out something flat and wrapped in leather. He turns around and holds it out to me, a smile on his face.

I'm touched that he's so thoughtful, and I can't stop grinning. A present feels like such a treat, especially since we're all being so careful with goods after losing almost everything to the cave-in. Even months later, "making do" has become the new normal. But we'll survive it, because we always do, and we'll eventually replenish everything we lost. "Are you sure?" I ask shyly, taking the leather-wrapped object from him. "I don't have anything to give you." I'm making him a soft, fur-lined tunic on the sly, but it won't be ready until the holiday.

"Just having you as my mate is gift enough," he says, and cups my face to give me a kiss.

"Aww, that is sweet. You're totally getting laid later," I tease, and my thrumming khui seems to agree. I pull the leather off the gift, and I gasp in surprise.

It's a skillet. It's not quite the same as the one I had before, but it's made similarly. It has a bone handle attached to a square piece of metal salvaged from the ship, with the sides bent upward to form a lip. The handle on my old skillet had been soldered, but this one is interlocking, with a bit of leather tied around to keep it in place.

"Do you like it?" Pashov asks. "Har-loh says we will have to change out the handle and the leather thong every few turns of the moon, but I thought it a small price to pay to get it for you again."

"It's wonderful," I say dreamily, running my hand over the surface. "And it's going to make cooking so much easier again." I give him a happy look. "You remembered?"

He nods, the expression on his face shy. "It is another memory that came back. Once I had it, I wanted to ask Har-loh about getting you another. I was lucky she had a few pieces of metal left."

"You're wonderful," I tell him. I'm truly touched—not just because it's the most thoughtful, perfect gift ever, but because more of his memories are creeping back. He's sensitive about them, because I know that he's frustrated it's taking more time than he wanted, but we're together and happy, and his nightmares have stopped now that we sleep in the furs together every night. I don't mind waiting a little longer for the last of his memories. And if he never gets them back, I don't even care anymore.

I have my Pashov. That's all that matters.

"I wanted to make my mate happy," he says simply.

"You do. Every day, you do." I set it down on my stool and move forward to put my arms around his neck. My khui's purring furiously and I'm feeling more than a little turned on—and it's not just because of the gift. It's because he's so thoughtful and wonderful and utterly sexy and I love the way he looks at me.

He pulls me against him, and I can feel my breasts bounce when my body hits his. His khui is loud, too, and I reach between us to caress his cock. It's hard as a rock already, even through the leather of his breechcloth. "I see someone's been thinking long and hard about his reward for making his mate so happy," I say playfully, my voice a throaty purr.

"I cannot help it. You are irresistible to me." He leans down and grazes his mouth over mine in a gentle kiss. "Shall I see if Asha can watch our son for a time and give us some privacy?"

"So I can show you how much I like your skillet?"

His eyes gleam. "Yes."

"By . . . making you eggs?"

His mouth curves into a wicked smile. "Only if you allow me to eat them off of your stomach."

"You strange, kinky man," I say with a laugh. "It's open for negotiation."

He leans in to kiss me again, and suddenly . . . I feel it.

Resonance.

The loud, pleasant hum of my khui changes tone, becomes louder, more insistent. His sings loudly to mine, the joined song so loud it feels as if it's filling our small house and shaking my body.

I gasp, clinging to him. "Resonance! Again?"

"Again," he says happily, and claims my mouth in a ravenous kiss.

And oh god, it feels as if my face is going to melt off from the fury of that kiss. It's wicked and delicious and so deep and wet that I can feel my entire body turning into an inferno. I know what to expect from resonance now that it's the second time around, but time hasn't dampened the feeling. The ache between my legs is insistent and intense, and my nipples feel like tight, aching little buds that are just begging to be licked for a few hours.

Pashov groans as he kisses me. "You. Are. Incredible." Each word is punctuated with another heated kiss. "We will have another kit," he marvels. "A daughter this time. One that looks like you."

I laugh, rubbing his cock through his breeches, because I can't help myself. "Or another son. I'm fine with either as long as it's healthy."

"Or twins, like No-rah."

"Okay, slow it down there, big guy," I warn. "Let's not count our chickens before they hatch."

"Mmm, I do not know what you just said, but it is arousing." He leans down and traces his tongue along my earlobe. "Shall I take our son to Asha, then, so we can get to work making our next kit?"

I cling to him, because his tongue is doing magical things to my ear, and I might just collapse into a puddle of overheated goo if he continues. Not that I ever want him to stop. "Ask her to keep him overnight. If she can't, then your mother."

His eyes gleam as our gazes meet. "You think it will take all night?"

"Well, we just want to be sure," I say coyly, and give his cock another stroke. He's rigid under my grip, but he can throw on his winter leathers and no one will notice the stiffness under the layers. "Hurry, though."

I have never seen a man move so fast as he scoops up our son and the small pack we keep full of his loincloth changes and toys, and flings his leather wraps on before hurrying out the door. I giggle, watching him head down the cobbled, icy street, and then I touch my belly.

Another baby.

Another kit.

My perfect little family is growing, and I'm excited. No, ecstatic. I think of the pleased look on my Pashov's face and pull the tie free from my braid, humming happily to myself.

Memories aren't a problem, I've been realizing over time. We can always make new ones. And as long as we're together, every day is a new opportunity to love and be happy.

Sometimes, that's all you need.

BONUS NOVELLA

AFTERSHOCKS

Rukh

My mate has been sitting at the wall again all day.

"Come away," I tell her, putting our kit into her hands. "Rukhar wants his mother."

She looks up at me and gives me an absent smile. "I'm obsessing, aren't I? I'm sorry." She gets to her feet, but glances back at the wall with its flashing lights and clicking buttons. "It's just . . . I don't like things I can't fix, you know?"

I grunt acknowledgment, because the way her mind works is a mystery to me. I know things I can touch and taste. My world is in this moment, with her and our son. I like doing things the way they have always been done. I do not like change. My Harloh is different, though. She constantly thinks of ways to improve how our people live. To create new things to make changes for the better. She does not see limitations. To me, the thing she stares at all day is just a wall. To her, it is full of ideas and concepts that can help, and she sees herself as the one that must unpack them.

And as her mate, I must be the one to pull her away and remind her to eat, and to take care of herself.

Har-loh cuddles Rukhar, pressing kisses on his brow as she gets to her feet and moves close to the fire. I have put on a bit of meat to roast for her, and some of the roots she prefers. If it were up to her, she would eat nothing but roots, but I make her eat good red meat. She needs to stay strong.

Always, I think about how fragile she is. How close I came to losing her. I must protect her in all ways.

"What are you working on today?" she asks absently as she sits near the fire. She opens her tunic, revealing one breast, and Rukhar immediately leans in to nurse. "Still trying to fix those hides?"

I get one of her little bowls that she likes—she does not wish to hold handfuls of food as she eats, a concept that is still strange to me—and fill it with more meat and roots than she normally eats. I do not want her getting thin with the brutal season coming. I sit next to her and pick up one of the cubes of fresh meat and offer it to her lips. "Eat."

She rolls her eyes but smiles at me and obediently eats a chunk, her lips brushing against my fingertips. "You're so pushy."

"Because you forget," I tell her. "Always forget."

She smiles at me, warmth in her eyes, and my chest burns with sheer joy. My sweet mate. Every day with her is a gift. "I'm lucky I have you to keep my head on straight."

I frown, eyeing her. "Is not straight?"

Her laughter is like a warm blanket. "It's a thing humans say."

I smile at her. "Then I like it on straight."

I love it when she smiles. I watch her, feeding her another cube of meat when she swallows. She nurses our son, who is old enough now that he watches her with interest and pushes his hands against her teat as he feeds. He eats a mushy version of Har-loh's roots sometimes, but his fangs are small and not yet ready for meat. I watch as she smooths a hand over Rukhar's hair and strokes his horns. Sometimes I am jealous of the attention she gives our son, because I want her to look at me and only me with so much love. But then he looks over at me as he feeds, and a silly, milk-wet smile curves his mouth and I feel my chest squeeze with affection for my son.

"He looks like you more and more every day," Har-loh says. "Don't you think?"

Eh? I gaze at my son. He looks like me? I rub my jaw. I have never seen my own face. "My nose has . . . bumps." I reach out and touch Rukhar's small nose. "His like yours."

"If you say so," she teases. "But the rest of him is all you."

I find it odd that a creature as small as my son would have my face. I thought I would look like my brother, the way Pashov and Salukh have similar features. But my brother Raahosh is ugly and scarred. Am I ugly to Har-loh? Disturbed, I push another chunk of meat into my mate's mouth.

Rukhar finishes nursing and she wipes his mouth with a bit of soft fur and then sets him down on his favorite blanket. He crawls about, reaching for a carved bone toy, and then pops it into his mouth, biting it.

"Do you think you can watch him a little longer?" Har-loh asks. "I need to keep working on the computer. It's a puzzle I can't quite figure out and it's bothering me." Her reddish brows pull together. "It's like there's something missing that I'm just not getting."

"Missing?" I offer her another chunk of food.

She takes it absently, chewing slowly. Her thoughts are

clearly with the com-pyew-tor. "The dates are all wrong. I just . . . I don't know. It's a hunch I have. Everything says that the sa-khui have been here for almost three hundred years, but when I crunch outside data, it just doesn't add up."

"Do what you need," I tell her. "Rukhar and I will work on the skins."

Her mouth twitches with amusement. "He'll help you like he did yesterday?"

I grunt. My son is too curious. Instead of staying on his blankets, he gets into things. Yesterday, he got into the bowls of offal that I use to tan a hide. I recently learned this from Hemalo and wished to create a soft blanket for my mate for the brutal season. All of the furs I know how to make are tough, scraped clean but not very soft. Hemalo's hides are soft like my mate's skin. I want the best for her.

But now that Rukhar has spilled all of my tanning fluids, I must figure out another way to make the hides soft. I do not want to waste them. "I will work despite Rukhar's help."

Har-loh's peals of laughter echo in the strange cave. She gets to her feet, and I do, too. Her arms go around my neck and she leans in close, her eyes soft in the way that makes my cock ache. "Maybe after we put him to bed, you can give me a tour of the furs."

I like that thought. "I can put him to bed now."

She giggles at my teasing and gives me a kiss. "I will leave you two to your work, and get back to my projects."

I brush her arm as she goes, desperate to touch my mate again. Sometimes it is difficult to let her work when all I want to do is grab her and pull her leathers off her body until she is naked and under me. I rub absently at my own bare chest, glad that we are away from the tribe and I am free to dress how I please—in not much more than a loincloth.

"Da Da!" Rukhar calls out and raises his arms for me.

"I am here," I tell him, and heft him into my arms. My son. Did I think my life was not complete without my mate? I feel the same fierce love for my small son, but in a different way. He is my heart, just like my Har-loh is.

My "heart" gurgles at me and slaps a hand on my jaw. "Da Da!"

"Da Da work now," I agree, tucking him under my arm. "Come. We make leather."

Working with a small kit underfoot is not much work at all. Rukhar has a soft blanket that I place him on to play while I scrape the large dvisti skin I have stretched out in the snow. Since I do not have the brains and guts of the creature, I have been rubbing the skin with fat and then scraping it to try to soften it . . . in between retrieving Rukhar. My son is now crawling and uses every opportunity to race away.

I retrieve him out of a nearby snowdrift and place him on his blanket again. It is a game he likes to play. He crawls away, and I put him back. He crawls away. I put him back. He crawls away. I put him back. Rukhar finds it fun.

And even though I cannot get much work done on the skins, I also cannot be mad when he smiles up at me, mouth full of drool and his gums punctuated by two small, crooked fangs.

"Stay for a little while," I tell him again. "We play game later." The suns will be going down soon, and I will have to pack up my projects and bring them back inside the cave. It is a messy task and so I do it outside, in the snow a short distance away from the cave entrance.

I sit down at my skin.

Rukhar immediately crawls away.

I sigh and crawl after him—and a shiver swells through my legs. I sway, rolling to my back, confused. Is it me? Why is my body trembling? Why do I have no strength? But then Rukhar lets out an angry wail, and I realize it is not me.

It is the ground.

It shivers again and then begins to roll and tremble. I scoop up my son, ignoring his frightened screams as I stare at the world around me. Everything is shaking. The trees in the distance move back and forth like they are caught in a windstorm. The ground shakes beneath my feet. I hear the sound of ice cracking, and a massive gorge splits the earth a short distance away. It starts out small and then grows and begins to snake across the snow, widening as it does.

Har-loh. My mate.

"Har-loh!" I scream, looking to the elders' cave. As I watch, the crack moves toward the cave. I race after it, but then the ground shifts away under my feet and I lose my balance. I roll carefully, cradling my son close so my weight does not crush him, and protect his body with mine. All around me, the world groans and shudders, and the snow shakes wildly underneath me.

What is happening?

The world grows dark and I hear the groan of something new. A crunching sound. A thick fall of snow cascades over my body, dumping from above. I shake it off like a dvisti and look up. The cave has grown in size, the strange rock it is made from uncovered. And it is . . . moving. I frown at it, surprised. Did Har-loh do this? Did she learn how to make it move?

The ground at my feet shakes harder and gives a strong shift, and I am knocked backward. Dazed, I pick myself up off the snow. Rukhar is wailing, his face flushed with emotion, and he raises his arms for me to pick him up again. I do so, crouching low in the snow. I dare not stand and be knocked down again.

As I hold my frightened son against my chest, the shadow rises. The crunching sound gets louder, and as I watch, the cave slides into the gorge.

No. My mate. She's inside. She's trapped.

"Har-loh," I scream so loudly that I feel something burst behind my eyes. I want to approach it as it slides, but my son is in my arms. I am torn—can I save my mate? What if I put Rukhar down in the snow and wild metlaks grab him? I cannot! I race forward, plunging through the newly deep snow, praying it does not cover new cracks or hidden dangers. All the while, the cave slowly slides backward into the gorge. As I watch with horror, the entire thing tilts and upends like a bone disc, revealing the guts of the cave on the underside and leaving a black scar underneath it where it used to be.

The entire thing is going to disappear into the ground and carry my mate with it.

I must do something.

I race forward with Rukhar, holding him tightly. With every step I take, the sick feeling in my gut grows. I wait for this moment to get worse, for the cave to slide away entirely into the ground and disappear.

It heaves upright, like a finger pointing in the air, and then gives a great shudder. It stops.

Everything stops. The ground no longer shakes with anger.

"Har-loh," I bellow again, pushing forward. I must get to her. Is she hurt? Is she waiting for me to rescue her? Is she . . .

I think of my father, his dead body lying so still as I put rocks over it.

No.

No, not my Har-loh. Not my mate.

My thoughts are growing wild. Rukhar screams in my arms, but I put a hand on his head to calm him and do little else. I am focused on my mate. I must get to her. *Now.*

The entrance to the cave is now high in the air. I can climb to it. I set my wailing son down in the snow at my feet . . . and then immediately pick him back up again. I cannot climb with him in my arms . . . but I cannot leave him, either. I howl with frustration, and he howls with me. I must do this. I must.

For the first time, I wish the people of the tribe were here to help out. Normally I am glad to leave them behind because there are so many. Today, I would do anything for an extra pair of hands.

Rukhar grabs a fistful of my hair, wailing. "Ma Ma! *Ma Ma!*"

His frustration is not helping mine. I must think, but my mind is frantic. I see visions of my father's body and imagine putting rocks over Har-loh's smaller form . . . and another howl of grief escapes me.

No.

Please, no.

I cannot lose her.

I cannot be alone again.

She is my world. She is my everything.

I grip my son fiercely against my chest and he screams anew, furious at me and scared. I am, too. I press a kiss to his forehead like Har-loh does, trying to think. I need a wrap to hold him to me. I look back, but the leathers I was scraping are long gone, buried in snow or shifted beneath the broken earth. The only thing I have is my loincloth.

I rip it off a moment later. It is not long enough to act as a sling to carry my son, so I grab one edge between my teeth and rip. The leather rends in two, right down the middle. I set my son down and tie the two lengths together and then pick him up again and tie him to my chest. I place one hand under his bottom, holding him tight against me, and then I begin to climb.

There are not many footholds on the outside of the cave, but there are small cracks. I force my fingernails into them to act as a grip, ignoring the pain that shoots up my fingers. My pain does not matter. Only Har-loh matters.

The climb seems endless, but I make my way to the entrance and then surge to the lip, holding on tight. "Har-loh!"

Lights flicker. It is dark inside, the fire having gone out. More of the strange lights flash here and there, and the cave itself is now one long pit. The lights flash again . . .

And then I see my mate.

Her body is cast down at the bottom of the pit, resting on what used to be a wall.

There is blood everywhere.

She is not moving.

"*Har-loh!*" I scream, and something inside me breaks.

Harlow

A low growling breaks through a haze of pain. Everything hurts, but I force my eyes open. There's something sticky dried across my face and my back feels like one big bruise. When I suck in a breath, a sharp, stabbing pain radiates from my middle. But I'm alive, so there's that. I'm disoriented, and it feels like there's a heavy weight on my chest.

It's dark. I blink my eyes slowly, trying to adjust to the low light. There's a bright spot high overhead that hurts my eyes to look at, so I avoid it and look for the source of the growling. It's there, at my side. Rukh is next to me, shifting back and forth as he crouches on his feet. He's hovering so close that his tail flicks against my shoulder and I can feel the warmth radiating from his body. Something shifts on my chest, and I realize Rukhar is lying on top of me. "W-what happened?" I ask, not quite ready to get up and face the pain yet.

Rukh just makes a low snarl in his throat. *"Har-loh."* The word is guttural and . . . savage.

Fear slices through me, not for myself, but for him. I force my body into a sitting position, ignoring the protest of my ribs, and hold Rukhar close to me. I reach out to touch Rukh gently, my hand caressing his knee. "Are you okay?"

He sucks in a deep breath but doesn't answer. He touches my face. "Har-loh."

I'm growing worried. His glowing eyes are bright but there seems to be something . . . brittle inside them. Like all is not right in his head. "Rukh," I say gently, rubbing my thumb over his knee. "I'm here. We're okay."

He doesn't say anything, just continues to stroke my face.

Uh-oh. I run my hand over his jaw, making sure he's not wounded. My mate has never been a huge talker, but this silence is worrying me. I pick up Rukhar and offer him to Rukh. "Can you hold him?" I'm going to try and stand up and see what the situation is . . . and I want to see how he reacts to our son. It's clear something's wrong, but it's also clear that wherever we are, we can't stay here. Something hard is shoving against my hip and it's dark. It feels claustrophobic. I can't quite place where I am, and I feel like I should be able to. I feel like there's something I'm missing.

But I'm most worried about Rukh. He's my rock. He's my world—him and Rukhar. If something happened to him . . . I shudder because I don't want to think about that.

Rukh takes the baby from me and holds him gently against his chest. His focus is still on me, but that's all right. One step at a time. I keep my hand on his leg as I try to get to my feet—and fail. The moment I rise, I get dizzy and have to sit down again. My body breaks out in a cold sweat.

And my mate starts growling again.

I sink to the ground again, pressing my forehead against Rukh's arm. "I'm sorry. Give me just a moment."

"Har-loh," he rasps, and I hurt all over again at the pain in his voice.

"I'm fine," I tell him, even though I'm not. The stabbing pain in my side isn't going away and I want to cry because everything hurts so much. My brain feels scrambled and it's hard to focus. But we're alive. I have vague memories of being inside the ship when everything shook and then—

I gasp, sitting upright again and looking around. In the dark, it's hard to make out anything. I'm aware of the floor underneath me, though, and I can feel a few familiar squares that seem like keyboard keys.

Oh my god. This narrow, dark pit? This is the ship.

"What happened?" I ask Rukh. "Tell me."

He pulls Rukhar close and ignores the baby's smacking fists. He presses his mouth to the top of Rukhar's head and I think for a moment he's not going to answer. But then he speaks, slowly, as if trying to remember the words. "Cave . . . move."

The ship moved? I peer up, to the bright spot that hurts my eyes. I try to force myself to look even though it makes my head throb. It's the door we use to come in and out of the ship . . . and it's about a hundred feet up.

The ship is *sideways.*

I'm suddenly terrified. If the ship is sideways, what is it resting on? We might be in danger even now. "Rukh, we have to get out of here."

He growls again, and I'm hoping it's acknowledgment.

I stare up at the doorway and wonder how we're going to get there. We have Rukhar and I'm having a hard time sitting up, much less climbing up a wall. Hot tears threaten, but I swipe them away. Now is not the time. I have to save my baby and my mate. "Can you carry Rukhar?" I ask him. "I don't think I can carry him up the wall."

"Carry," he rasps, and touches my cheek. "Har-loh carry. Rukhar carry."

He wants to carry me? It's sweet but I want them to get out first. "I can manage," I tell him, crawling to hands and knees. If I go slow, maybe I can do this. Heck, I don't have a choice—I *will* do this. "Everything is going to be fine, Rukh."

My mate pulls my son close to his chest and tucks him into what looks like a leather sling. He gets to his feet and then looks down at me, waiting. It's clear he's not leaving without me.

Okay. I need to move, then. I slowly get to my feet. Once I'm there, everything seems to hurt worse and my rib feels like it's stabbing a hole in my gut. I need something to lean on, and am grateful when Rukh is there, cradling me close. *"Har-loh."*

Rukhar starts to wail.

"I know," I say, trying not to breathe in too deep. "I'm coming. Take Rukhar out of here if you can. I'll be right behind you."

He puts an arm around my shoulders, ignoring my request.

"No," I tell him, pushing away his touch. It hurts—both physically and mentally—to do so, but my little Rukhar is screaming and I'm worried for him and my mate. I need them safe. Being in the belly of the ship while it's turned on its side is terrifying me. I need them out so I can concentrate on rescuing myself. "No, Rukh. I need you to take him to safety. Get him out of here. *Now.*" When he hesitates again, I continue. "If you love me, you'll do that."

Rukh makes a pained groan, and I can hear his tail flicking against the floor angrily. He's mad at me—and hurt—but I need them to be safe.

"I'm right behind you," I promise him. Somehow I will be.

With a snarl of frustration, he flings himself away, and I watch as he moves to the wall and begins to climb it with effortless ease. Rukhar's wails grow stronger, and my body vibrates with anxiety. My need to be a mother and protect him wars with my need to tumble back to the floor and take a break from standing. I'm already exhausted, my legs strangely weak. But I can't stay here.

I watch as Rukh climbs, and as he disappears into the sunlight above, I get a flash of bare ass and a glimpse of his sac swinging between his legs as he climbs out. Naked? Wonder what happened there. The sight of it is enough to make me smile, though, and it rejuvenates me. I can do this. I need to be with them. Rukhar needs me desperately . . . and Rukh might need me even more than that.

I take a shuffling step forward. Pain lances through my body and I double over, which only causes more pain. Everything hurts. Everything. I'm starting to worry I might not be able to make it up the wall. Floor. Whatever.

Rukh did it, I remind myself. He's out there with your baby, waiting for you. You don't have a choice.

And I don't, so I push forward another step. Then another. I make it to the wall and put my hands on it, feeling around for a handhold. There's not much, but I manage to wedge my fingers into a crack and pull myself up. Just a little. The next handhold is even higher up, so I heave myself forward to reach it.

My entire body protests. My head swims. The world goes black.

Georgie

I'm worried about Vektal.

It's hard being the chief. And normally my mate handles everything with calm, with a fair gaze regardless of his personal feelings. Exiling Hassen? It weighed on him because he understood Hassen's reasons. He understood the soul-crushing loneliness of wanting a mate. And Hassen was a friend. But an example had to be set for the tribe. I know it kept him awake many nights, worrying if he was destroying his friend. If the punishment was just. Being chief means he's responsible for everyone. That in a time of crisis, they look to him to fix everything.

And I don't think this can be fixed.

I look over at my mate, who's busy tying what few goods we have onto a makeshift sled. Others are standing around in the early morning, trying to ignore the cold, or the ash that's falling like snow. Nearby, Analay cries despite Ariana's soothing of him.

"Cover your mouth, little one," I tell Talie as she pulls the leather bib off her face again. I replace it carefully, letting it hang off her nose so she can breathe, but it has to go on. I point at my own bib. "See? Like Mommy."

"Da Da," she tells me.

"Not like Da Da," I say. Vektal's not wearing a mouth cover, even though I've suggested repeatedly that he should. I don't like the thought of us sucking in all this ash. I also don't know that a piece of leather over our mouths is going to do the trick, but we don't have any other options. Talie ignores my request and tugs on the bib again, and I put it back. Again. It's a game we've been playing all morning. I'm trying not to get upset at her, because she's a baby. But my patience is strained thin and I'm just as worried as everyone else.

We're homeless. I look back at the wreck of what used to be the cave. It's completely collapsed. The cave that everyone lived in. The cave that my daughter was born in. The cave that Vektal brought me to because it meant safety and family and home. It's nothing now. And the shock I feel can't be anything compared to the shock that the sa-khui must be feeling.

At my side, Claire bursts into sudden, noisy tears.

"Are you okay?" I ask, rubbing Talie's back. She's still at the age where if she sees someone crying, she starts to cry, too.

"I don't m-mean to be cruel, Georgie, but that's a s-s-stupid question," Claire blubbers, wiping at her face. She's got a small bag of supplies in her arms. It smears ash all over her cheeks, leaving dark streaks. "I'm homeless and hormonal and pregnant. Of course I'm not okay. Where are we going to *live*?"

Poor Claire. Her belly seems to be growing by the day, and as it does, her anxiety is ratcheting up. I don't blame her—the timing is not great. But I can be reassuring. "There's a runner out to the South Cave right now," I tell her in a firm voice. "We can winter there. It'll be a tight squeeze but we'll manage. And in the spring—sorry, the bitter season—we can look for a better home, or fix the one we've got." I move forward and pat her shoulder. "It's going to be fine. I promise."

It's a lie, of course—I don't know if it'll be fine, but it has to be. We don't have any other options.

"Oh sure," Claire says, sniffling. "God, I'm such a mess. I didn't realize how crazy I would get when pregnant."

"We all had those moments," I tell her. I think of the baby in my own stomach, a secret for now. Vektal and I recently resonated again, and I know I'm carrying. A second resonance is a little strange. You still resonate to your mate off and on after the first initial "song," but when you resonate a second time, it feels different. The song itself feels pitched differently, though you're just as horny. I think that's the reason why we've been able to keep it a secret so far. No one knows but us.

Now's a bad time to think about that sort of thing, though. We have to focus on the tribe. This baby's not coming for at least thirteen months, so there's plenty of time to worry about it later. For now, I have to keep my tribe together—and that means being a cheerleader to my human girls, even when I want to sit down and bawl like Claire. "Are you ready to travel? Where's Ereven?"

"He's helping Kemli and Borran make a second sled. I told him to leave me alone because I needed a moment." She wipes at her face again. "Clearly I need more than just one." She gets all teary again and clutches my arm. "Tell me we're going to be okay, Georgie. I need to hear it."

"We're absolutely going to be okay, Claire. It's a cave. We made it out and that's all that's important." I look over at Warrek, who's struggling. Not all of us made it out alive. His elderly father, Eklan, was crushed in his own bed. Grief threatens to clog my throat at the thought. Eklan was sweet. Gray-haired, still strong but starting to fade, and always kind. He made the fur blankie that's around my Talie right now.

And Pashov . . . we still don't know if Pashov is going to make it. I can't think about that right now, or the fact that Stacy might be a widow soon. I hug Claire close and give her a reassuring smile. "As long as we're together, nothing bad can happen."

"Ho!" someone calls in the distance. I turn, and as I do, Vektal rushes past. He's racing toward Haeden and Josie, sent out to check the South Cave yesterday.

Was it only yesterday? We've been homeless for almost two days now and it feels like eternity.

Please have good news, I silently beg. I watch Vektal sprint through the dirty snow toward them, and I can practically see the tension vibrating through his big blue body. We need a win right now. I watch them speak, and then a moment later, Vektal bows his head.

Oh no.

My heart hurts for my mate. I can see an almost imperceptible slump in his shoulders. The news isn't good. We'll manage, then. We'll figure something out. I hold Talie tightly as Vektal returns to our small camp with Josie and Haeden. His face is grim, and I can tell by the firm set of my mate's mouth that he's unhappy. "Bad?" I ask, moving forward to meet them.

"Gone," Vektal says in a gruff voice. He reaches out and brushes his knuckles along my jaw. I'm not sure if he's trying to comfort me . . . or himself. He ruffles Talie's curly hair and then looks at me. "We wait no longer, then. We go to the elders' cave as planned."

I want to ask questions. I want to see where his thoughts are, because I can tell he's not happy. I want him to open up to me and let me share his burdens. But everyone's looking at us and we need to be strong and take charge right now. So I nod and turn to the cluster of people standing around. "Everyone have your things ready to go within the hour. Let's get packed up. We can be at the cave by nightfall if we hurry."

Vektal gives my shoulder an absent squeeze and I feel his tail flick around my waist, almost like a hug. "I must go help the healer ready Pashov to travel."

"Do what you need to. I'm fine." I smile brightly at him so he won't worry about me. "I'll round up the others and get everyone moving."

He gives me a smile that doesn't reach his eyes, and then bounds away, heading to the makeshift tent where Pashov and Maylak have been huddled for the last day and a half. I watch him go and then turn to the other humans waiting nearby. Claire has been joined by Ariana and Josie and Megan. They're all looking to me like I've got answers. So I gesture at the spread of gear by the firepit. "Let's get this together, all right? Ariana, take Talie so I can help pack things up, would you? And let's make sure someone grabs Stacy's things, because I don't want her to have to worry about them right now."

And then we're busy, and there's no time left to panic, because there's too much to do.

Vektal sees the broken, lopsided carcass of the elders' ship before I do. He's dragging a sled of supplies behind him and I'm holding Talie as we walk. He's everywhere as we travel, trying to take care of the tribe. He takes over for Taushen when Pashov's litter gets to be too heavy. He helps Kashrem pull Maylak's travois for a while—because the healer is too exhausted to walk. He carries infants, drags sleds, and heads to the back of our group to help stragglers catch up. He's everywhere, with a seemingly endless supply of energy.

He's a good leader, my mate. He's hiding the fact that he's just as worried as the rest of us. I know that later, when he and I are alone, all of that positivity is going to come crashing down. But until then, he's putting on a brave face. I've been watching him closely, and that's how I know something's wrong. His steps slow, and then all the color drains from his face.

"What is it?" I ask. I turn to see what he's looking at . . . and then I feel sick.

Over the next ridge, something is sticking out high into the sky. Something black and metal. I realize after a few moments that it's the elders' ship—and that underneath all the snow and ice that coats it, it's black. And it's on its side.

Oh no. "Harlow and Rukh?" I ask softly. "Rukhar? Do you think they're all right?" I don't think we can bear to lose more people. Not Harlow, with her sunny attitude and freckles. Not Rukh, who's still getting used to people. Not their sweet little boy, Rukhar. If the ship is destroyed, we've lost so much with the loss of the computer . . . but right now all I care about are the tribesmates. "You don't think they were inside, do you?"

"I do not know," Vektal says. He drops the sled he's dragging behind him and then takes me by the arm. "Georgie, I must go ahead—"

"I know," I tell him in a soft voice. "Go and see. We'll catch up with you." Our little party is slow to travel, and something like this feels like it can't wait. If Rukh and Harlow are in trouble, every second might count. "We'll meet you there."

He nods and takes a step forward and then pauses. He rushes

back to me and grips me tight in a bear hug, squishing Talie between us. My heart nearly breaks for him. My mate. I want to help. I want to fix this, but I don't know that there's anything that can be done except to ride out the aftermath. "I love you," I tell him softly.

Vektal presses his forehead to mine, caressing my cheek. Then he steps away. "Haeden! Ereven! To me!" When the other two jog forward, he continues. "We must go ahead and check things. Georgie will lead the others to the elders' cave." His gaze fixes on me.

"I got this," I call out. "You guys go ahead."

My mate nods at me and then the three men are racing across the snow. I pray that they find Harlow and Rukh alive and well. I pray that there's not anything bad on the other side of this cliff.

First the home cave. Then the South Cave. Now this.

We could really use a win right now.

Vektal

I did not think that things could get worse.

Clearly, I am a fool.

We find the elders' cave. A giant crack has opened up in the ground, and it looks as if the cave has pulled itself from the ground and slid into the hole created. One end hangs high in the air, casting a shadow over the snow underneath. The entire valley has changed. It looks ripped apart, the snow churned as if many herds of dvisti stormed through. New cliffs have risen and the old ones are crumbling. The world has changed in an eyeblink, it feels. For turn upon turn, I have known this world. I have known every valley, every cliff, every cave, every mountain. Now I look upon it as a stranger, and I am worried.

We find Rukh in the shadow of the cave, clutching his bloody, unmoving mate to his chest while his son crawls nearby. Rukh is covered in ash and unclothed. Har-loh looks wounded, but when we approach, Rukh snarls and reacts so badly that we keep a safe distance. Haeden scoops up Rukhar and frowns in my direction. "What do we do now?"

"We retrieve the healer," I say, watching Rukh. He strokes his mate's face, caressing her cheeks. I do not think she is dead, but it is clear she needs healing. I am selfish, but I worry for the entire tribe when I see Rukh snarling and acting wild.

Now I have two hunters with no mind—Rukh and Pashov. I cannot afford to lose more. The tribe must eat through the brutal season, and we are rapidly running out of hunters.

I . . . do not know what to do. Where my people can go. Where we can be safe. There are so many kits to think of, and our mates . . .

My Georgie. My precious mate. Nothing must happen to her. For a moment, I feel as savage and wild as Rukh. If my Georgie was hurt? I would act the same. To lose home and mate both? It makes me feral just thinking about it.

I take Rukhar from Haeden and sit with him in the snow while Ereven and Haeden rush back to the group to bring the healer. I play with the kit, keeping an eye on his father and his too-still mother. Rukhar is my Talie's age, though she is larger than him. She will be tall, my daughter. I like the thought.

Rukhar sniffles and looks up. His face scrunches into an angry expression, and for a moment, he looks just like his father. "Ma Ma."

"She is asleep, little one," I tell him, and pull my sling off of my belt so he can play with it. "The healer will be here soon, and then your mother will awaken." I hope.

He plays with the sling for a time, but then flings it aside and begins to wail. At his cries, Har-loh stirs, but Rukh continues to hover over her, snarling at me as if I will take her from him. I am glad to see she lives, though I worry for her. And I worry for Maylak, who must tend to so many injuries she cannot possibly fix them all without destroying herself.

It is . . . a bad time. For all of us.

I cannot dwell on my worries, though. I must come up with a solution. A new place for my people to live. To keep my mate and my kit safe through the brutal season. To keep *all* of my people safe. It is my duty.

And I feel like I am failing them. All of them.

I comfort Rukhar as he cries. He is hungry, and cold, and tired, and scared. I am, too, but I can at least help where I can. I give him a piece of dried meat to gnaw on. He might be too young for it yet, but it keeps him quiet and occupied.

"Ho," a voice calls in the distance, and I pick Rukhar up and turn. It is Kashrem and Haeden and Ereven, dragging the travois behind them with the healer. They are racing over the snow, and in the distance, I see dark blots that tell me the rest of my people are not far behind. Good. Some of the anxiety tightening my chest loosens a bit. I head over to meet them.

Maylak needs help getting up from her seat on the travois, and her little girl, Esha, is tucked in next to her, baby Makash at his mother's breast. "Take me to him," Maylak says.

"He is not himself."

"He will let me near to help his mate," she says in a calm, firm voice. "I know it."

Kashrem collapses, panting and catching his breath while Ereven supports Maylak and brings her toward Rukh. I am handed a second kit, and Haeden takes Makash.

"Are we camping tonight, my chief?" Esha asks in her sweet, tiny voice. She grabs one of my braids to hold on to as she settles into the crook of my arm.

Haeden and I exchange a look. He knows as well as I do that it is not safe to climb into the elders' cave, even if we could reach the entrance. Not with it perched on the mouth of a deep crevice. "Yes," I say after a moment, my heart hurting. "Tonight we camp again."

She gives me a bright smile, delighted with this answer. "I like camping!"

Haeden snorts and rolls his eyes, but a hint of a smile tugs at his mouth. "At least one of us does."

Esha just beams at me, pleased.

I look over where Maylak is moving to Rukh's side. She kneels next to him and I see him stiffen in response. I tense, worrying that I will have to help Ereven pull him off of her, but Rukh relaxes a moment later, and then Maylak is at his side, her hands touching Har-loh's face. The expression on Rukh is one of terror and hope, and I ache for him. I know what it is to fear losing your mate.

I think of Pashov. My friend. A good hunter and always pleasant. I think of his mate, who has been beside herself with worry and fear. Kashrem comes to my side and there is strain on his face, his gaze on his mate. He worries she will push herself too far.

There are so many to worry about right now.

"Do you like camping, my chief?" Esha asks me, tugging on my braid.

I would give anything to have our cave safe and whole again. I think of Eklan, who cared for me like a father, and I feel a stab of grief. I could not keep him safe. As a chief, I failed him. I look over at Rukh, Har-loh, and Maylak and think for a long moment before answering. "I like my tribe around me," I tell Esha finally. "I do not care where we are at, as long as we are together."

Haeden grunts approval, and we both go silent to watch the healer work.

When the rest of the tribe arrives, no questions are asked. My Georgie takes one look at the elders' cave and then begins to direct the others to set up camp. There are a hundred things that must be done—food must be gathered, supplies protected from the elements, tents pitched, the injured tended—and everyone looks to me for answers. There is not enough time to do everything, but I cope as I can. I do not want to push anyone away or make them feel like I have no time for them. They are my people and they need their chief, so I must lead them.

My Georgie never ceases to amaze me with her bravery and courage. She immediately gets to work as well. While I am helping set up tents and doling out skins, she is taking control of the camp. She and a few of the human females build a big central fire, and as the hunters bring in meat, she sets others to work. When Claire starts to cry, Georgie hands her Talie and sets her near the fire. When Ariana panics, Georgie has her take care of Stay-see's little Pacy. Someone makes a stew. Another begins to make warm clothes for Mar-layn, who got out of her cave with little more than her kit and her mate and has nothing. By the time the suns go down and it grows dark, most of the tents have been set up, food is cooking, and everyone is gathered by the fire. My mate has it all under control, and she is leading her females and keeping as many as she can busy while I work with the others.

I check on Maylak; the healer has collapsed again, her kit taken out to be nursed. Har-loh is on the mend, sleeping peacefully. Even Rukh looks calmer, and I suspect the healer has put her hands on him as well. He sleeps beside his mate, and Rukhar is out with Kemli so they may sleep. Maylak and Kashrem are curled around each other, sleeping as well. I must remember that we should save them food for when they awaken.

I move to the next tent, where Pashov is resting. A nest of furs has been set up to keep him comfortable in the small tent, but he looks the same as ever—his eyes are closed, his face is bruised and swollen, and one horn has been broken off. It will grow back, but the sight of it makes me wince. Stay-see is at his side, her hair a mess and her face paler than usual. She holds his hand tightly in hers. "How is he?" I ask.

"He hasn't woken up," Stay-see replies, voice soft. "He's sleeping and he's breathing fine, but he just won't wake up."

"He will," I tell her in a firm voice, and give her shoulder a touch. "Do you need anything?"

"I need my mate to wake up," she says, voice wobbling. "That's what I need."

"We all do. He is my friend as well. I would like nothing more than for him to wake up and laugh with us."

She sniffs and swipes at her cheeks. "Right." She nods, her gaze never lifting from her mate. "I'm okay, but thank you for asking."

"Would you like to come by the fire for a bit and eat?"

"No, I think I'll stay here. I don't want him to wake up and be alone." Her voice wobbles again. "Is Pacy with Georgie still? Does she need to bring him back to me?"

"He is taken care of. Watch over your mate. Let me know if you need anything."

"I will. Thank you." She lifts Pashov's bigger hand to her mouth and kisses his knuckles. "You've seen this kind of thing before, right? Where Maylak healed someone? He's going to live, isn't he?"

I do not wish to lie, but . . . I do not know what to tell Stay-see.

I have seen many live, and I have seen others die from less. "If he can be healed, she will fix him," I tell her. "For now, we must wait."

"That's a terrible answer," she whispers. "But thank you for not lying to me."

I leave the small tent behind, aching for my friend and his mate. By the fire, Farli is braiding cords with Meh-gan, her little dvisti pet in her lap. Georgie looks over at me and gives me a little nod. Things are under control.

For now.

There are not enough tents to go around. Even though the sa-khui make use of all parts of the animals we hunt, we have lost much of what we owned. The tent that Georgie has claimed as ours is small and barely big enough for the two of us and Talie to squeeze into. Add in that Pacy is sleeping with us tonight, as well as Esha? It is very . . . crowded.

Georgie puts a finger to her lips as I open the tent and join her. It is late, and the fire is dying down. One of the hunters will stay up all night to keep watch over the camp and ensure that the fires remain burning to frighten off any curious metlaks. Everyone else is going to sleep and try to forget for a few hours.

I would like to forget, myself. And I can think of no better place to do this than in my mate's arms. She is curled up in the furs, an enticing sight. I strip off my leathers and tug off my boots, not an easy task given that I cannot stand upright. My mate checks on the kits—all three bundled together on the side of our furs—and then holds a hand out to me.

I join her, sinking into her arms. She is warm and soft and smells like smoke and wind and milk. I love the scent and breathe in deep, nuzzling against her teats. Some of the stress I am carrying falls away.

"How are you holding up?" Her voice is a mere whisper. She strokes my mane, her small fingers dragging through the tangles.

I close my eyes and just hold her for a long, long time.

"That good, hmm?" She caresses my jaw and then traces her fingers over my brow ridges. "It's going to be okay."

"I do not know if it will be, my sweet resonance."

She cups my jaw and then forces me to look up at her. She is beautiful in the low light, her smooth human face perfect in the shadows. I love her round cheeks, her flat forehead, her strangely curly hair. I love everything about my mate. So much that it hurts to think of her lying still and lifeless, like Pashov. I am lucky she was one of the first out of the cave. "It's hard right now because you are the leader," she tells me. "But you are doing a fantastic job. I promise. No one could ask for more."

I grunt, because I do not know that I agree. All I see is more to be done, and my people are yet sleeping in the snow. "I do not know where we can go."

"We'll figure something out."

"I wish I could do more." I think of Stay-see, holding Pashov's hand with a desperate fierceness. Maybe she needs more furs—it is cold tonight. I start to get up—

—Only for Georgie to pull me back down against her once more. "Stay," she murmurs. "You're allowed to take a few hours for yourself. And it'll all be there in the morning. You need your sleep."

I hesitate.

She tugs at my arm, trying to pull my larger body against her, and I give in. It is too nice to hold on to my mate. After the day I have had, nothing gives me greater pleasure. I sink into her embrace once more, letting her wrap her arms around me. As our bodies press together, I can feel the low hum of my khui singing to hers.

Even in all this, our bodies remember each other. I stroke her soft skin, thinking of our second resonance, which we had just a short time ago. Then, I was filled with joy. One kit is a gift beyond words. Two seems like an incredible bounty. And yet . . . now that we have no home, I am filled with worry. Will I have someplace safe for my Georgie and Talie to live during the brutal season? They cannot stay in tents. Georgie's human body is much too fragile, and Talie is too young.

My tribe has grown an enormous amount in the last few seasons. I do not know how we will manage. There are so many humans and kits to protect, more than ever before. They must be protected at all costs.

"I can practically hear you worrying," my mate whispers. "Harlow and Rukh and their kit are alive. It doesn't matter that we lost the elders' cave. We'll find someplace new to live. Give the runners a chance to come back and tell us what they found."

"You sound so sure."

She chuckles low. "Oh, I've had my share of freak-outs. Sometimes I look around and just want to scream and throw my hands up and wait for someone else to fix things. But you know what? That's not going to happen. And did you see Maddie just jump in and start taking charge? I saw her do that and I realized I can't sit around. You are the leader. I'm your mate. That means we have to lead, together."

"You are not frustrated?"

"Oh, I want to scream and cry as much as the next person. But our tribe needs a leader, and you can't do it all on your own. I'm trying to pick up the slack where I can and help out."

I am humbled. I hug her tightly to me. "You are the best of mates."

"We're in this together, you and I." She strokes my cheek again, her caress loving. "It's all going to work out. I've been in worse situations. Remember when we humans crash-landed here with nothing but a pair of pajamas? At least now we have food and blankets and, well, a clue." Her chest shakes with a suppressed laugh. "We got through that, and we'll get through this. All of us. Together."

Perhaps she is simply telling me what I need to hear. Perhaps she is giving me the same emotional support she gives the tribe. It does not matter, because it is what I need to hear. My mate has all the confidence in me. That I will not fail us.

And I will never let her down.

Harlow

I watch my mate sleep next to me. Rukh's face is relaxed in slumber, but there's no hiding the dark circles under his eyes. I'm guessing he hasn't slept in days, and it's all because of anxiety over me. I love my mate, but I'm worried about him. He hasn't been himself.

Then again, I suppose I haven't, either.

I only have vague memories of my injury. Just a lot of pain, a conversation with Rukh down in the belly of the ship, and then a lot more pain. Flashes of warmth and Maylak's kind face.

Maybe it's good I can't remember. I think about the ship being broken, being lost to us. It's our only connection to technology, and within the depths of the near-incomprehensible computer, there's so much information and so much that can help us make our lives better here, if only I can get to it. It's obsessed me for the last six months or so.

But then again, maybe it's a good thing that it's gone. I know I've tried to make new equipment for the sa-khui, only for it to be met with wariness. A space heater? No one wanted it. No one trusted it. My stonecutter? No one used it but me. The language download is the only thing that anyone found useful, but they didn't trust that, either. Sometimes I feel like I've been pushing what I want on the tribe versus what they actually want for themselves. So, yeah, if they're happy with spears and slings and fur blankets, maybe that's what we leave it at, then.

My breasts feel achy and full, and I know my son needs to be fed. Somewhere outside of our small tent, a baby cries. It's not him, but my body reacts just the same—my breasts start to leak.

At my side, Rukh stirs, blinking awake at the child's cry. He focuses on me, and then a fierceness comes into his gaze. He wraps his arms around me and holds me crushingly tight against him. "Har-loh."

"Hey there," I murmur, sliding my hands over his bare shoulders. He feels tense, as if he's still carrying the worries of the world inside his chest. I feel my khui thrum in response to his nearness and his responds. I smile. "Listen. We're singing together. We must be feeling better."

The look he gives me is full of hurt and worry. His big hand caresses my face. "My mate. You . . . hurt? Healer?"

At least he's speaking again. I'm relieved, and at the same time, I suspect that while Maylak was working on me, she might have worked on him a little as well. "I'm fine. Leave her alone. I'm sure she's tired."

The look on his face grows stubborn. "If you need—"

"I don't," I promise him. "Truly. What I need to know is if you and Rukhar are all right. Where is our son?"

He rubs a hand over his face, as if struggling to focus. He still looks exhausted, poor thing. "With . . . Shorshie. She helps."

I make a mental note to thank Georgie later. I can relax, then, if he's with her. She'll make sure he's fed and kept happy. My focus turns to my mate. "How are you feeling?"

"I no matter. You—"

I press my fingers to his mouth to stop his words. "No, I'm serious, Rukh. Are you okay? You scared me."

His eyes widen and then a scowl crosses his face. "I scare *you*? You . . . you . . ." He threads his fingers through my hair and then buries his face against my shoulder. "I nearly lose *you*."

"I'm fine," I tell him, though I'm downplaying how I felt. Before the healer got here, I wasn't fine. I was pretty out of it. "I know you're worried, but Rukh, you worried me, too. We have to think of Rukhar. If you have to choose between him and me, always choose him—" I break off when he growls low in his throat, like an animal.

So I smack him on the arm, because I've had enough of that shit.

He sucks in a breath and looks at me with a shocked, wounded expression.

"I'm mad at you!" I tell him. "How dare you fucking lose your shit! We have a baby! Our son! He needs us!"

Rukh's look of pain doesn't sway me.

"How do you think I feel, knowing that when I was hurt, my mate totally lost his mind and endangered my son? It's not just you and me now, Rukh. We have a child to think about. I know you were scared and worried about me, but you have to, have to think about Rukhar. I don't know what I would have done if something had happened to me and you weren't able to take care of him. I can't bear to think of our son alone, just like your father left you alone."

He flinches. My words hurt him. I feel like the meanest, cruelest mate ever, but all I can think about is my little Rukhar, left without both parents—me dead, and his father gone feral. It's not a pretty thought.

"Did you not think about Rukhar? We have to be strong for him, even when one of us is in trouble. He has to come first."

"I think of him," Rukh tells me in a gruff voice. "I think of Rukhar. Always. But then I think of my father, and how he did not live after my mother die. All day, he move. But he not *live*." He presses a hand to his chest. "I no want to do to Rukhar. But . . . without Har-loh, I no *live*."

Tears burn my eyes. I reach out and touch his face, because I love the big guy so much and it hurts to see him in pain. "I love you, too, and I wouldn't want to go on without you, either. But we're parents. We can't be selfish and think just about ourselves. Would you want to do to your son what your father did to you? Leave him alone in the world? To fend for himself?"

He shakes his head slowly. "All I could see was you . . . and blood. I not think."

I nod. "I love you and I would never leave you if there's any other chance. Any at all. You know I'd follow you anywhere. You wouldn't even have to ask. Just know that I'm always at your side."

Instead of my words comforting him, he looks further troubled by them.

"What is it?" I ask.

He smooths a big hand down my arm, then my side, as if he has to touch all of me and make sure for himself that I'm all right. "I think . . . many times I think about go back to cave. By ourselves."

"The sea cave?" I ask. It's where we spent last year.

Rukh nods, still moving his hands all over me. It feels good.

I'm too tired and spent to be aroused, but just his touch feels wonderful. I could never get tired of it. "Sea cave," he agrees. "But . . . no healer. Har-loh . . . strong but not."

Strong but not? "My health has been a little fragile at times, I know." I think back to Rukhar's birth, when I was so sick I could barely stand. And then I think of my brain tumor, kept in check by my khui. Okay, maybe he's got reason to worry over me so much.

"Har-loh must stay near healer," he says in a low voice. "Always."

"Always?"

"I no lose you." His big fingers trace my jaw. "So I live with noisy tribe. Because I live with Har-loh. I no live if no Har-loh."

Tears brim in my eyes again. Damn it, I'm always weeping, aren't I? I grab him and pull him against me in a fierce kiss, and I don't even mind that our teeth clash a little. "I love you, too," I whisper to him. "I don't live without you, either."

He says nothing, just holds me close. We lie in my furs for a while, just wrapped in the blankets and feeling together. I have to be more careful, I realize. Rukhar depends on his mommy, but Rukh can't lose another person he loves so dearly. He's lost so much in his life already and been alone for so long.

That decides it. Harlow stays with the healer. Maybe it's time to give up on my one-woman quest to restore the ship's computer. Kinda moot now that the ship is on its side and looks like it'll slide into the new gorge at any moment. But if Rukh can give up his dreams of peace and quiet because he worries over me? I can abandon the computer dream.

It's something that can wait for another day, or another human. We live in the here and now, and I need to accept that. If the sa-khui are happy with bone spears and fur coverings, then who am I to force space heaters and stonecutters on them? Not that those are operational anymore anyhow. I sigh.

It feels, to me, like being stranded all over again with the loss of the elders' cave, but in the scheme of things, I suppose it is very small. We are all together. We are healthy. Nothing else matters.

A baby cries again, and my breasts respond. I pat my mate's shoulder. "Want to go get our son so we can all three snuggle together?"

He nods and presses a kiss to my cheek. "You stay."

"I'm not going anywhere, big guy," I tell him softly.

And I mean it.

Georgie

"He's awake?" I look in the direction of Pashov's tent. People are streaming toward it, including his brothers and Farli. "Is he all right?"

"I don't know," Josie says. She puts her arms out to take Talie from me. "Farli was yipping about it as she ran over there. You want me to take over so you can go say hi?"

I give her a grateful look and hand her the long femur I've been using as a soup stirrer. We're doing our best to make every bit of meat stretch, so that means soup for everyone—even the sa-khui, who aren't big fans. One quill-beast can make enough soup to feed the entire tribe, though, so it's a wise move. Plus, there's fruit to be shared afterward. Rokan and Lila are back with more bags of fruit, and we're carefully saving seeds and pits to replant, and drying the rest before it goes bad.

But I want to see Pashov, just like everyone else. So I hand Josie both stirrer and child. "Back in a flash."

I head over to the tent and peek over the shoulder of Farli, who's holding one of the door flaps open. Kemli and Borran are next to Pashov's bed, his mother gripping his hand and beaming with pleasure. Across from them on the other side of Pashov is Stacy, who's wiping her eyes over and over again. She looks tired but relieved, and I'm so happy for her.

Pashov is thin—he hasn't eaten much in the days he's been unconscious, and his cheeks are hollow, his color a pale blue. He smiles at his parents and then at his sister. "I am fine, truly. My head hurts, but that is all."

Stacy sobs a little, and Pashov's brows go down, his smile fading a bit, as if her reaction confuses him.

"My son," Kemli says, squeezing his hand in hers again. "You must never scare me like that again. I have aged three hands of seasons every day you slept."

He chuckles and then presses his free hand to his brow.

The tent goes still, everyone looking concerned. As I watch, Stacy trembles, her fingers pressing to her mouth.

"I am all right," Pashov says. He rubs his forehead and then gives us a rueful smile. "It is no more than a headache after drinking too much sah-sah. Do not worry over me. I shall be out and hunting again in no time."

"No," Kemli says firmly. "You will stay here in camp with your mate and rest. Just because the healer fixed the worst of it does not mean you are completely healed."

But Pashov is frowning, his smile gone. "Did you say . . . mate?"

I hear Stacy suck in a breath.

Everyone is quiet. Pashov looks at his parents again and then at Stacy, and I realize the confusion on his face is for her. Oh my god. He doesn't recognize her.

Kemli is the first one to speak. She nods. "You have a mate."

"Who?"

Stacy seems to flinch all over.

Kemli nods at Stacy. "She is your mate. Do you not remember?"

Pashov gazes at Stacy for a long moment, then shakes his head. "I . . . do not see anything. I have a mate?" His eyes widen in alarm. "Is . . . Did I resonate?" He looks at the human in surprise. "To you?"

Stacy jolts to her feet. A broken sob escapes her and then she pushes out of the tent, barreling into the snow.

Pashov tries to get up from his bed, worry on his face. Multiple sets of hands immediately pull him back down. "Rest," Kemli orders him. "You must rest! Give her time."

"But—" Pashov begins, casting a pained look after Stacy. "I . . . do not want to hurt her."

"There is no way this cannot hurt," Kemli says. Her face is worried but she presses her hand firmly to her son's shoulder. "But you must stay here and rest. You almost died, my son."

"I shall get Maylak," Farli says, casting me a worried look. She darts off.

I head out after Stacy, because how can I not? She's one of mine, and she's a close, dear friend. The person that should be supporting her and helping her through all of this *doesn't even know she's his mate.* I try to imagine how it would feel if Vektal lost all memory of me and shudder.

Oh god, and he didn't even remember his little son, Pacy.

I find Stacy sobbing, collapsed behind a nearby tent. Her fists are covered in snow, and as I watch, she slams one into the ground.

"Oh, Stacy." I kneel next to her, putting my arms around her.

She flings herself into my arms, crying as if her heart will break. My own tears start, and I stroke her hair as she holds on to me, soaking the front of my tunic with her tears. "He d-doesn't remember m-me," she chokes out between sobs. "Or Pacy. The last two years we've spent together? Our resonance?

It doesn't exist to him." Her hands clench my leathers. "Georgie, *he doesn't remember me*!"

"It's temporary, Stacy. It has to be." I rub her back. "He suffered a terrible head injury. He was near death. These things take time." It seems like a shitty way for the universe to reward Stacy's unflagging devotion. She hasn't left her mate's side since the cave-in. Now he's awake and . . . still not quite whole. "I can't imagine what you're going through right now. Anything you need, you just let me know and we'll make it happen."

She sobs for a little longer and then looks up at me, her eyes puffy, the blue glow edged with red from her tears. "I need someplace to sleep."

"What?"

"I can't stay with him, Georgie. I'm a stranger. My baby's a stranger." Her words are bitter and her voice shakes. "I can't have him look at me . . . like he did earlier. Like it's a big blank. I'll die inside."

"You can stay with me tonight," I tell her firmly. "And as many other nights as you need. You know we'll take care of you."

"I wanted him to take care of me." She crumples against me, sobbing anew. "I wanted him to wake up and take my hand and let me know everything is going to be all right. And . . . he's not even my mate. Not anymore. How can we be mates if he doesn't remember anything?"

"It'll come back to him," I say fiercely, hugging her close and stroking her hair.

It has to, doesn't it?

Hours later, Stacy's sobbed herself to sleep on a pallet of furs in Vektal's and my tent. Pacy's curled up next to her, and now that

Stacy's quiet, I can finally put Talie to bed. I snuggle her in the blankets with me, imagining what it'd be like to lose home, security, and mate all at once.

I decide I'm the luckiest because I have my Vektal.

As if my thoughts summon him, he peers into the tent a moment later, his eyes a glowing question. He looks tired, but he also looks so handsome that my heart aches with all the love I have for him.

I put a finger to my lips and gesture at Stacy, then stroke Talie's hair as she sleeps.

He nods and removes his boots, then crawls into bed with me. Careful not to disturb Talie, he still manages to somehow pull me and her against his big, broad chest. Comforting us, the way Stacy longs to be comforted and can't be. Even if Pashov hugged her right now, it wouldn't be the same because he doesn't know her. She's a stranger to him.

My heart wrenches for her and I suddenly feel like weeping all over again.

Vektal presses a kiss to my brow and then whispers, "Is she well?"

"As well as can be expected." I look over but she's not stirring despite our low conversation. Too exhausted. "It's been a real blow."

"He is upset as well," my mate says. "He has hurt her and feels badly. He is confused, too. His memory has many gaps in it. Maylak says it is not something she can encourage his khui to fix. That it will take time."

"But the memory will come back?"

"She cannot say."

Oh, poor Stacy. Poor Pashov. I hold my mate and my kit, closing my eyes. "God. Please let him get his memory back."

Vektal presses another kiss to my brow. "Is this the time that I tell you everything will be all right, my mate? As you did to me the other day, when I brought you my sorrows?" His big hand strokes Talie's curls and I melt at the sight of father and daughter, so peaceful. "You kept me going when I wanted to collapse. I will do the same for you now. It will all work out, my mate. Pashov will remember her . . . or he will not. But give them time to find their path. We can be a friend to both until they are ready to talk."

I sigh. "You're right. I just want to help her, to fix it. She's suffered so much."

"We are all suffering. Stacy knows this. She would not ask you to bear her burdens. Just like I would not ask you to take on all of the tribe's suffering. We are in this together, my sweet resonance. We will find a home again soon. We will ride out the brutal season, and we will emerge as a stronger tribe. No . . . as a family."

He's right.

Things are hard right now, but they will get better. Already, things are looking up. We have the fruit cave. We have Pashov awake and mostly whole again. The runners will return with more supplies. We'll figure something out. As long as we have hope and our tight-knit community, we'll be fine.

Stacy gives a hiccuping little sigh in her sleep, and I hurt for her.

If she can't have hope, then I'll have hope for her.

Everything will be all right in the end. We just need to take it one day, one hour, at a time. And until then, we lean on each other and we hold tight.

ABOUT THE AUTHOR

RUBY DIXON is an author of all things science fiction romance. She is a Sagittarius and a Reylo shipper, and loves farming sims (but not actual housework). She lives in the South with her husband and a couple of goofy cats, and can't think of anything else to put in her biography. Truly, she is boring.

VISIT RUBY DIXON ONLINE

RubyDixon.com
RubyDixonBooks
Author.Ruby.Dixon